THE OTHER SIDE

A HORROR ANTHOLOGY

DANIEL WILLCOCKS

DEVIL'S ROCK
PUBLISHING

OTHER TITLES BY DEVIL'S ROCK PUBLISHING

Serial Fiction, "When Winter Comes"

The First Fall (Episode 1)

Buried (Episode 2)

Black Ice Kills (Episode 3)

Masks of Bone (Episode 4)

Into the White (Episode 5)

Winter Comes (Episode 6)

Anthologies

The Other Side: A Horror Anthology

Keep up-to-date at

www.devilsrockpublishing.com

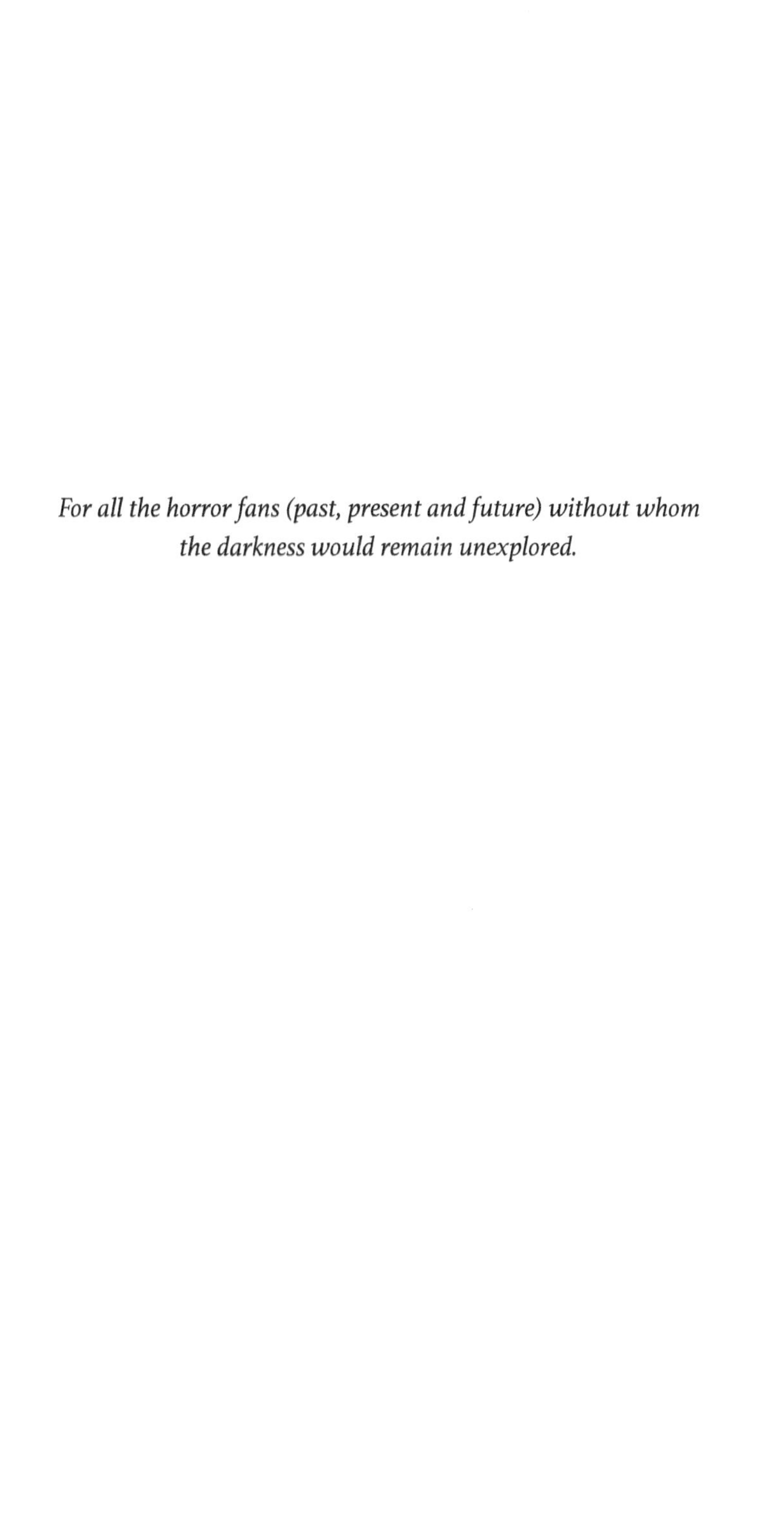

For all the horror fans (past, present and future) without whom the darkness would remain unexplored.

CONTENTS

FOREWORD

 "The process of dying is falling asleep. The process of death is waking up."

— J. Adam Snyder

"Death." To some, it marks the final chapter. To others, it marks the next.

There have been theories around the Great Beyond since humans were first intelligent enough to think beyond our own existence and ask the great questions. The Egyptians, the Mesopotamians, Greeks, Romans, and virtually every sub-sect of religious faith believes in some form of afterlife. Whether with Hades in the Underworld, or in forms of reincarnation within Buddhism, Christianity, and Islam—to name a few—the exploration of Death has a colorful and varied past. Stories of Death are written in every culture and in every language. The one thing that we, as a global community, all agree upon, is that everyone must one day die.

But what truly lays beyond the curtain? Is there another

dimension to our existence? What of the belief in ghosts? Is the paranormal just fiction, or does it hold some semblance of truth in our own realities? Are the sinners punished? Are the just rewarded?

The Other Side aims to showcase just a glimpse of some of many possible scenarios of the afterlife. When assembling the impressive band of writers you have before your fingertips, I had one focus in mind: to find original, unique, and innovative stories that could bend the reality of what you believe the afterlife to be.

Boy, did they deliver. In order to sift through the submissions to give you the cream of the crop, myself and my submissions team waded through hundreds of stories and hundreds upon thousands of written words to find those printed in the pages ahead. These truly are the crème de la crème, and I'm excited to present them to you here.

This collection will take you to the farthest reaches of your realities, pulling you apart piece by piece until you're left questioning your own existence. We sniff at the repercussions of the living in the wake of a close family member dying, we visit graveyards and say hello to witches, we go to far-off realms, as well as those oddly familiar, and all of these tales have one thing in common.

To see what lays beyond The Other Side...

Daniel Willcocks
October 5th 2020

THE OTHER SIDE

DIRT

BY TOM GARBACK

Mom's bookcase has so few paperbacks on its top shelf that I can count them with all three of my left hand's fingers. The other two digits are somewhere in an east Pennsylvanian landfill, I'm told. She insists it was an accident with the car door, but I wouldn't know, having only been four or five at the time. I've always thought that, if it had been the car door, doctors would have sewn me back together. By now it's clear that your pointer or middle finger is so small a thing to learn to live without.

On the shelf sits Poe, the sexist, and Lovecraft, the racist, and Stephen King, your average guy, if no genius. "The dumbest men are the luckiest," Dad would say, the little he does. Mom likes to call that shelf "the upper crust." In her mind, there's something made of graveyard dirt in all things, including people. "You come from dirt, you're gonna be dirt. See those books up there? They've got none; they're clean. The upper crust of our mad, mad world. It's about honesty. Nothing's got more dirt than a liar. Those books tell life like it really is." Her voice puts bruises on my eardrums, even just the thought of it. "Why suffer a soul made of dirt when you can scape it out whole and call yourself clean?" She's always speaking cryptically, distantly, like the past has won her over, cast its shade across her eyes.

That's how I imagine it, anyway. Same way she might, but with less invention, through long, stretchy folds of time that pile up like ice blocks left on the beach, their opalescent fractures all vanishing on the absorptive sand. That was a game Alison and I played in Ventnor, back when we took family vacations. "Wait and watch them melt," she'd say. "You can't stop an ice cube from melting. It's its nature, once you toss one in the sun."

Mom sets steak knives next to our plates, knowing Halloween's next week, reminding me of the chef's knife that's been missing for months. Dad brings out the charred pot pie. "I'll need some extra time to tame him tonight, so eat up fast." Alison didn't need to be asked twice, but I was a slow, picky eater. "It'll be rough. He gets angrier every day. He fears All Hallow's Eve. Losing control of himself." I think of how the paranoia behind lost control is precisely what looses it.

Mom is talking about the ghost, the one that lives in the room above the stairs. Not the house stairs, but the iron spiral stairs propped on the back porch, with its swirly, spiked railing, just as spiked as the high metal picket fence below, gothic enough to stab out Mom's anxieties of trespassers, its sandy ring the cold announcement of bad fortune. It wasn't too dangerous, she'd decided, because Alison and I weren't stupid little kids who might leap from a second-story window, in escape, perchance, and worsen their untimely blow with picket fence impact.

The steps, though, they wind up to the guest room on the third floor, where Grandpa would have stayed, had he lived long enough to finish moving in with us. All that had remained was his personal luggage and himself. Mom wanted Grandpa here years ago, maybe from a spot in her heart that had opened up into a hole and wanted filling. This space was as empty now as that room on the third floor.

The owners before us tore down the inside staircase and threw up a wall, for whatever weird reason people put up walls, like dumb superstition, being set in some ways. Not when it came to houses, evidently; just fears. My parents were weird, too: went the cheap route, ignored housing regulations, and other mannerly things. They got the iron stairs from the old, dying couple down the street who used to offer us games of penuckle. My parents possibly stole without the couple knowing or lasting the night to catch their stealth, tied it to their truck, dragged it over, balanced it on its hind legs like a circus act, stuck some nails where they could fit them, and called that climb the kind of obstacle Grandpa deserved, a fair welcome. And they were right.

Every day, for maybe twenty minutes, Mom sneaks up after dinner as the sun's descent turns the sky to muddled berries. She takes the key tied to her ankle bracelet and locks herself in. "To tame the beast, to clean him out." Whatever that means, and whoever the ghost is supposed to be. Mom's never said. Alison's too scared of the possibility of a phantom to not believe, and Dad and I are too scared of Mom to not at least pretend that we believe.

So, we eat; Mom sipping pills, Dad his beer, our knives untouched and words unspoken, or maybe it's the other way around, and afterwards Mom goes to tame her beast, and

Alison takes a bath again, and Dad drives to the bar, and I lay in bed to watch men, making sure to wear my earbuds this time, remembering last night's incident, with Mom walking in and marking the worst humiliations of adolescence. I'd wondered all day how she'd punish me, or at least tell me that she was angry, but by now it seems she hadn't, after all, been able to tell the moans were men in love, and I wondered if she'd even heard anything at all, or if she'd ever heard the sounds of love, or if her look of nausea from my door was just another way of saying that life hurts.

You're bound to think strangely, living with my mom. Flashes of the past stab through the canvas of the present. Once, she said, "We live on the permanence of things that've already happened, Michael." That was before she made the decision to move us near a Levittown, where we'd get a fresh set of neighbors. She'd be more private, swear off fights in the grocery lanes or box office lines. That old scent of 1950's suburbia, white rubbing off old picket-fences, and apple pies left in the window to mold. We were home.

Before the move, standing from her bathroom window, looking over her half acre one more time—an acre that would turn to half its size in the house we now inhabit—she saw me on the deck below, sunning up nutrients for the last time, and said, "Nothing's harder than breathing. Some moments can do you in. But once you've mastered breath, everything else is easy." She must have been thinking about swimming lessons with Grandpa when she was a girl, which she's yet to tell me the truth about, though she'll mention them during her worst attacks, when even the pills have worn off, and I must, as always, "be there for her."

Our house sat somewhere, somehow, still unrecognizable in the great scheme of what makes up a state, particularly one in the haunted east of our nation, so prone as it was to nightmares of the Gothic past. My own started a few months after the move, near the time Dad's drinking felt its cruel ascent and all our lives closed the doors on themselves.

My nightmares came for other reasons too, of course, but I won't think about them now. They'd turn my head into one huge bruise, its pooled blood beneath staining all my young, healthy skin blue.

I CAN'T SLEEP. All I see are the undersides of eyelids, mine or not. Like movie screens, they show me shapes, and I can make out one of them as Greeks did the constellations, the eight cookie-cut sides of a spinning lamp shade, and it's Mom getting run over and over by Grandpa's car, and how pathetic and hilarious and awful, and I see beside them what must be veins, and I think of how slimy human bodies are, like swamp creatures. We can never get outside of them.

So, instead I wait, knowing that, when I do sleep, I sleep as sound as the dead, despite the house's stench. All families have a unique set of scents dictated by detergent, raw produce, and hormones. Ours came from mystery, perhaps the ghost, after all. It lingered, particularly rank these days, accented by a sickly sweet odor and stocked with gassy sour, eggs left out, toilets unflushed. It seemed to precipitate from some vengeful heaven set to warn us we had all died already.

I hear the clock strike twelve, calling out Grandpa's anniversary and commencing the witching hour.

A year ago today, he leapt off a goddamn lighthouse. I remember Mom telling me how his old, wrinkly body must have been unrecognizable by dawn, when a fisherman found him because he thought another guy had chummed the waters already, which was illegal in that area, and I remember wondering what kind of animals tear their victims without consuming them, and I remember never seeing his death on the news or releasing an obituary or having a funeral or telling any family, and that was mostly because there wasn't anyone to tell, let alone anyone who'd care.

I'm sure he never wanted to live with us, to plop himself down the way he does on his yearly visits, complains again and again about how he can't sit right because his dad shot framing nails into his ass as a boy whenever he bullied kids at school, and how his backside's like the night sky in negative, that the doctors never got all of the nails out because of how deep they were, of how embarrassed he was telling them he'd accidentally done it to himself in the shed. It always makes me think of the metal bar Mom got placed in her chest from the time Grandpa ran her over with a car for trying to run away in open daylight. "Nothing gifted to me by him has ever been more *mine*," Mom says of that bar.

That raggedy grand-bastard came over a few days sooner than expected, or a few days after, but never on time, and that made Mom mad more than anything, which was Grandpa's goal, more than anything. He scrubbed the halls with cigar smoke, raided the overstocked medicine cabinets, mocked us at dinner by asking me if I liked any girls yet, for high school was a whole new chance to start clean—"Don't you speak of clean," Mom'd interject—asked my sister if school was treating her any better, for junior year was the most important one, asked Mom if the marriage counselor had lowered her rates, for the wages of a self-employed accountant and a much-too-old auto mechanic didn't allow these kinds of luxuries, you know.

Grandpa had jumped to his death, and we'd dodged a framing nail.

HOURS LATER, Mom stands over the tub, her bloodshot eyes as red as the water. Alison holds her groin, saying how sorry she is, but Mom's voice is drowning her out. "All Hallow's Eve is up to no good upon you, now, is it? You've never been strong enough to finish it, have you? Before screaming and waking me up? And Michael this time, too." I don't breathe. "Put more pressure on it, will you? I'm sure you're well practiced in squeezing yourself. We were all girls once."

"I'll call for help," I say, just to make her stop, to wake us up from this otherworldly distortion. "I'll get towels. I'll get Dad." I alternate lifting my feet up and down off the tiles to feel how sticky they are with icy sweat.

"Don't do that," Mom says. "Her cuts aren't deep, not with the dull razors we got, and that area won't bleed too much, 'cause she missed the artery."

"Stop it!" I yell, but she doesn't take a throw at me, because she doesn't hear me, because I haven't actually said anything, and nothing's alright.

"The water'll clean things up," Mom goes on. Sweat drips down my thigh, and the warmth makes my heart stop, and I know it's not a wetness as clean as sweat. "As for your father, he's out, per usual—quit whimpering, Alison. Blood's a part of growing."

"The ghost hates me most," my sister pleads, the porcelain light of the tub on her face, and I stop myself from thinking that her eye whites have poured out through her tears. "He made me do this 'cause he wants you to hate me as much as he does. As much as I do."

"Don't blame this on the ghost," Mom says. "It's a matter of attention. I was a teenage girl a hundred years ago. I know how it feels to want to cause a scene, hog the limelight, and it is a matter of hogs when you're a teenager." Is there steam, or are my eyes clouding over? "You'll have to jump off a skyscraper to outdo your grandfather, understand? And, until then, I'm not giving in and letting you have all the attention that you don't deserve. It'll help you in the long run. So, press yourself now, and close the lips on your face, too, before something slides out."

"Please—" I start, and Mom flicks her head toward me, her hand needing not raise to tell me my place, and Alison stands, the red cascading over prickly shins, the cliffs that separate reality from intolerance, and escaping into the water like a portal to someplace safer.

"Go back to bed, Michael. These things are womanly troubles."

Then Alison screams, the blade pinched between her fingers, a privilege I can only envy, though at least I'm a boy, for a growing girl would surely miss her fingers more, particularly the middle, and Alison's arm is swinging out, and Mom is turning around, catching a nick in her night-gown, the breasts beneath flashing under the brightness of the room.

"This is your fault," Alison says. "You'll never get your dirt out, will you?" Mom steps back in reply, faltering.

Then she's steady. "Try and cut me again, bitch. Our ghost will eat you up. He'll do anything to protect me. He's mine. Remember Emma?" I push that sweet name from my mind, and Allison falls back against the wall, vanquished, and slips down with a cold and soundless splash.

Mom walks out, stepping around me in the same way that she steps around the toilet and the trash. The door slams. "What can I do?" I ask, shaking and shaking, watching my few fingers wobble in mid-air, then looking at my glossy mess on the tiles, knees bent to my heart.

"Leave," Alison says.

So, I go, and I still don't breathe.

AND I DON'T STOP THINKING of Grandpa. Mom hates me for taking his death so lightly, for never shedding a tear or cracking my voice for as much as a syllable. The real reason she cried was for the guilt of never mending things, and if I didn't have that to regret, what reason was there to cry for someone you couldn't feel safe being alone with? Mom could only share a room with her father if we were around, or they'd start a boxing match.

Last Halloween, a little over three months ago, she hit me for buying a costume, as if life dare to make a joke of sick things, or just move on. My glow-in-the-dark skull mask was covered in the blood, lit up like a lava lamp. Mom cried until I calmed her myself, and then she went to the room above the stairs an hour early, and I finally got a minute to wrap my nose in gauze from the kit I hide in the trunk of my Nascar bed, which I outgrew before we'd even moved in.

I don't blame her. After years of tax fraud and gambling, Grandpa had left some debt, and Mom and Dad couldn't afford their therapist anymore, and they don't see her even now, regardless of being able to afford it. All relationships eventually pass the point of no return.

One time at dinner, no more than a week after Mom told us the news—however she'd heard it, cause Grandpa lived alone—she tried giving some sort of commemorative speech, as if to make up for never having a eulogy, about how her childhood wasn't so bad after all, how Grandpa had, in fact, taken her on vacations after Grandma's death, when Mom was an infant, how he hadn't instead stayed home and scarred her with leather whips, strung her to the wall by chains, beat her after she'd passed out, how that wasn't Grandpa's favorite part, to play with things that looked undone. He hadn't cut the Child Services lady upon first meeting her, and she hadn't blamed Grandpa for years and years, letting the hate fester to blooming infection. "Dirt's a powerful force," Mom said, stretching her mouth wide, but not smiling, and that was when I laughed, coughed my Campbells across the hardwood, appalled at her audacity to attempt amends with a monster. She fumed.

That evening, Mom hid my blankets and pillows in her closet. I eventually got everything back as my birthday gift that spring. Dad wrote the card; *To Michael* and *From, Us*. In the meantime, Alison, the only person I could trust, making for the only healthy tie of loyalty this semblance of a family possessed, gave me a torn green horse from the bottom of her toy chest. It was all she could do with Mom locking us in our rooms by ten o'clock. She didn't just work from home, where no one could count the anxiety pills she prescribed herself, but snooped from home too, so I kept the horse in my schoolbag. Classmates were too polite to snicker or point. Instead, they talked, and that mattered more in the long run of having friends.

Nowadays, Mom forgets to lock us in our rooms, but we no longer have the interest to leave.

"I WON'T BE TAMING him anymore," Mom says, setting down the knives, which haven't been washed, haven't been used. "Not after last night. He's too angry, now, with All Hallow's Eve so close. I've come to seeing that our ghost is trying to help. He's told me if we don't start acting good, there'll be repercussions. He's never been this angry. I couldn't tame him if I wanted to." All of us look to keep her going, as much as we hate it. "No more secrets, or else he'll use my body to fix our mess. We're more similar than not, he says. Possession would be easy."

Dad laughs so loudly despite his hangover that he needs to leave the kitchen, and I think of how that's the only way 'like father, like son' applies to us, and I expect he won't return. Maybe it would have been easier if Dad didn't live with us at all, and maybe that was the way we lived already, and maybe he was the real ghost of our house. How unromantic, how anticlimactic of the afterlife, to offer us the disposable snore in the corner, the guy we knew we'd be better off, more coherent and comprehensible, without.

Alison sits up straight. Mom nods to nothing, washes her pills down with milk. "We must do whatever it takes to make this house clean. Before our dirt spread up to our brains." We're far beyond that, I know.

"We could just move," I offer.

"The dirt's inside of us, Michael. It follows." So, Alison and I nod along forever until sunset, and I end up being right about Dad.

THAT NIGHT, finally able to sleep again, I'm gnawed by dreams of Emma's fur. She'd come to us from the pound, a gift on the recommendation of the school psychologist to keep Alison distracted. It was clear then that this dense specialist would never pick apart what Alison (and I) had been trained to hide, and a big part of the meaning of hope was lost to me from that point on.

The decision to get the pup came easier than expected. I wouldn't be surprised if my parents' therapist had, at some point prior, unaware of Mom's hatred for meek creatures, suggested they get a pet to refresh their intimacy through the feeling of something newly born. And how pointless it all was, because now there was just the atmosphere of something newly dead. But I can hardly blame that on Emma.

ALISON WAKES ME UP AGAIN, but not all the way from the bathtub. She sneaks into my room, sits on my bed. I fold into a ball beneath the quilt to cover my groin. My underwear is on the frigid radiator, where I tossed it hours ago, given that it's 4 a.m.

"You need to tell Mom you're gay," she says, and I feel struck dead. "No more secrets."

"I don't know how to get you to believe that ghosts aren't real."

"Since when did you start thinking that? I know we hardly talk anymore, but—"

"I grew up. So should you. Besides, if professing our secrets is what saves us from the wrath of hell or whatever, then you've got to come clean about the reasons you cut yourself."

She slaps me, thinking it could possibly hurt a kid raised in this house, and she stands up, folding her arms tightly across her abdomen. "Let me deal with my own issues, alright?"

"Then how could you think it was your place to stroll on into my room and say what you said?" I ask. "You're dumb to be afraid. Of ghosts, at least. We're not being haunted."

"You're right; our ghost doesn't haunt us. He makes us haunt ourselves and watches from the room above the stairs." I clench my teeth. "Don't you ever want to get clean?"

And that does it for me. "I actually thought you were better than that. I thought Mom's bullshit sermons on dirt had nothing on you. What kind of fucked up life is that, anyway, huh? Thinking you're stuffed with mud? We ought to be orphans."

I try and try to find something in Mom that makes her sympathetic to a stranger. That's what I dream of on the loneliest nights, and I know that's what she deserves as much as anyone. But the cold and stubborn truth is that, in my eyes, there is nothing sympathetic there. I owe her no sympathy, nor a depiction of it. There is only the nihilist one-side, the black and white of my inability to see anything soft behind the milk glass of her soul. And I have no apologies for that.

Instead of slapping me again, Alison walks out and shuts the door cleanly behind her, cutting off more than the hallway light.

In middle school, Allison tutored younger girls in math and history every weekend. She ordered drinks without ice. Red before hot pink, scooters over bikes, and an allergy to latex. She was prepared to beat down anyone who dare speak against her family, be it school counselor or High

Judge. I have always loved my sister. But I know nothing about her anymore.

I take out my phone and earbuds, and a part of me is wondering if maybe there is something like dirt around my lungs, between my ribs, in other places that pound hardest with each heartbeat.

By the time I'm out of breath and closing my eyes, I try to think if dirt is always dark like soil, and I toss my wet tissue, but it can't go very far when you've only got two fingers and a thumb.

THE NIGHTMARE RESUMES, and I recall the time five weeks ago when Dad found Emma frozen to the spiral stairs, hind paws down a step from the front two, half her head chewed off. Not that I know this is true. I didn't see for myself, and Dad gave no more details after that first one, because I'd thrown up burnt pie on the potted flowers, thinking, too, of Grandpa in the ocean. Alison blamed the ghost. Dad blamed an eagle. I thought, *He's not telling the truth. But why lie for a ghost?* Back then was when I still believed in such an easy, childish form of monster.

I'M WOKEN ONCE MORE, but not by Alison. Someone is chanting through the door, and I run out to the hall. Mom's a few yards off, her figure blurred by shadow, the boning knife in her hand reflecting the moon's alkaline glow from the window behind me. She turns to the stairs, nearly falls as she descends, and shouts, "He said he'd take me to the island for my birthday. I can't tame my secrets anymore. I hate him. I've tried and tried to hold them in, tried to make excuses for him, for me. Taking out your dirt is hard, Michael. It hurts. Wake your sister, Michael. You're stronger. She woke me up screaming again. Father made promises. I've made excuses. Lies. Wake your sister. She broke dams this time. Mommy made promises. He said we'd see the top of the island."

I almost follow her down, almost say, "Let me hold you, alright? That always helps," but I don't want to this time because of that tear in the nightgown, and maybe she'd make me hold her anyway, but hadn't I offered to? And I can't say what strange desires she'd request of me once in my arms, and me held to her tenderness.

That's the last image of tenderness I will ever have of Mom, and it only ever existed in my head.

When I go into Alison's room instead, she isn't in bed, so I check our bathroom across the hall, next to Mom and Dad's open bedroom door, the cave inside stuffed with shadows, but here's where she is, inside the tub of course, and the water's so thick that I can't see her legs. And I grab her shoulders and shake them, and they're oiled dough. "Was it what I said?" I say, my breath surely gone for good this time. "Mom!" In her silence, I run downstairs, where Dad's headlights are rolling across the walls from the windows.

"I tried to wake her," Mom says, rounding the corner in a flash, her nightgown whooshing open at the tear. "But it was too difficult. I thought you'd be stronger. Our ghost will be so angry. He'll want to see me now, to do things his way. It's time. His."

My eyes see nothing, as am I—numb, numb, numb. Dad busts in the front door, lurching to the left, his eyes half-closed, his keys slipping and cracking on the ground, and Mom is still running around aimlessly, her knife out like a sword, her eyes on everything. "He said he'd take us to the very top, to the lighthouse. Father made promises. I made excuses. I made up stories. I brought him to the top of the island, in a way, in my head, and pushed him off. It was a better death. I built him a eulogy made of lies." Dad is rubbing his nostrils, moaning.

I go to the phone and peck the numbers for the police, number, number, number, tell them that my sister is dead, and that's when Mom's in the living room, tearing her paperbacks from the shelf, slashing at the ancient pages, tossing them into a monochrome cloud, and Dad has noticed, has begun to growl in his drunken delirium. Mom twirls around, shoots through the back door, Dad following, angry mumble, mumble, mumbles.

I go, too, and when I'm on the porch, shivering, Mom is ascending the stairs, meeting each preserved snow print perfectly, by memory. "You ole bitch," Dad slurs. "You come down or fall. I dare you." He starts his way up, swinging back and forth against the railings to keep his balance, hands up to block the floodlights from his eyes. "Tell me what you did." I think of how hard he holds his liquor to hold her secrets, the heavier sedative, and then I think of tonic clearing the six senses, bubbling over. "Tell me, girlie, or I'll throw you down." She does.

"I let him back into my life. I made excuses. I thought past meant dead." How sober she is, I see, though my eyes are pointy with spots and quivers.

Dad reaches the window, still swaying violently, like he's pouring his anger out on those iron stairs. The metal cries against his striking thunder. "Come back down, both of you!" I call up, my chest and throat so tight that I'm not sure I'm making any noise, and I wouldn't ever know for sure, because my ears are off, aren't they, because my parents' words can't be real.

"They put me in an orphanage. He tried to find me. I was a teenage girl. I wanted to die. Our ghost is mad. The past can't die. The world is mad, mad. Time's run out. Mad, mad, mad."

Dad is still not moving, but the steps are popping, crackling, the sounds of small explosions where the metal meets the house. But Dad is moving then, backwards, his mouth agape, his eyes transfixed by what's inside the room above the stairs. "Don't tell them what I've done," Mom's saying, her voice furthering itself. "I'm full of dirt and darker things. I tried to kill myself. I was just a girl. She was just a girl. You are just a boy." It's almost mute by now, and maybe her words are mine, because that's how well I know her now. "Father broke our promises. I made excuses. I wanted to die. My body is his. Here is Heaven. Finally, the lighthouse. Goodbye, goodbye."

Then the black room behind the window is silent, and the staircase exhales a raspy, fiery series of snaps and groans, and all the Earth leans forward, the stairs and Dad stuck still. I jump to the sliding doors, close my eyes, feel the air and the great falling thing. Dad is wailing, passing through the air as the stairs toss him off, or Mom is moaning, or everyone's been fast asleep, and I'll wake up to Alison apologizing soon, and I'll say sorry, too.

The ground shakes once, sure of itself. A cold, sandy ring, quickly halted. Mom is whispering to the wind, but I can no longer make out words, for they aren't really there anymore, though I wish they were. I open my eyes and look up. She's entirely gone, the window closed, everything quiet and still. Across the deck and onto the yard is where the iron staircase lies, half concealed and still, stabbing the snow that glitters with the start of things, unwarm fire in the sky. Stabbing the dark stuff underneath, too.

Dad must be half in the yard, half without, the derisive picket fence between all things, and he is too drunk to cry out his final cry, dragon's dying flame, and he hangs, a plane in Pentax, balanced for once in his life, above all, still. At least the way I picture it in my head.

I can't move anymore, not so much as eyes, and I hinge on breaths alone, alone.

WHEN THE AMBULANCE ARRIVES, it doesn't drive away with one body bag, or two. They set a ladder against the house, and when they find Mom inside, when I've climbed up behind them, both policemen shaken off my shoulders, I see she's taken after Alison, hacked into her own motherly place, so deeply that everything inside's been tugged out, the muddled berries of the sky. Somehow, she's fished up to her metal rib, yanked it loose, wrenched it all the way out. I must be imagining. She couldn't have lived through that. All I can do is hope that she was happy getting clean of her faux bone, and I wonder, if I'd been given faux fingers, would I now take up the knife and debone my own dirt, perhaps excavate even further?

Grandpa's bulging luggage is by the door, and seashells scatter the bedside table, surrounding the grimy chef's knife we've been missing, and the back wall is lined with stacks of paperbacks, their boxes barely broken down, set aside. I can't see the covers in the dark, but I doubt they'd be Mom's taste, because Grandpa hated horror. He'd always say that nothing was scarier than real life, and there was no point in trying to outdo it.

The ambulance doesn't drive away with three body bags, either. I sit at the curb, the gentleman with the notepad asking questions, my mind in the past, as it's always been.

One of the authorities had grabbed me, tried to pull me from the window, and I know that this is when I see the other body—the thing that's hardly a body anymore—the furry set of bones strung to the wall by oxidized chains, the green ooze soaked into the stiff carpet beneath, the ivory hairs and teeny tiny framing nails mixed in, half-dissolved from tens of sad years, the stiff pieces on top that must be cartilage, the flies and maggots and fungus and putrescence.

I also see the worn whips on the bed, and the stained rubber gloves, and the rusted handsaw, and the mallet with shallow, bite-like dents on top, and I think of all the time Mom's spent up here, taming our ghost. There aren't handcuffs or blindfolds or rags for gagging. There is no sign of struggle or beaten life, but only of the deathless dirt that follows. And I think of deathless things for the rest of the day and night, be it waiting on the greyed curb or laying under heartrate monitors, and then for years, for all those that must so stubbornly come, my mind undone, but never not numb, my tongue and nostrils stale, even now still stale, within their cruelest pores lying dormant evermore, the remnants of blood and spoiled meat.

I FIND myself reading Shirley Jackson too much. Maybe it's that Halloween is drawing near again. They've got so many more books here than Mom ever did, and none of them are sorted into a hierarchy, but only by doctor's warnings.

I curl up on the sill, look out through the bars at the city below, imagine Alison's in the bed across the room, bandages on her wrist and other places, where they should've been all along, and I read my hours away, and the nurses don't mind, and it somehow makes me feel like dirt is trickling out of each and every one of my sore crannies, from my bruised ear drums to the stubs where my fingers should be, so that when I'm out of here, either in the shadow of some lonely middle-aged pair or more suitably on my own, a requisite birthday card from the staff in my back pocket, who as my only points of social interaction feel obligated to bring me cake and let me throw it up too, indeed when I'm out, maybe I'll be clean of what was born inside of me, from the foul rib of Eve, and I just hope that when this happens, I'll feel clean of what I used to be, and what used to be done to me, and I'll never cry when I ejaculate or feel the sun set too fast, and I'll never see Mom where she bleeds whenever I blink or wake from dreams of chains and leather whips.

MARVIN'S TAVERN

BY HEINRICH VON WOLFCASTLE

I

Marvin's Tavern stands somewhat crooked and has for about as long as anyone can remember. The plaque hanging near the front door says it was built sometime in the late 1800's and, once you're inside, it sounds every bit its age with all of its creaks and groans. It's old—scenic, maybe—with a long lake at its back, but it's not remarkable. If you didn't know to look for it, you might not even find it. It's kind of like a man pointed to a hill on a whim one day and thought to clear a space between the trees and build a bar there. I suppose that is what happened, and that man's name was Marvin.

Marvin was something of a local legend—fame or infamy, maybe a little bit of both. In its prime, Marvin's Tavern was an evening fixture, a place to stop for a drink or to end your night. Marvin would serve as bartender while catching up with the local folk about the latest happenings.

They hung a photograph of him in the bar from his younger days, candidly captured wiping down some glasses with his serious expression hidden behind a formidable mustache.

He only had one child; a son named Maurice. From what I understand, Marvin's wife, Beth, was killed in a horse and buggy accident some years into Maurice's childhood. Some say it was a highway robbery and that she was targeted as Marvin's wealthy wife. Others say that *she* was actually the one doing the robbing. Verdict was never really reached on that one. Either way, Marvin wouldn't remarry or seek out other female company. He claimed that she was his one and only true love, and he seemed to bring up her smile at every opportunity that he could. He even commissioned an artist to paint a picture of her in mid-laugh—an uncommon practice for the time. He hung the picture behind the bar, where I imagine it still sits today—a bit dusty and a bit worn, maybe.

Maurice didn't have the charm that his father had. He was born mostly deaf, which made it hard for him to make friends. He could lip read and understand others well enough, but he had a real bad speech impediment. The town folk would talk about him behind his back and make their jokes, but no matter their gossip, he had a way with tools and carpentry that silenced even the cruelest of town critics.

Thing about Maurice was, being unable to hear and all, Marvin learned to become real protective of him, making sure that no boy of his would be seen as a town fool. He would harass the boys and girls that came near the tavern, just assuming they were there to mock Maurice. So, eventually, some of the local boys thought to get a little payback at Marvin's expense. They came into the bar one afternoon when Maurice was by himself and a few jokes turned into an all-out fight. From what legend says, the boys were making fun—earning their trouble that Marvin was giving them anyway—when Maurice tried to defend himself. He might've gotten a few good swings in, but he was outnumbered. They managed to get his arms behind his back and pinned him to the ground. While he was held down, the leader of the group took a knife from the bar and cut Maurice's ears off. "You don't use 'em anyway!" he cackled. A real sick bunch, these kids were.

Well, when Marvin returned to the bar, the boys were standing over Maurice, laughing and holding his ears up to his head and taking them on and off again. Grasping the scene, Marvin took the claw side of a hammer and caught the leader in the back with it. While the rest of them were scuffling out of there, he also caught one of the slower ones by the hair. They say the boys' faces were unrecognizable when they were found. Neither of them survived, and that changed public opinion of Marvin—not that it was too high to begin with.

The dead boys' fathers came back to the bar that night with a few other men and intended to kill Marvin, 'eye for an eye' kind of stuff. Something snapped in Marvin and, according to the survivors from that night, he wrestled two of them to the ground and strangled them to death one-handed each. He fought off another one of them, too, shattering the man's face in different places, and he died from his injuries some days later.

The boys may have started the fight, but Marvin sure finished it. Some suspected the police would arrest him but, for one reason or another, they hardly investigated the murders. Some said that Marvin had them all in his pocket, and others said that what Marvin did was justified—simple as that. Either way, it wasn't good for business, and the toll it took on him seemed to accelerate his aging.

In his last years, Marvin's black mustache turned white along with his wild eyebrows. He would hobble around, hunched over, muttering about his body falling apart. Something in the bar would need repair, and despite his best efforts to attend to the issue, Maurice would ask him to step aside so he could do the fixing. Marvin spent his final years trading glances between his painting of his laughing Beth and his own wrinkled and shaking hands.

After the controversy, there were no more customers for the bar, though it couldn't have happened at a better time since prohibition was just getting started anyway. Some thought that would be the end of Marvin's Tavern but, apparently, the two men managed to find a new line of revenue to keep the place afloat. No one could quite figure out what it was. Weekends and weeknights, out of town characters would show up, dressed to the nines, to close the place out. Everyone just assumed they were liquoring up the cops or paying forward political favors.

At the same time, they say Marvin passed away after accidentally falling down the stairs into the bar's cellar, and Maurice had something like a mental breakdown and became a recluse thereafter—seen less and less often outside the bar until he just disappeared altogether.

Towards the end of those years, just about everyone in town had forgiven Marvin's nefarious history and connection to the place—well, except for the last of those boys' fathers. Just as business started rolling again, he threw a bottle bomb through a window and set the place on fire. He admitted his guilt and didn't fight the charges, though he wouldn't discuss what compelled him to do it. Some considerable damage was done, including handfuls of deaths, but nothing to wipe the place away completely.

Marvin's Tavern really is the best kept secret in town, and its complicated past splits public opinion; either the town folk frequent it, or they change the conversation when you talk about it.

The first time I saw the place, my girlfriend and I had spent the night out drinking at the lake under the hill—just blowing off steam on spring break. We had this little wooden raft that we'd throw out into the water and drift around on until we returned to shore. It was the kind of thing we'd done a hundred times before, but that night we ended up in a spat. She told me that she got accepted into a program for teaching abroad, and she was talking about how she was going to live her dream of teaching English to kids from other countries and whatnot. I don't know what happened, but something about the idea of her going off to another country while I waited for her to come home— failing out of my gen ed classes in the meantime—I guess I snapped.

We were screaming at each other, and I was yelling that I wouldn't let her leave me. One thing led to another, and before I knew it, I had my hands on her. I was squeezing her neck and watching her change colors—starting to wonder if her head might pop off—when her knee came up and struck me in the groin. I rolled off of her so fast that I accidentally tipped the raft and knocked us into the water. While I was trying to right the thing, she swam her ass to shore—probably for the best. I could hardly stay afloat, so I gave up and headed to shore, too. But I was all turned around and I came out right at the base of the hill. Anyway, after I made it out of the water, I thought to go up and over the hill to the main road, rather than taking the long trek back around the lake. Sure enough, as I crept over the top of the hill, there was Marvin's Tavern in all of her glory. And, God, did I need a drink.

That night, and for the rest of my spring break, I drank and made a nook for myself amongst the locals, learning the sordid history of the place. But that bar, she's a deceptive one; having a drink there was like having a drink in your own grandmother's living room, if only your grandmother's house were built over Satan's den.

2

THE FUNNY THING about having a drinking problem is that the details—those little facts, the pieces of truth on wheels—seem to always be rolling away when you reach for them. When I look at the few details I managed to hang onto from my last night at Marvin's, the picture they paint is a bleak one.

I was thinking about calling Nicki—you know, trying to find a way to make things right—and I wanted to be sure I was in the right headspace for that kind of a conversation. I was parked at the wobbliest stool, just a little bit right of center at the bar, with my favorite bartender, Ellie. One lesson my foster dad taught me early on was that when you're going for something, "Go all in and go in good company." Ellie was about as good of company as you could find.

She looked like she was in her late twenties, but she would tell you stories about what her twenties were like when she lived them more than twenty years ago. Some people hire a shrink to talk to. Me? I had Ellie. Like her drinks, her words of wisdom packed a punch. And, let me tell you, you don't learn to swing like that until you've been around the block a bit.

Next to me was my favorite new drinking buddy, Hank. Under that gruff beard of his was always a frown but, I swear, he meant it like a smile. He was the sort of guy you'd fear breaking into your house in the middle of the night with a shotgun or something. I liked to remind him that he would probably die alone for that reason; his goddamned grimace scared away the women. He'd thank me for the advice, calling me a "motherless son of a bitch" in return— but always with a pat on the back.

So, there we were, finishing our first round of drinks, when Hank thought to ask Ellie for something special. After some consideration, Ellie poured him something she called, "Death in the Afternoon."

"Listen, absinthe gets a bad rap, but it makes for a nice night. You just enjoy the drink and don't tell anyone who poured it," Ellie explained. "Capeesh?"

"Capeesh," Hank said with a wink.

"Hey Ellie, what if I wanted to try something a little less *safe*?" I asked.

"I think a little 'Death in the Afternoon' would do you just fine, too," she replied.

"No, I mean, that's good and all," I began, "but you've made me that before. What would you be pouring for you, if you were me?"

"You really want to know what I would make for me?"

"Yeah, what would that be?" I asked.

"You really want to go for it, huh?" Ellie asked. She paused, tilted her head, and let out a deep sigh.

"Absolutely. Give me something ominous," I said.

"Listen, if you think you're ready for it, I've got something for you. But I'm only making you one, and if you tell anyone about it, I'll deny it."

"Shit, Ellie, what's in it?" I asked.

Without answering, Ellie grabbed a glass from the counter and took it behind a closed door in the back. I turned to Hank, "Is she serious?" I asked.

"I've learned to not mess with her," Hank chuckled.

Ellie returned from the room with a miniscule amount of some kind of foaming liquid in the bottom of a glass. She proceeded to mix a few other bottles into it and then slid it across the counter to me.

"Listen, Ryan, you drink this slow and just enjoy the ride," she cautioned.

"What is it?" I asked.

"It's a family secret," she winked. "I only give it to my favorites, and it comes with a coffee at the end of the night so you can tell me all about it."

I held the glass in my hand and swirled the drink a couple of times, imagining that I knew what to do to appreciate it. It had a pungent odor to it; something was hiding under the smell of the other liquors—tequila and whiskey, I think they were. I put it to my lips and noticed nothing unusual, except for the taste. If drinking scotch had hints of smoke flavoring, then this was like drinking dirty rainwater out of a fire pit.

"Wow, Ellie, this is awful! This is what you make for your favorites? I want my money back," I joked.

"Just take it slow, young blood," she smiled.

"Want a sip?" I asked Hank.

He waved my offer off with his hand. "Ellie's already made me one of those. One was enough," he chuckled.

Hank must've had five or six drinks before I finished my first. We played a game of chicken to see who'd be the first to have to get up to hit the John. I don't remember the score that night, but Hank was the first to break the seal. By the time I had to go, I was a bit off balance, to say the least.

I hobbled my way to the bathroom, cautiously bracing myself against the wall to not tear any of the fraying wallpaper. Once I got to the door, I kind of fell inside.

I went in there to take a leak, but I couldn't find the urinals. They were all taken off the wall or something and replaced with stalls. I don't like to make a habit of sitting in public restrooms but settling for a stall didn't seem like such a bad idea in my condition. It was only then, when I was already sitting down, that I realized I was in the women's restroom. That was all right, though, I thought it would make for a funny story to remember the night by—something to add to a future catalogue of "Remember that time when…" But that was the last part of the night that resembled any kind of normalcy.

I was considering leaving the stall to head to the men's room, when the bathroom door swung open. A woman walked in, wearing a bright green dress that clung to the best curves on her body, and she carried a small bag with her. I peeked out from a crack between the stall and the door to see her remove some kind of black band and feather from her head. I didn't mean to be watching her, but I couldn't leave the stall, either. The last thing I wanted was for someone to call the cops about a pervert hanging out in the women's bathroom. I tucked my legs onto the toilet and sat as quietly as I could while waiting for her to leave.

Instead of leaving, two more women came in after her—each one just as stunning as the first, and each with her own cloth bag. The second woman wore a red dress with tassels and had multiple layers of white pearls hanging from her neck. The third woman wore a black dress with gold chains dangling from it. My first impression was that these women must have been celebrities or movie stars, but what would they be doing at Marvin's Tavern?

The three women watched themselves in the mirror while removing their ornate pieces of jewelry and headbands, placing them with care into the small bags that they had brought with them. They didn't speak or even acknowledge one another as they removed pieces of their outfits.

The woman in green reached to the bottom of her dress and pulled it up over her head, exposing her bare body, with exception to her underwear and bra. I wish I could say I had the decency to look away, but I did not. Aside from admiring her form, I was taken aback by the design of her undergarments. Believe me, I had seen enough women in different styles of underwear before to know that what she was wearing was strange; she was like a vintage model. The woman in red removed her dress next, revealing something like a tight nightgown. The woman in black also wore some kind of slip beneath her dress. Each of them removed those layers as well and placed them in their bags.

The three women stood together silently, pausing to gaze at their naked reflections in the bathroom mirror. Next, the one that had been wearing the green dress brought her hand to her face and looked to be digging her nails into the skin under her jaw. I put my hand over my mouth to keep from gasping as I saw little trails of blood drip down her arms. I wanted to burst from the stall to stop her from hurting herself, but the other two women started doing the same thing. They each pulled the skin back from under their jaws and unraveled the flesh from their faces. They were muscle-tissued and red. Systematically, as if going through routine, each of them continued to skin their bodies with their nails. Each made her way down her neck and shoulders and arms and torsos and legs, leaving a puddle of blood at their feet.

The room began to spin, and I thought I was going to pass out or puke—maybe both. As much as I wished to look away, I was captivated by their grotesque bodies. After skinning themselves, the women reached into their bags for long black gowns and placed them over their bloodied masses, losing their form and figures under thick layers of robed cloth.

Finally, the women brought out headpieces from their bags to complete their outfits. They appeared to be long and leathered beaks—the kind of thing doctors wore during the Black Plague. They placed the masks over their faces, obscuring their mouths and expressions, and then took turns securing them with laces and belt hooks. Without words, they stood in front of the mirror, lifted their hoods from their robes, and walked single file from the restroom.

Once they left, I stumbled my way out of the stall and crashed into the bathroom sink, having slipped on the trails of blood that coagulated into one pool of crimson. I thought to look through their bags but began to gag on their iron-laden smell. Dizzied, I pushed the bathroom door open and became lost in the hall. The entire bar had gone silent—no music, no chatter, no nothing.

I leaned on the wall for support and began to make my way in the dim hallway towards the bar. As I went, my hands traced the wall until it gave way with the weight of my body. Something like a secret door flew open from the hall, revealing a long set of wooden stairs, which I proceeded to tumble down, head over heels.

I awoke at the bottom of the stairs with aches and pains shooting up my legs. It was dark, but I could make out a series of glowing candles flickering in a large circle. As my eyes adjusted, I could see a group of individuals in leathered beaks surrounding the configuration of candles. There appeared to be no edges between their robes and the darkness.

In the middle of the circle was the bent body of a man lying next to a skeleton. They rested on an etching that was carved into the ground. I thought to call for help but could not find my words. By the time I could process what I was seeing, I realized I was shrieking and already scrambling to find my way up the stairs. In my raucous fumbling, one figure broke from the formation and removed the beak and hood from his head. The last image I have of the night was a skinless man without ears.

I told you, my memory of that night was bleak.

3

THERE ARE hangovers and there are hanged-overs. I woke up the next afternoon to a blistering fever, having somehow been passed out and up all night at the same time. The worst thing about a fever is that it makes your bones ache, your blood boils, and everything is sensitive to touch—like you have no skin.

I never did get that coffee from Ellie at the end of the night, or maybe I did, and I didn't remember. I spent the next week or two as a zombie, just puking my brains out; I remember that. Classes and finals were missed and, before I knew it, I was a community college dropout with nothing to say to anybody—not hard to do when you grow up a foster kid, always a 'son' with an unspoken asterisk.

In the days and weeks and years that followed, there had

been thin stretches of sobriety, but there had also been profound stretches of walking the highway and kicking stones in a drunken stupor, like some kind of demented animal on the prowl. As weeks bled into months and years, I lost my home, my friends, and my so-called family. I never worked up the courage to talk to Nicki again, either. In those days, well before cell phones, it was easier to just disappear, and I made a habit of it. I did well to stay away from Marvin's though; the idea of going back was about as good of an idea as sending a werewolf to live on the moon.

But, eventually, I saw the thing I always hoped for and dreaded at the same time: a 'PROPERTY FOR SALE' sign. Apparently, Marvin's Tavern was going to disappear. I guess I decided that if there were ever a reason to go back, it was to say goodbye.

4

I TOOK the long walk to Marvin's, trekking up the backside of the hill and taking my time to remember what it was like when I first found the place—my clothes soaked, my body exhausted, and totally out of breath. I couldn't decide if I hoped to find Ellie still working there or not. Even if she did still work there, would she remember me, one of her *favorites*?

I made my way around to the front, admiring the construction that two hands had built, and two more hands maintained for so many years—at least in the places where you could see the original work. A cold sweat broke out on the back of my knees; I wasn't sure of what I was hoping to find or do when I opened the door.

No, I knew the answer to that: have a drink.

Touching the doorknob, I remembered the image of Maurice—the bloodied man without ears from the cellar. He had taken up residence in the back parts of my mind over the years, a reminder that I just might be clinically insane. God knows what happened down there that night or what was in my drink. I turned the knob and had to kick it in a bit—stubborn as ever—making for more of an entrance than I intended. I closed the door behind me and was greeted by a round of applause from a full room of patrons.

"Hey, there he is, the guest of the hour!" one of them yelled. Men and women across the bar rose to their feet in a gradual wave and continued to clap for me.

I was dumbfounded by the reception I received—half unsure if I was hallucinating, or if I was standing near someone else who recently arrived and deserved the celebration. I was most struck by the sameness of the place, as if I had walked into some kind of living, breathing, time capsule. The whole thing was like walking into a dream. I've been called delusional before, but, I swear, they were waiting for me.

Cheers continued to follow and deflate as I smirked and nodded, doing my best to hold back the sense of panic building in my chest. Something was wrong. Something was oh-so-very wrong.

"For you, Ryan!" a guy named Ed called out from the entrance of the bar. He lifted his drink and took a swig. I remembered him; he was the local dancing drunk.

"Oh, c'mon. What is this shit?" I muttered under my breath. I was ready for the Marvin's Tavern experiment to end immediately. I hustled to turn back to the door but was blocked by a couple wearing what looked like party clothes from the 1920's.

"It's for you, Ryan!" they answered with obscene smiles.

"How do you know my name?" I asked in a whisper. I shrank back in an effort to distance myself from the attention. A pit of nausea rolled in my stomach, and I tried to make my way again for the door. But, no matter how I turned, the whole tavern seemed to bend and turn with me, giving me the feeling I had been drugged and dizzied. The bar was the only way forward.

A man seated at a booth tipped his hat to me. "Up there, Ryan," he said. He pointed to the stool a little right of center from the bar and nodded.

"Don't let them bother you. We're just happy to see you is all," another voice called out.

It was like someone stuck me on pause while everyone else around me was allowed to keep moving—drinking, cheering, celebrating. A woman in a navy blue dress approached me and gave me a kiss on the cheek. "Drink with us, Ryan," she said.

"Ye-yeah," I stuttered out, finding my voice. I scanned the room in detail, taking in the worn, wooden flooring and pinstripe wallpaper still splitting at the edges. The odd assortment of customers in the bar looked to be attending something like a decade party with everyone in costumes from the 1920's and on. Regardless of their outfits, all eyes were on me, encouraging me to make my way towards the stool that seemed to be waiting for me. I walked to it with hesitation, skimming my hand against creaky tabletops along the way.

As I approached the bar and my old, wobbly stool, I saw Ellie posted behind the counter, still looking as young and spry and joyful as ever. We made eye contact and she patted the place at the bar in front of her. Something about her calmed the waves in my stomach.

"What'll it be tonight, young blood?" she asked with a smile.

"Whoa, hold on," I exclaimed with pause. "What in the hell is going on here?"

She laughed. "It's good to see you again, Ryan," she said.

"I mean it. What the hell is going on?" I stammered, looking at the countertop and back to Ellie. "And look at you, what is your secret?" I asked, dragging out the words.

"Just breathe, Ry Guy. Here's a gin and tonic. Let's ride that train for a while," she said.

I nodded, forcing a false sense of ease.

Ellie poured my drink, slid it to me, and then took a swig off the bottle. "Don't tell," she said and winked.

"Yeah," I replied with a sneer. How was it possible that this place, that these people could look so much the way I left them a decade or so ago? The question had me scrambling to make sense of my sanity.

"Nothing they can do to you, now," the man to my left said. It was Hank. I was so distracted by seeing Ellie, I didn't even realize he was sitting right there with me, looking not aged by a day since our last night together.

"Goddamn, Hank!" I reached over and shook his hand, surprising myself with my own enthusiasm.

"Goddamn yourself," he chuckled, still grasping my hand. "It's been too goddamned long." He gave my arm another shake.

I surveyed the place from over Hank's shoulder, noticing a cluster of crooked pictures adorning the wall—still not straightened since I last saw them. Out of the corner of my eye, I caught a glimpse of Ellie watching me with a look of warmth and concern. A part of me wished to let my guard down, wished to admit that—despite my questions—it just felt good to be back.

"Alright, let's have a round for Ryan here, a drink in his honor!" a man called from a table in the back.

"Cheers to that," a woman next to Hank said, and took a sip of her beer. She was wearing a green dress that left me feeling unsettled—a reminder of the night when everything unraveled. The resemblance was unsettling.

"Cheers!" Ellie returned.

I sat back firmly on my stool and took a sip from my drink. "I just don't understand any of this," I started. "How did any of you know I'd be here? How do you all look the same?"

"We're just so happy you're finally here with us," Ellie smiled.

Hank nodded after taking a sip from his drink.

"Why is everyone saying that?" I asked with rising tension in my voice.

"C'mon, Ry Guy. Don't be like that. This is your night," the woman in green encouraged.

"My night? I don't have a night." My frustration was building again with every statement that avoided my questions. Nothing made sense—the round of applause, everyone knowing that I'd be here. "How do you know my name?" I asked her. "How does everyone know my name?"

"Poor bloke's confused. Still doesn't know, does he?" a man replied from behind Ellie. He reached for a bottle on the top shelf behind the bar, presenting his back to me. "If he doesn't know, he can't see the world as it is," he continued, reviewing the handwritten label on the bottle in his grip.

"What are you talking about?" I asked.

He turned around and placed the bottle on the counter. Pound for pound and mustache for mustache, it was the man from the picture wiping down the glass; it was Marvin.

"Should someone tell this poor bloke what happened?" he asked.

"This is impossible!" I yelled. "Y-you're impossible," I stuttered in disbelief. The pit of nausea in my stomach rose with immediacy. Something was brewing in my gut and it was just moments away from pouring out of me.

Marvin placed two glasses beside the bottle. "Welcome to my tavern," he said with arms raised, presenting the bar to me.

"Maybe you should tell him," Hank suggested to Ellie.

"You can't be here," I muttered to Marvin, to Ellie—to all of them. The sensation in my stomach continued to churn.

Ellie let out a sigh. "Ryan, Ryan, Ryan," she said after a deep breath.

I stared at her blankly, wondering if I would make it to the bathroom in time to throw up if I had to. Even if I could make it, I decided I'd rather puke all over the countertop than to see a bathroom in Marvin's Tavern ever again. "You can't be here," I repeated.

Marvin poured two drinks from his mystery bottle and pushed one towards me, taking a sip from the one he poured for himself.

"Is the bar closing?" I managed to ask, pushing the drink away. I didn't know where that question came from, but it felt important to ask—otherwise, it was like I had fallen into a spider web.

"We *are* at the end of our lease, I guess you could say," Marvin returned with a laugh. He glanced to Ellie and waited for her to fill in the blanks.

Ellie caught Marvin's gaze and turned back to me. "We hoped the sign might get you to come back," she said. Ellie took a deep breath before continuing. "Do you really want to understand?" she asked.

I nodded. Every part of my body was crawling with dread. This was definitely an oh-so-very-bad idea to come back here. I had officially shipped a werewolf to the moon.

"The last night you were here, you asked me for a special drink. Do you remember that?" she asked.

I nodded.

Marvin pointed to the drink he poured me.

"So, I gave it to you," she explained, "but the drink I made you was a concoction of sorts—something that allows the user to see through time and space. I was trying to break the news to you, hon, because I didn't think you knew."

I couldn't find my words. "Knew w-what?" I choked out.

"Well, that you're dead, hon," she continued.

I gasped for air and could find none. The rush of nausea in my stomach took over and pumped waves of vomit out of my mouth. But it wasn't thick or heavy or acidic; it looked like water.

Marvin snatched my glass away with haste. "This," he said, "would've helped with that." An air of disappointment stood out in his voice.

"I'm sorry, Ryan," offered the woman in the green dress.

"But, but–" I stammered between bouts of heaving, looking to Hank.

"Yeah, Ryan. When you were out on the lake," Hank started, "I think you drowned." He put his hand on my shoulder and nodded quietly.

A trail of water drooled from the corner of my mouth.

"My tavern is for the dead. You can't find it unless you've already passed on," Marvin explained. His words pulled the wind from my lungs. The lights above the bar wavered and burst with a blast of electricity, forcing me to shield my eyes from the raining broken glass. I turned back to Marvin; his neck looked like it had bent and broken sideways. He watched me from an impossible angle and smiled. "It burned down after the bottle bomb in the '20s," he continued. His voice was strained and pressured, attempting to speak at his contorted angle.

I turned my gaze to look back at Ellie. Her smile and warm cheeks were replaced by divots in her skin and gaping holes of missing flesh. I gasped and fell off of my bar stool. As I hit the ground, the entire tavern devolved again. It was charred and black, and it smelled of death. Water, again, welled up into my throat and mouth.

"Old places like this, the Muslin curtains over the windows, they burn quick and easy," Marvin continued. "No fire escapes, no emergency lighting, just a bunch of burning people trying to pull open a jammed front door with bodies blocking the way." He struggled to make his voice heard through his crooked neck.

The top of the bar cracked and fell to the ground with a thud, sending smoke and ash into the air. I scrambled backwards on the floor and pushed away from them. Ellie was riddled with bullet holes and missing pieces of her body.

I crawled backwards and bumped into a man at a table. He looked down at me with a grotesque smile, his teeth pressed through bubbling and decayed skin that hung melted over his mouth. "Here, let me give you a hand," he laughed. He extended his hand down to me and it was nothing but burnt bone and tendons. His clothes had welded to his body, making it impossible to identify charred cloth from skin.

"But the people downstairs!" I managed to say. Water ran from my mouth with every word, choking my breath. "They were real!"

"No, honey, not anymore. Not when you were seeing them," Ellie answered. "Places like this, they gather memories of the things that happened, and they like to dwell on them from time to time. I was trying to show you the coven meetings that took place in the cellar during the prohibition years. I wanted to help you make sense of things—of me and my family." Blood sprayed from her mouth with her every word.

"Your family?" I asked through a series of muffled attempts. Water pooled in my mouth and nose.

Marvin put his arm around Ellie's vibrant corpse. "This is my Beth," he explained.

"Ellie is short for Elizabeth, Ry Guy," she replied. "And the memory of this place that I was showing you was *that night*. I wanted you to see. I wanted you to know!"

I looked back to Hank on his bar stool. His beard was scorched, and his skin hung from his body like loose sheets drying in the wind. "It's true," he said. His eyes looked as if they had boiled in his skull and dripped down his cheeks.

"What night?!" I wanted to scream but couldn't get enough air into my lungs. I scooted myself back into another table and knocked a pile of bones to the floor. Footsteps approached from behind; it was the skinless man without ears from the basement. The muscles in his face pulled to form a smile.

"You met our boy, Maurice," Ellie went on. "During those prohibition years, after Marvin died, Maurice wanted so badly to have his family back that he found a way to do it! Every night, he hosted coven meetings in the cellar. He gave of his flesh to resurrect his flesh—just like the others taught him to do, you understand?"

Maurice reached his red and fleshy hand down to me to pull me to my feet, but the strength had left my body and I fell back to the floor in my puddle of watery vomit.

"And he kept at it until we could return to him," Ellie

went on. "But, by then," she chuckled, "there wasn't much of him left."

"W-what night?" I stammered again.

"The night Maurice finally succeeded!" Ellie answered. "The night we were *reborn*." A ball of maggots fell forth from one of the holes in her neck. I wanted to shriek but gagged instead.

"Oh, you'll get used to the pain of it," Marvin said in his cracked voice.

"Good to have you with us, Ryan," a voice called out from the front of the bar. It was Ed. He was smashed against the front door where he had been hoisting his beer bottle only moments ago. Burnt bodies littered the ground around him and on top of him.

"We didn't mean for you to find out like this," the woman in the green dress said. She stood and approached from behind Maurice. The skin was missing from her entire body. "I'm sorry, Ry," she offered.

I crawled to my feet and attempted to worm my way across the ash-laden ground towards the door. With every effort, the door seemed to stretch further away.

"How do you know my name?!" I choked through mouthfuls of water. "Why me?!"

The skinned lady continued towards me, wincing as her vulnerable flesh made contact with ash floating through the air. Maurice joined her, both of them standing side by side in front of me.

"She's your mom," Ellie explained. "She and Maurice, they're your parents. But the government took you away from her when they found out about some of the things she did." Ellie paused and smiled revealing her blood-stained teeth. "But we wouldn't let them keep you from us forever, Ryan. We're your family."

"Once you found us, we were finally all together. And it was so good to be all together, Ryan! Wasn't it? We waited here for you for so long." Ellie looked fondly to Maurice. "But then you left us, and we were so afraid that you were going to find the light—that you might leave us for good." She frowned with blood-stained lips.

"I didn't worry, Ryan," Marvin grinned. "The men in our family, nah—there's no light for us."

"We had to keep our doors open while we waited for you to come back," Ellie continued. "We are a respite for the dead, and we wouldn't close our doors before you returned to us." She motioned to the bar around us. "As you can see, it was getting so crowded." Corpses and bodies riddled the entire tavern in piles—disembodied heads enmeshed with the rotten limbs of man, animal, and insect, alike. "You're here, and you won't leave us now, Ryan. You can't find the light here."

"I'm not dead!" I called out between gasps for air. "I'm not dead," I repeated. Water splashed to the ground from my mouth as I turned to crawl towards the door again, but it moved back with every motion I made towards it. "Why are you keeping me here?! I'm not dead!" I choked again.

"You are, Ryan," Ellie answered.

I looked down at my body drenched with lake water—bloated, soft, and full. "But—" I started.

"We all are," Ellie said, motioning to the corpses throughout the tavern. Maurice, the skinless woman in the green dress, and Marvin joined Ellie behind the bar where they stood in their states of morbid decay. "And in death," she said through her bloodied grin, "our family can finally be together—forever."

CORPSE FOREST
BY JULIE HINER

Afterlife

Voices whispered through Willy's ears, the haunting tones crawling their arctic fingers down her spine. Imaginary threads sewed her eyes shut. Her sacral senses pulsed. She didn't know where she was, but she knew she wasn't in her sunny apartment. The last thing she remembered was the knife, held by her own trembling hand, slicing into her neck, and the hot gush of blood that followed.

The whispers intensified, kissing her earlobes, whipping into her ears, weaving through her insides. Words escaped from the blended sound of dozens of phantom voices melded into one.

Escape.

Suffer.

Afraid.

Slice.

Maim.

Kill.

Willy gritted her teeth and squeezed her eyes tighter. She inhaled deeply. The Drakkar Noir remnants of her last one-night stand had been replaced by rot and decay. Where was she? Why was she here? If she looked, would it all become real?

A tear tore free from the corner of Willy's eye, slithering down her chapped cheek. The whisper of a child told her he'd taken his own life. Was this the afterlife of those who stopped their own beating hearts?

A young voice separated from the melting pot of pleas. "I'm here because I took Mommy's pills. I saw her do it. I wanted to sleep, too. I couldn't take another belt lash to my back. I just couldn't."

Then, she belonged here. But did they know the truth about her?

She swallowed hard against the fear clawing up the inside of her throat. She knew she had to look.

Taking a deep breath, she forced open her eyelids. Locks of chocolate curls obscured her vision. She lifted her pale arm, the skin thin and rotting. She brushed her hair from her eyes. Nothing could have prepared her for this.

Putrefied corpses swung back and forth, each wearing a coat of translucent flesh over skeletal frames of black bones. Charcoal trees loomed, dripping with silver witch hair. A purple-blue hue painted the entire forest, as far as Willy could see. Rotting remains hung from tree after tree with no clearing in sight.

Her eyes darted along the never-ending collage of hollow faces. Empty eye sockets filled with dark space reached for her. In unison, the pairs of black caverns widened, thousands of small, skeletal hands sprouting from deep inside. The sea of bony fingers swam toward her, prying her mouth open until her skin split across her face and pain seared through her skull. Rough nails raked down her throat, scraping her insides in their frantic search. Her screams stifled in the stern of her jaw.

Her mind exploded in a rant, yelling at the hanging carcasses, "What do you want?"

The sighs amplified, echoing around her. In a flash, the hands retracted in a single slice from her gut to her lips. Her insides stretched, then collapsed against her bones. Thousands of murmurs blended into one solitary soft voice like a winter breeze. "Why are you here?"

She looked across the ghost faces, the explanation of each fate clear from the unhealed wounds. A pair of wrists slit deep, an unending red river running from them. A hole blasted through a skull, exposing a mess of pink-red brain-blood mush. A winding rope mark burned into a neck in purple, black and sickly yellow lines.

The kid. The one who had whispered to her, swung from his tree, his insides transparent, a pile of pills stacked in his stomach. His face blue, his eyes black, his skin pallid.

Willy licked her lips and swallowed. Two drops of saliva forced their way down her parched palate.

She spoke, her voice raspy and weak. "I sliced my throat."

It wasn't a lie, but it wasn't the whole truth either. The knife reappeared in her trembling fingers as she relived the horror of her self-inflicted end. Pain shot across her face as she poked the tip of the knife into her skin. Her hand guided the handle across her neck, the blade slicing a thick slit into her flesh. Blood poured over her hand, down her chest, soaking her ivory negligee. Terror pierced every organ. She pulled her hand away and looked at her shaking arm, the bath of blood, and the shiny silver blade. Her scarlet-soaked nightdress stuck to her skin.

"Why?" the kid-corpse inches from her whispered.

She jolted. How did he get there?

How could she answer that question? Did any of them know the truth? Was this a test?

The ghost with the slashed wrists materialized closer to her. A woman with long, dark hair. She whispered, "I cut my wrists and bled to death. I couldn't take one more day in the depths of loneliness." An empty hole opened in the woman's stomach, stretching into a dark and bottomless well.

White light shimmered as the ghost woman vanished. The man with a smoking hole in his skull glared at Willy, inches from her face. Brain matter mixed with blood floated through the air around him. His deep voice echoed off the trees. "I pulled the trigger. One single shot to end the pain. I watched my child die. A sickness took her. I couldn't take the constant pain any longer."

A flash of pink light as the ghost man vanished. A third appeared. The young woman with a winding purple-black mark around her neckline. "I hung myself. I couldn't take one more needle." She turned her arm, exposing a collage of blood-tipped punctures. Toxic fluid seethed through her veins, bubbling her skin.

A blue haze took the rope-marked woman. The kid ghost full of glowing pills appeared. His cold breath sliced Willy's cheeks as he blew a whisper, "Why?"

Willy froze. What could she do? These others—these ghosts—their reasons for taking their own lives all seemed... justified.

The icy breath cut her cheeks again. "Why?"

"I couldn't go on one more day." The dryness in her

throat smothered her words into a croak. It wasn't a lie. It was a partial truth.

The small face of the kid ghost inched closer to her. "Why?"

She stared into his dark, cavern eyes. Hands of fear wrenched her heart. Her voice barely audible, she said, "I was afraid. Every day. I couldn't live with the fear."

The faces stared. The kid vanished, then reappeared, hanging again from his tree. No more whispers. No more stares. All the spirits seemed satisfied with her answer. They hung still, their void eyes staring vacantly into nothing.

The knife sat in Willy's blood-soaked fingers. Her red-stained negligee clung to her thighs, heavy and wet. Her neck throbbed. Fingers of pain wove through her face and down her arms. Sickness swirled in her stomach at the realisation that this was her end. Would she hang here forever, swaying back and forth, soaked in blood and pulsing with pain? No relief had come when she slit her own flesh. At least not for her. Maybe she had spared others. How many would she have hurt?

She hung. She swayed. Her mind numb, her body shivered in cold blood.

Cycle of Whispers

THE CORPSES SWUNG GENTLY BACK and forth from the tall, dark trees. The bruised hue of the forest clouded Willy's vision. The ghost whispers followed a cycle. As if on cue, their mouths moved, their eerie voices echoing off the trees, winding deep into the pit of Willy's ears. She couldn't tune it out. Cries of pain seeped through her for what felt like an eternity until they finally wound down and the forest became silent again.

If she mustered up the energy to whisper her own plea, the phantom voices would muffle and the knives of pain slicing through her would ease to a dull rub. As soon as she stopped, the voices swirled through her mind, contorting her brain and seizing her skull. Pain sliced through every part of her body, amplified with each sway.

She forced her cracked, cold lips to move. The desert in her throat filtered her voice to a raspy whistle. The half-truth of the reason for her arrival in the corpse forest dripped from her lips on repeat.

"I am here because I slit my throat. I bled to death. I couldn't take it one more day. I was afraid."

As the last word seeped from her lips in a slow crawl, a deep sigh sunk through her. The thought of hanging from the tree, silent and swaying was a welcome image. She longed for a deep sleep—to no longer hear, see, *feel*. Even the slightest pause between the end and the beginning of her next script claiming her spot in this corpse-laden forest resulted in the first knife slicing her inside. She chose the grueling rewind and repeat of her cry over the over-whelming pain of a thousand blades.

She wanted to tell the whole truth. A desire swelled within her to spill out every detail—not just of why she was here, but of why she had taken her own life. Maybe if they knew, she would be spared the pain. Could she be allowed to rest if she released a full confession? She clung to a tiny granule of hope that this was possible. Yet, something deep in the bowels of her gut told her if she vomited the words of truth, a fate far worse than a whispered plea on repeat would befall her. Unsure of the outcome, she stuck to what she knew, whispering to numb the pain.

A crack in her bottom lip split suddenly. A warm drizzle of fresh blood trickled down her chin. Did it hurt? She wasn't sure. Her mind was numb, her motions robotic, her ghost body heavy with exhaustion, all her focus on her lips to keep them moving.

After an eternity on the clock of death, the haunting murmurs faded. Silence descended. The blue tinge waned. The forest turned black. The ghosts took their hiding spots behind the cloak of night.

Willy succumbed, entering the sleep of the dead, in which there was nothing but pitch-black and silence.

~

Mittens

THE GHOST BOY materialized a mere inch from her face. Willy jerked. She was on edge, unable to get used to the barrage of surprises in the forest of corpses.

The kid's blue lips moved, his cold breath leaving icicles across her face. "Why are you here?"

Willy swallowed, saliva slipping through the slit in her throat and drizzling down her neck. "I am here because I slit my throat."

"But, why?" the boy enquired.

"Because I was afraid."

The empty eye sockets of the dead boy swirled, black, purple, blue. A small hand reached out of one of the cosmic caverns. Long, bony fingers grasped for Willy's face. She flinched. The skeleton hand missed her face, stretched out over her head, and pierced her skull. The hand plunged straight through her brain, the bony fingers scraping against her gray matter, causing a painful itch. Her body juddered. Her mind froze. The bone fingers scratched and scraped, then stopped. They wrapped around a series of neurons and squeezed. She gasped. The corpse forest vanished.

Soft grass tickled her bare knees. Warm sun baked her face. Soft fur grazed her fingers. She looked down at her hands. Her stomach clenched as the puzzle pieces clicked together. She was back on her childhood street. It had been a long time since she'd been back here. She stared at the small, brown kitten settled into the palms of her hands.

It purred, a vibration buzzing through her arms. A tiny *mew* escaped from its mouth. Mittens. Missy Wilton's new pet. Missy had lived three doors down from her. Missy with her perfect blonde hair that always shone and her pretty pink dresses with matching shoes. Willy stared down at Mittens.

Willy tightened her grip, finding the kitten's neck with her fingers. She wrenched the tiny neck. Bones cracked. Raspy gasps seeped through Mitten's tiny mouth.

The kitten went limp.

Willy set it on the warm grass. She slipped a pocketknife from her back pocket and clicked it open. The blade slid into the fur and through the warm skin with little resistance. She pulled the knife down the length of the small, limp body. Warm blood spurted over the kitten, matting its fur. Willy wiped the knife on the grass, snapped it shut, and slid it back into her pocket. She stared at the slimy organs, wondering what they would taste like. Her mouth watered.

Snapped from her post-mortem reverie by the voice of

her mother, she listened to the dinner call. "Wilhelmina! *Wilhelmiiina!* Dinner time."

She looked down at the bloody carnage. A drop of terror trickled through her. What had she done? What was wrong with her? She abandoned her fresh kill and sprinted home.

Mid-run, her childhood street vanished. Pain sliced through her. She swung back and forth, from her tree, in the corpse forest.

The dead boy floated in front of her. The hand retracted from her brain and returned inside the dead boy's empty eye socket. His dark eyes stared into her. He knew about Mittens. Is that all he knew?

In a flash, the dead boy was back, hanging from his tree. Willy pondered what this all meant. What was he searching for? Did he want to know the truth about her? If he found out, would she be sent somewhere even worse than this morbid forest of swaying skeletons? Could it get worse than this? The ball of fear in the pit of her gut told her it could.

She could still hear the cracking of Mittens' bones as she wrenched its little neck. Missy was a mess when she found poor Mittens dead and slit open, lying in a pool of blood on the grass in her backyard. Missy cried in horror, putting on quite a show. She wouldn't calm down until she was bribed with a new pink dress. How many pink dresses could one little girl own?

Despite Willy's jealous jabs at Missy, something sick swirled in Willy's stomach when she thought of Missy's terror-stricken face.

No one had suspected Willy. She'd always been a well-behaved little girl. She'd been discreet with her un-girl-like tendencies. Even more so as they followed her into adulthood. Poor Gerald, living five houses down, was the target of blame for Mittens' unfortunate end. Gerald had always been weird. He was jittery and stared at the other kids like a creep. Willy knew there wasn't anything actually wrong with Gerald. He wasn't... like her.

When Gerald was questioned about Mittens, his anxiety got the better of him and he froze up. His lack of response was interpreted as guilt, and he was sent away to a specialist for assessment.

Something had washed through Willy that day when Gerald was sent away. A dark weight in her stomach. Did she feel bad Gerald was gone? Was she sad Missy was so upset? She didn't know. But she wanted to tell someone what really happened to Mittens. She had walked down the stairs into the kitchen and found her mom baking chocolate chip cookies. When she opened her mouth to confess to the one who would nurture her no matter what, something clicked in her brain.

She couldn't remember what happened next. There was a period of nothing. Then, next thing she knew, she was sitting at the kitchen table with a warm chocolate chip cookie in one hand, and a cold glass of milk in the other. What had she said to her mother? She'd never know. She'd been too afraid to ask.

Acid-laced bile swam in her stomach. Why did she have to relive all of this? She took that knife to her own flesh so she could end it. No one had told her that, when you died, you didn't die. You became something else. Swaying back and forth from her tree, she'd morphed into a skeletal ghost coated in her own blood, her self-inflicted wound searing in never-ending pain.

Lindsay

THE DEAD BOY'S twin abysses explored Willy. His cold whispers chilled her cheeks. "Why?"

She racked her brain for the right words. Why did she take a knife to her own flesh? Because she was scared of what would happen if she didn't. He wanted to know more. The holes of his nothing eyes spun in a swirl of red, orange, yellow, and purple. Before she could say a word, a little hand reached skeletal fingers through the kaleidoscopic grotto.

The bony fingers pierced her skull again. This exploration was rougher than the last one—fingers of hard bone sliced into her brain matter, sending sharp spikes of pain through her.

The corpse forest vanished. A forest of firs engulfed her, tall and green, spattered in fresh pine cones. She trotted along, pine needles crunching under her sneakers. Wafts of citrus swirled around her. The knife in her back pocket pressed against her.

A girl with long, red hair skipped along in front of her. Her heart froze. Lindsay. The only best friend she'd ever had. This wasn't right. Why did she have to relive this? Why did they want to know?

Lindsay chirped over her shoulder, "How much further?"

Willy heard herself respond, unable to stop what she knew would happen. "Just around the next turn."

The sun bathed the circular clearing. Willy sat next to Lindsay, both cross-legged. Willy reached out, taking Lindsay's soft fingers in her own.

"Close your eyes," Willy said.

No. Don't show me. Willy searched for the sapphire

mouth. The dead boy was nowhere. She screamed to be back in the corpse forest.

A soft vibration moved through her throat as she sang to Lindsay. Lindsay smiled, her eyes closed.

Willy couldn't control the words slipping from her lips.

"Lindsay, Lindsay, lovely Lindsay."

She placed Lindsay's hands together, resting them in her lap.

"How does your garden grow?"

Willy slipped the knife from her pocket and clicked it open without a sound.

"With blue bells and cockleshells, and Lindsay lying in a row."

That last word wrapped its death fingers around her heart. She tried to protest.

Her hand shot out, stabbing the knife into Lindsay's heart. Scarlet syrup seeped over her hand.

Lindsay's eyes popped open in shock and disbelief.

A click echoed through Willy's mind. She expected the blackout to come, like it had on that day. The sun shone bright, the green trees stood in place. The blackout didn't come. Instead, something washed over her, seething, an animal-like instinct through her veins.

Lindsay found her voice and cried out in terror.

Willy stared at her with curiosity. In a sudden movement, Willy flung herself over Lindsay and mounted her. Lindsay fell hard against the ground. Tears welled around her eyes. Her lips trembled.

Willy pulled the knife from Lindsay's heart, flesh tearing and blood pouring. Turning the knife and positioning her hand above Lindsay's neck, she plunged again. The blade slid into Lindsay's neck.

A fresh burst of blood sprayed over Willy's face. She

licked the liquid from the corner of her mouth. A tang of copper clung to the back of her tongue. Pulling the blade down, she tore Lindsay open from neck to navel. Lindsay's eyes went glassy, her cries simmering to a slight whimper.

Lindsay's chest rose and fell. The movements became more subtle until there was stillness. Small organs wet with fluid were exposed as Willy pulled away skin in two large flaps.

Her brain clicked.

A flash. The carcasses hung, staring at her with their empty eyes.

Willy's stomach churned. Digestive juices clawed up her throat. She swallowed hard against the vile revolt. The dead boy hovered as the hand retracted back into his eye socket.

"Why?" she muttered. "Why are you forcing me back there?"

The blue lips remained nothing more than a thin line. The boy vanished.

Willy's mind raced. Her temples throbbed. Why couldn't she just be a ghost hanging here in forever-pain for the wounds she had inflicted upon herself? Why did she have to relive what she knew she was but fought not to become?

Steamy, salty tears trickled down her face. Her nightdress was now crusty with caked blood. The slice in her neck was gooey and throbbing.

Lindsay. She'd never lived what she'd done to Lindsay. Until now. On that day, as soon as she'd stuck the knife into Lindsay's heart, she'd heard the click in her brain, and she'd blacked out. When the light returned, she was covered in blood, hovering over Lindsay's gutted body. She ran to the river and swam in the clear water until she was clean. She threw her knife in a dumpster in a back alley on the outskirts of the park. She ran all the way home and pretended to be napping when her mother came in from the grocery store. How she knew to do all these things, she wasn't sure. All she knew was she'd stabbed Lindsay, blacked out, and woken to a scene from a slasher movie.

Wasn't it enough that she had taken her own life to end it? Wasn't it enough she was here, a swinging ghost under the scrutiny of the bottomless black eyes of a dead boy?

Was she the only one afraid to tell the truth, clinging to this horrific reality in fear of a worse one? She wished she could sprout a skeleton hand out of her own eye socket and examine each and every one of the scraggy figures hanging around her. She closed her eyes, dug deep inside, and searched. To her surprise, she could see inside of herself. She took an internal tour, scanning down her oesophagus, over her still heart, her translucent lungs, and her empty intestines. There it was. A bone hand, nestled beside her kidney. She focused her mind, concentrated, and willed it to move. The skeleton fingers twitched. Her scalp tightened. She sent neurological nudges to the twitching bone fingers. The hand flung up inside of her, out of her eye socket, and toward the blue boy. His corpse body seized as the hand pierced the top of his head.

A glimmer of light produced a vision. The young boy, in a small kitchen, holding a syringe in his hand. Droplets of clear fluid created small ripples in a circle of brown, housed by a floral teacup. A discarded tea bag, labeled orange spice, lay on the countertop.

A sweet voice trickled down from an upstairs bedroom. "Timmy. Is my tea ready?"

The boy looked up from his task. "Almost, Momma."

"Thank you, dear."

A yellow flash followed by the piercing cavern eyes of the corpse boy. Willy's hand retracted. The blue-lipped boy stared. She returned his glare, refusing to flinch. He had his own secret. He wasn't an innocent child. Willy could see it all—the droplets of poison, the sick mother in bed, the guilt that led him to swallow all those pills.

The boy returned to his tree. Her brain settled at the realization that she wasn't the only one whispering half-truths.

The silence of the forest drowned all else. The ghosts swayed back and forth, sending an icy breeze through her bones. The dark-blue hue dimmed into complete darkness.

Serpent

THE FOREST of hanging corpses vanished. Black nothingness cloaked Willy. Where was she going now? Thick silence clung to the cold air. Her breath pierced the dark in a white puff as she exhaled. The soft cloud vaporized before her eyes. Heat broiled her skin. The sun seared her eyes. Her feet sunk into hot sand. A vast desert opened up around her. The cry of an eagle shot through the silence.

Something scintillated, right in front of her. A small man walked along a dirt trail, black hair slicked back from his tanned face. Ahead of him, two young women wearing backpacks and sturdy boots chatted as they trekked. He approached them. They stopped to consider him. Willy couldn't hear what they were saying. She could only watch from where she floated, a phantom imposed on a desert scene.

A flicker of worry in her gut told her something was off.

Digging into his own pack, the man produced two cans of pop, cold droplets sprouting over the tins. The girls licked their lips as they reached for the refreshing gifts. Two snaps echoed through the silent desert followed by the hiss of carbonation escaping into the hot, dry air.

Willy watched as the girls tilted the cans to their mouths, gulping back the welcome liquid relief. They chatted with cheery voices to their new-found friend. A minute later their smiles turned to worried frowns. They dropped the cans into the sand, the moisture mixing with dry granules into a dark paste.

The girls fell to their knees. The man hovered over them. The blonde-haired girl crawled away until the immobility climbing up her legs reached her arms. The brown-haired girl froze in fear, clawing at her face. Blondie fell back against the sand, desperate wails seething from her pink lips.

What was happening? Willy looked down at her hands, the pale skin flaking away from her bones. She was still dead. Were these hikers ghosts, too? Why were they so scared if they were already dead? She thought of all the fear that had stricken her since she had died. Were they reliving their own horrific ends?

A tornado of questions whirled her mind into a haze. She longed to be surrounded by the corpses swaying from black trees. At least that made sense to her.

Hot air circled around her as the desert shimmered. The man hovered over the paralysed blonde girl. His skin peeled away from his face, exposing viridescent scales. Terror shot through Willy. She shook her head, silently crying, "No, no, no." She couldn't watch any more of this.

A translucent layer stripped away from the man's lips. A long, pink tongue slithered from his mouth, the end split in two prongs. Hissing drowned out the panicked cries of the blonde and the brunette. Cold crawled through Willy despite the desert heat. Her still heart came to life, beating hard against her skeleton chest.

The epidermis husked from the man in one long strip down his arms and legs. Shedding all that made him human, he became a massive serpent, sliding easily over the sand toward his helpless prey. Willy trembled, begging to be returned to the corpse forest.

A click rang through her head. The switch had moved to *on*. The blackout didn't come. Willy's body stilled. Her mind cleared.

The reptile weaved over the sand, circling around the girl. Its thick, scabrous physique wrapped around the girl's neck, winding itself down the girl in a death coil. Bones cracked.

Willy's arms tingled with electric energy. Her dead heart beat with excitement. The girl's screams competed with the hissing of the two-pronged tongue. The scaly body tightened its grip, suppressing the shrill cries into mere whimpers. The girl wheezed her last few breaths, then went limp. Willy's brain buzzed as she licked her lips.

The serpent unwrapped itself and slithered in circles around its kill. The brunette, still alive, whimpered. Large fangs were exposed as the mouth of the viper stretched wide. Scaly lips wrapped around the girl's blonde curls. Flesh punctured as the fangs bit into the girl's neck.

Bones crunched and crackled as blood oozed over the pale skin. A metallic tang clung to the back of Willy's tongue as if she were the one feasting on the girl. Her stomach growled. Her arms tingled. Was this what it would be like if she didn't black out?

The serpent worked its way down the length of the body, swallowing its meal in digestible chunks.

Could the man-serpent see her? Would he come for her? No. She knew he wouldn't. The familiar click echoed through her mind. The switch went off. Fright coursed through her veins. Her stomach churned. What had happened to her?

Charcoal trees etched into the dark background. Her eyes darted across the swaying figures. The ghosts were quiet. She settled into the lull of swinging back and forth, home again in the corpse forest.

Wolf

A WHISPER WOKE Willy from her corpse sleep. Blue lips floated in front of her face. "You have to choose."

The silhouettes of black trees gleamed as they vanished. A quiet street appeared. Willy floated in the cold dark of the night. A streetlight buzzed as the dim bulb blinked off and on. A young woman walked down the street, puffed up in a winter coat, a thick woolen scarf wrapped around her head.

Willy exhaled. White vapor misted the night air, little icicles forming around her lips. A voluminous moon hung high in the ink sky, casting a silver glow.

The woman walked briskly along the sidewalk. Willy hovered and watched.

A police cruiser rolled up the street. The car pulled alongside the curb, next to the young woman as she passed under the broken streetlamp. The window on the passenger side rolled down. A deep voice echoed through the quiet. "Can I offer you a ride, miss?"

Worry writhed through Willy. Something was off. Again. This was going to be another scene she didn't want to watch.

The woman climbed into the police cruiser. The car pulled away from the curb and drove on down the dark street.

Willy's stomach churned. The switch in her head moved to *on*, sending a loud click through her. The click was louder than usual and had a tone of finality. Worry evaporated from her pores, leaving a concoction of excitement and electricity coursing through her veins.

A cloud of white, frosty mist floated over the dark street. As it dissolved, the police cruiser rolled by a small, brown house. Willy could hear the young woman protesting from inside the vehicle. "Officer, my house is right there."

The officer remained silent.

The cruiser gained speed. A dark forest appeared, looming over the small car. Not a single soul, dead or alive, was in sight.

The cruiser rolled into the forest, bouncing along a rough, dirt road. The panic-laced pleas of the young woman intensified. The tingling in Willy's stomach crawled through her, down her legs and into her arms.

The cruiser stopped at the side of the dirt road, under a massive tree. The door on the driver's side opened. The officer emerged, unfurling to his full stature. He casually strolled over to the passenger door.

A rattling echoed through the silence as the young woman frantically worked at the door handle. The officer leaned over and looked into the window at his frightened catch. He slid a key into the lock and turned it with a *click*.

He opened the door and grabbed the woman by her rich, red hair.

Willy's fingers tingled.

The officer yanked the woman from the car by a handful of ruby locks and dragged her along the dirt. Her boots shuffled awkwardly over rocks as she tried to gain control. They approached the massive tree stretching over the police cruiser. The officer smashed the young woman's skull into the rough bark. A sound rung through the forest, pinging off the trees. A sound like no other Willy had ever heard.

The crunch of thick bone mixed with the tear of hair from scalp. A shiver of delight trickled down Willy's spine, one vertebra at a time. Her arms shook in anticipation. The switch in her head hammered *on.*

Ruby hair streaked with dark crimson flew through the air in wild chunks. Flesh-brain jam oozed over the exposed skull as the officer smashed the woman's head over and over into the solid trunk. The woman's manic cries crawled up Willy's insides, fueling the adrenaline-soaked blood pumping through her veins.

All those memories that were blacked out throughout her life at the click of a switch—would she be able to live them all, now? She supposed it had been a defense mechanism of some sort. She couldn't handle what she did, so her mind took over and shut her out. Now, she'd never felt so alive, watching the horrific demise of an innocent being.

How could she go back to the pain of her self-inflicted wounds and constant whisper of a lie as she swayed back and forth in the corpse forest?

The woman lay limp on the dirt ground. The officer stood tall, hands raised, head tilted back, face turned to the celestial sphere high in the night sky, black strips of cotton clouds seeping through the silver glow. He shimmered as he changed. His lips peeled back into a snarl as long, razor-sharp teeth grew from the sides of his mouth. His nose protruded into a long snout, his nostrils sticky with mucus. His chest heaved with muscles, ripping his officer's uniform free.

The pin holding the golden badge to his shirt snapped. The badge hit the pebbly ground with a tinny echo. Thick, black fur sprouted over his skin. His fingernails grew into shiny ivory claws. He crawled to the woman on all fours. Saliva dripped in thick drops from his mouth as his lips stretched wide and he plunged his snout toward the fresh meat. A ferocious feast of flying flesh ensued, blood drowning his face and matting the thick, black tufts of fur.

An ocean of saliva swelled in Willy's mouth. She longed to savor a slab of buttery fat melting on the back of her tongue.

Sharp fangs bit into warm flesh. Blood oozed over chunks of human meat. Willy's teeth nattered, pulling her to the fresh kill. Rooted to her spot, floating over the dark forest, a mere spirit, she couldn't move.

She watched. She waited. The desire within her mounting. What was she?

A flash of light as the dark forest vanished and the hanging carcasses returned. She was home. Or, at least, what she'd called home since she sliced herself open.

The dead boy hovered, frowning. He blew icicles over her face as he spoke. "You have to choose."

Willy hung and swayed. She waited for the switch, but it didn't click.

～

Willy

WILLY STARED at each hollow face, pondering the fates of all the others who had ended their lives by their own hands. The corpse forest was dark. If she concentrated hard enough, stared long enough at one skeletal face, her eyes would adjust, and she could make out the wounds.

She knew they were sleeping—or, at least, as close to sleeping as the dead could get. They were still, their swaying halted for the period of time deemed to be night in this death realm. She homed in on the man with the smoking hole in his head. He'd said he put a bullet through his skull to stop the pain of watching his daughter die of a sickness. Had his pain really stopped? She looked at the mess of brains and blood, a thick goo oozing over his bony skull. Her mouth watered.

Since she'd been back from the visit to the ice-cold night where she watched the policeman morph into a savage beast and feast on a young woman with luscious red hair, the switch in her head hadn't clicked back to *off*. Had she made the choice the ghost boy told her she had to make? Is that why she was still *on*?

All she knew was that she was no longer afraid. She stared into the hole, looking straight into the man's brain. She relished the thought of devouring the pink, meaty mush spilling out from the wound in his head.

A longing to uncover the secret behind the smoking hole overtook her.

She closed her eyes and looked within herself, finding the bone hand once again. Gathering a ball of neurons in her mind, she willed the electrical sphere to jolt the skeletal fingers to life. The bone hand twitched. It surged through her, shooting from her eye socket directly into the smoking hole of the man's brain.

Yellow light pulsed. An image of the man, his brains intact and safely housed within his unblemished skull, showed him peering into a dark closet. A small girl in a stained nightgown pulled her knees to her chest, pressing her back into the corner of the tiny space. Her head twitched. Her teeth chattered. Tears stained her cracked cheeks. The door slammed.

The yellow light pulsed, producing a second image. The young girl, motionless, on a gurney, her pretty pink night gown stained with red. The man watched, tears trickling down his face, mixing with saliva dribbling from his mouth. A police officer wrenched the man's arms behind his back and secured his wrists in tight metal cuffs.

The yellow light faded. The dark trees of the corpse forest became vivid. Now, Willy knew the secret of the man with the smoking hole in his head. He'd taken his daughter's life. He was the sickness that stifled her last breath.

The bone hand retracted from the smouldering hole and settled beside Willy's kidney.

She swept her gaze across the corpses and found the woman with the slit wrists. She recognized her by her long, dark hair. It took a few moments until she could make out the details of the body, hanging, dead, asleep. The constant crimson river ran from the open gashes in each of the pale wrists. Willy swallowed against the dryness in her throat, longing for the soothing sapidity of an ore-tinged moist merlot.

Her stomach grumbled. Her mouth parched, her stomach empty, she longed for a real meal.

Her pain had numbed. A deep longing swelled within her.

If she had chosen, where would she go? Would she be able to sate her needs? She had no idea what would be ahead—in door number two. The urges within her were building as every moment passed, and her desire to satisfy them was driving her wild.

A whoosh whipped through her ears and ice cold hit her cheeks. The dead boy materialized out of nowhere, hovering close to her face. His whispers were colder than ever, leaving a crust of ice over her skin. "You have chosen."

The ice breath of the blue-lipped boy clouded around Willy. The corpse forest vanished.

Was she ready? Panic filled her. It was too late.

～

Epilogue: Raptor Morphosis

THE ICY, dead breath morphed into sweet white plumes. The wails of a rock god vibrated through the electric air. The sweetness of the vapor dissolved, and the room cleared. A pleather-clad man stood up on a stage, his long, raven hair cloaking his face and sticking to his sweat-soaked skin. A steel-studded belt hung low on his sinewy torso, muscles rippled up his abdomen. A scarf woven of glitter danced around his shoulders, clinging to his neck. The odor of barbaric desire clung to the hot air. Savage fans packed in tight, surrounding the stage like a wild herd in heat. She was back in her current life—the one she had taken herself from. Yet, she knew she was still dead.

She scanned the afterlife version of the familiar scene. Animal electricity seethed through Willy's veins. She clung to two glasses, cherries bobbing in the dark liquid. Her favorite sugar-infused, alcoholic concoction.

She stalked through the tightly packed, hot bodies, inspecting the herd. Tall black boots up to her thighs secured her sturdy steps against the liquor-soaked floor. A long, dark cloak flowing over her shoulders amplified her slight stature. The clank of the buckles littering her shiny boots vibrated with the guitar riff seething from the stage. Tight pleather packed her curvaceous legs. Her glossy chocolate hair, wild and teased in a crazed mane, poked into the corners of her eyes.

Working her way through the crazy crowd, she examined each specimen. They looked human. They seemed oblivious.

A shimmer caught her eye. A tall man with dark hair hovered behind a beautiful blonde woman. Glitter shone from her crop top as she pumped her hips to the primal beat. The man's physical being flickered like a fluorescent tube on the brink of burning out. One second he was there, and the next he wasn't.

His materialisation toggled between a human-like man and something out of a horror film. His long fangs protruding from the sides of his mouth hung close to the blonde woman's milky skin at the nape of her neck. His green scales iridescent under the purple-blue light bouncing off the stage.

Willy knew he was like her, in more ways than one. Dead. Ready for a feast. In his serpent-like manifestation, the red glow of his eyes caught her gaze. She nodded and kept moving through the heat of the packed bodies.

All the questions whizzing through her brain as she hung in the corpse forest had dissolved. The pain had vanished.

Drinks in hand, she wormed her way through the broiling bodies. Sweat trickled down her back to the nape of her crack where it clung. She halted her prowl with a stomp of her boot. She saw the one she was seeking. The girl stood two bodies ahead. Soft, bleached-blonde curls wild and free around her face. Tight, acid-washed jeans encasing her shapely legs like a perfectly packed butcher's cut, and a lacy white tank top clinging to her perky breasts. Willy slid up next to the white tank top and lightly bumped the girl's shoulder.

The girl jolted.

Willy coated her voice with sugar. "Oh, I'm sorry. Tight crowd."

The girl blushed. "It's okay."

"Are you alone?" Willy enquired.

"Uh, yeah. My friend was sick, so she had to go home. I didn't want to miss the show."

"Would you like a drink?" Willy held up one of the cherry Coke cocktails.

The girl eyeballed the drinks with suspicion.

"I have an extra. My dick of a date ditched. Hasn't been touched."

The girl smiled. "Oh, that sucks. Sure."

Willy handed the girl a drink. "Great show."

"Yeah. These guys are always so good." The girl smiled sheepishly, her cheeks flushed.

Willy moved to the music, watching the girl out of the corner of her eye. The girl danced and drank her special cherry Coke.

"Are you from around here?" Willy asked.

"Not exactly. I'm stuck."

"Stuck?"

"Oh... are you new here?" Empathy bled from the girl's

eyes.

"Uh, yeah."

The girl placed a hand on Willy's arm. "You know you're... dead?"

"Yeah."

"Yeah. I do."

"You might be stuck, too. When I... died, I kept living my life. But here. I can't seem to get out of this strange world. Crazed monsters appear sometimes. And people disappear."

"Scary."

"Yeah..Always good to have a friend nearby."

"Good idea." Willy took a sip of her drink. "I think I'm stuck too."

The girl nodded. "I've been watching the others. I think we have to be patient. Wait until we move to where we're supposed to be."

Willy pondered the words.

The girl looked back at the stage and kept dancing. After a couple of tracks, she leaned on Willy. "Oh, I'm dizzy."

"It's hot in here. Let's get some air," Willy said.

The girl nodded.

Willy led the bleached-blonde out the door and into the parking lot. The frigid air slapped her cheeks and stung her lungs. Despite the chill, the girl drooped her head and struggled to keep her eyes open. Willy smiled. She mixed the drink perfectly. She guided the girl across the dark parking lot and along a sidewalk.

Across the street, under the dim glow of a streetlamp, a police cruiser slid up alongside the curb. A young woman, wrapped in a woolen scarf, halted her walk through the cold night to lean over and speak to the driver. As the woman climbed into the car, the driver stared out the window. His arctic wolf eyes glared. His chiselled face shimmered, turning from that of a man to that of a savage beast, mucus dripping from his snout, his sharp teeth stained with blood. Another monster of the night on the prowl in this death realm.

A few blocks later, she steered her frail prey onto a dirt trail, into a forest of tall, dark trees.

Willy laid the bleached-blonde down in a circular clearing in the trees. The thick, moist grass left droplets over the goosebumps pricking the girl's arms. The midnight sky twinkled with stars. The bulbous, silver moon cast an eerie glow over the forest.

Willy slid her knife from inside her tall boot, strapped against her thigh. The rhinestones studding the golden handle glimmered in the moonlight. She admired the special tool.

Willy knelt over her catch and moved strands of bleached-blonde hair away from the creamy neck. She wrapped both hands around the heavy, golden handle, and raised the knife over her head. -She drove the knife down into the heart of her prey. The girl's eyes popped open as she gasped. Blood trickled out of the corner of her mouth. Her wild eyes stared as she wheezed.

Willy stood tall, black cloak draping her body, boots rooted into the thick grass.

The dark night spun around her, a crisp whirlwind prickling her skin. She looked down at her body. Her torso shimmered, transparent one second, solid flesh the next. White mist seeped in small clouds around her. The tips of her fingers tingled.

She looked down at her hands. Her fingernails surged into obsidian talons. Her teeth slid down her chin as they protruded from her gums into pointed fangs. The dark cloak fluttered, thin material thickening into a black velvet, hanging heavy from her shoulders. The pleather encasing her legs stretched, ripping open, exposing her meaty flesh. Plumes of feather-like, soft, onyx fur sprouted from her skin.

Animal blood coursed through Willy's veins, broiling her insides. She knelt down over the acid-washed prey. Wrapping a black clawed hand around the golden handle, she pulled the knife from the heart of her kill.

Blood oozed over thin, white cotton, steam rising as the heat of the liquid hit the icy air. A metallic tang taunted Willy's nostrils. Soft wheezing whistled through her ears.

Willy placed the tip of the blade against the creamy neck, and with the utmost precision, sliced a long slit deep enough to sever the windpipe. Wheezing turned to gurgled gasps. Willy's ears perked. She waited for the silence.

With the obsidian shard protruding from her pointer finger, she ripped the limp body from neck to navel. Flesh parted, exposing perfect organs shining with internal fluids, dark and ripe with health. A red bath seeped from inside the carcass, over the pale flesh. Willy swallowed down the rising hunger. Every particle in her body buzzed with life.

She had no idea if this would last. All she knew was that she had declared her choice, to accept who she was. Her afterlife reality turned from constant pain and exhaustion, whispering through cracked, dry lips a half-truth, swaying back and forth in a corpse forest, to a feeling of having all the time in the world to live out her ultimate fantasy.

She'd chosen to escape inflicting pain by slitting her own flesh. She'd chosen to escape the corpse forest by morphing into a night beast of the afterlife.

Were there consequences? She didn't know. Right now, all she cared about was relishing the meal laid out before her. A leisurely moonlight picnic.

WHEELS WITHIN WHEELS

BY DANIEL R. ROBICHAUD

Whathehelljusthappened?

Sensory impressions came in slow. A high-pitched keening, and below that the revving of an engine and a fast *whub-whub-whub*. Tires? Stink of burnt rubber with freshly mown grass. Steering wheel sitting akimbo. A car—he was in a car. Sensation of a belt, tight across lap and chest. A view through shattered windshield: the world turned upside-down and rocking slightly left and right and left again, moving dully like the pendulum on a dying grandfather clock. A single blade of wild grass reached up to tickle his nose. Small chunks of stone sitting over his head. Dust stinging his eyes. Something warm and wet on his face —blood on his hands, oh shit. Cold air on his scalp and neck, warm air blowing on his hands—the first came through the windows, the latter from the vents.

Whatthehelljusthappened?

Peter Ellis shook his head. The ringing in his ears would not quit. Moving foot off accelerator killed the engine and tire-rubbing sounds, thank God. He cocked his head to the left and then the right. Nothing he did turned the world right-side-up again.

One last desperate thought: *Whatthehelljusthappened?*

The clock on the dash glowed blue. Number flipped to five past twelve. Dark outside, so midnight. Midnight? So, he knew *when*. How about the other questions: Why? Where? What?

Answers eased through the panic, but they were broken into pieces the same as Peter's sensory impressions. Accident. Was driving I–75 South. Heading toward... Where? His brain called up south-eastern Michigan geography. So, Troy? No way he was even close to Ferndale and home. It was too dark around here. Some lights, though, off along the expressway. So, that would be Troy. Exit 69, Big Beaver Road —a laugh ever since elementary school. After that, Oakland Mall and 14–Mile Road. Then... a big gap until I–696. Out here, though? North of Troy? Big dark patch of nothing. No, wait. Not nothing. Coming from Rochester. From Oakland University. Memory clicked, and he remembered being at Oakland University for a late study session. He was tired, sure. Accident This was an accident.

No other cars around, though. No drivers. No one asking if he was all right.

Another piece in the memory puzzle appeared for him to turn over in his hands: an animal.

It appeared on the expressway, loping up from the island in the middle. Crossing from the east side to the west. An animal. What kind? Big. Bigger than a stray dog, bigger than a deer. Big as a moose? There were no moose in southern Michigan—those were upstate critters, upper peninsula beasts—but that's what it looked like. No, that was the size. Moose do not have sharp teeth or sleek snouts or powerful shoulders and lean bodies. Moose do not stare down oncoming cars, lips peeling back to unleash streamers of scarlet drool. Not a moose, but big. Animal.

An animal that might still be nearby.

Peter's hands fumbled with the seat belt, found the button, clicked it. It refused to release. He jammed his thumb against it, felt the sudden stinging pain of a bone shifting the wrong way before he heard the muffled crunch. Not from the buckle; that came from his thumb.

GoddammitJesusFuckingChrist! The pain made colors burst in Peter's vision. His hand was a gateway for sensation to come flooding back in. He realized his chest ached. Probably had been since the accident.

He lifted his thumb to see. Broken? Too dark. Too goddamned dark. He kissed the thumb, tasting blood and feeling a bulge where no bulge ought to be. Maybe broken, maybe not.

Something big ducked around the rocks to his left. The animal was nearby, all right. If it was an animal. If he wasn't just imagining things. Sitting upside-down, blood all rushing to his head. He might be seeing things. Sure, that was a comforting thought.

And the animal in the road? The big snarling beast Peter swerved to avoid? Not a hallucination. It was real enough— thus his predicament. It was a bad idea, swerving like that when speeding along at seventy-five, eighty, eighty-five miles per hour. Control of the car all but evaporated. Peter's Toyota Yaris bounded over the drainage ditch, rolled across grass, slammed through the fence.

What if it wasn't an animal to begin with. Then, what? Some twisted Devil's Night prank? Crazy jerk in a weird costume? Must have a death wish, come loping into the expressway like that. Maybe a robot or something. Automated. Kids in the weed with grins and an RC controller, antenna pointed toward their sick homeschool science project. That would be weird, huh?

Well, this was the place for weirdness. He was north of Troy, up by that White place. White Chapel. A cemetery for goodness sake! Wasn't that just the place for weirdness? Especially tonight. Wait. Halloween wasn't today. It was Devil's Night, time for the firebugs to go nuts downtown. Time for little devils to do the capital-D Devil's work. Half-remembered lines from a movie sparked him to announce, "All Hallows Eve ain't 'til mañana, crackhead!" His voice was an eerie croak. Besides, the clock rolled from 12:05 to 12:06, begging to differ. Crackheads might be celebrating Devil's Night, but it was officially All Hallow's. Like this mattered.

Must get out of here. Car might be leaking gas. Leaking gas might catch fire. Head might be collecting rushing blood. Collecting blood might damage things that didn't heal so fast or neat. His other hand reached for the button. Less optimal left. It found the buckle, jammed fingers on the button. It was wet and slick and resisting his efforts. Bloody, no doubt. Jesus, I hope I'm not seriously broken. Everything ached now. His knees and his elbows and his chest and his pelvis. Even his damned tailbone.

New sounds: a snuffling. *Shit.* Animal noises, sniffing the air. Smelling the blood. *Don't go shark on me,* Peter thought. Don't go crazy.

In the bent—but not destroyed—side mirror, Peter watched a shape break off from the shadows behind him and lumber toward the car. As it came into clearer focus, he saw naked feet. Bare ankles. Fuzzy legs. The shape hunkered down, knees popping like firecrackers and peeked through the broken windshield.

Mumbles and growls battled his own heart's pounding and the tinnitus. Animal growls. *Animal.* It was right here.

No, this was a man's face. Black man's features. White grin and eyes catching the Yaris' dashboard lights and all but glowing. He grinned there, waiting for a response.

Peter asked, "Huh?"

The stranger pursed his lips and repeated, slow and loud: "Had yourself a spill, huh?"

"Did you see it?" Peter asked in a sudden need to have his hallucination banished or validated. "The animal in the road?"

"You dodge a squirrel or something?" The man clucked his tongue, shook his head. Dreads rustled softly. He tapped the upside-down car's door, saying, "The real, unspoken price of PETA. Save a squirrel, get yourself wrecked." His laugh was almost a huff, a howl.

"Not a squirrel." Hurt to talk. Something was wrong in his throat. Still, he pushed the words out. "Bigger. Ani- *animal*."

The man turned his head in a slow negation. "Nah, man. Didn't see anything like that."

"You're naked."

The stranger wore a sudden expression of surprise and looked down at himself. There was enough light to see a lean body and dangling parts that were usually covered up in public spaces. "So it appears."

Peter forced more words up through his ravaged throat. They barreled over whatever rough patches the accident gave him, catching on sharp corners, losing volume and weight. "Why are you naked?"

"It's a nice night," the stranger said. Then a wicked humor drew his smile up even tighter. "No, wait. Wash day. Nothing clean." At this, he snapped his fingers four quick times.

Wasn't that from a movie, too? Like the crackhead line? Different movie, though.

"I'm trapped," Peter said. "Can you...?"

"Help a brother out?" the stranger asked. He hunkered there, knees wide and dangling bits swaying, grinning and making no move to help.

"Yes. Help."

The stranger stood up, tugged the door until it squealed open. The Yaris' dome light flickered on. A soft pinging alerted Peter the key was in the ignition. In the light, he saw the stranger's ankles and feet. Knicks and cuts and even a keloid.

The wind brought in a fresh stink of exposed car juices and blood. Fresh blood had no smell human could detect. *How long have I been hanging here?* Not long at all. This came from something else.

"Step one, done," the stranger said. "You got a phone?"

"Huh?"

"Call for help, man." He patted his hip. "Mine must've fell out my pocket." His laugh was louder and more hyena like. Animal.

Phone? Phone! Peter's mobile was connected to the radio by cable providing background noise while driving. Tonight, he listened to the Sawbones podcast, weird medical history factoids recounted by a doctor wife and doofus husband. Funny, funny shit. *Find the phone.* Several inches of severed cable hung from the plug and still jammed into the USB jack. The other end? "Where?" He looked, and there it was among the stones on the roof. Not far. He grabbed it, remembering too late his thumb's shape and whined as fresh pain burst in the digit.

"Let me get that for you, man," the stranger said. He

reached in, plucked last year's model iPhone off the roof and studied it. "You got a code?"

"Nah."

The stranger shook his head, tsk-tsk-tsking. "Not very safe to be unsecure these days." He fiddled with the screen, said "Hello, hello?" a couple of times and then shrugged. "Your shit's whack." He twisted at the waist and threw the phone at a headstone. It came apart with a loud crackle. "And the crowd goes wild!" He danced a bit, humming that annoying baseball music.

"The hell you doing?" Peter's hands pawed at the buckle. The belt sagged and he slammed onto the roof. The aches eased. Imagination? No way. Adrenaline flood, maybe. He could not right himself. Peter was stuck in a new contortion.

The stranger stood tall and proud at the edge of the dome light's range. No longer dancing, he stared deeper into the cemetery, head cocked and listening. "Yeah, yeah, yeah," he muttered, "Bitch, bitch, bitch." Then, he glanced back toward the car, his expression confused like he did not recall the mess.

"I was helping you, wasn't I?" the stranger asked. His voice then took on an ugly edge. "Well, let me help you."

The stranger closed the distance between them at a trot, heedless of the broken safety glass and debris he crunched beneath his soles. With one hand, he caught hold of Peter's shoulder and then plucked him free with no more difficulty than pulling a bagged suit out of a closet. When he was clear of the mess, the stranger let go and Peter dropped onto his seat in the cold grass and wrecked car debris. No one was that strong.

"How?" Peter asked. His throat felt better. Still rough, words needed to be pushed, but better.

The stranger waggled a finger toward the car.

Peter glanced inside and saw a bundle of clothes in the dome light in a jumble on the roof. Not just clothes, though. These were bulky, filled out. Peter realized he was looking at himself, a pulped body wrapped in bloody clothes.

"Guess your wreck finished you off," the stranger said. "Broke a neck or something."

I'm. That's. No. Peter's mouth may have tried to utter the syllables, but they stuck inside.

"It's all for the best," the nude stranger said. "Because we need a body, and I hate killing innocents. Way easier to pluck the soul out the corpse."

"What?"

"You heard just fine. You having a problem parsing because you don't quite get that you're dead. It's fine. No worries about Heaven or Hell, yet. It being Halloween and all. Go haunt someone. You got almost twenty-four hours without consequence."

A shadow shape eased up past some of the headstones on the other side of the stranger. Its yellow eyes glistened in the glow of the car's headlights. Not animatronics. Not a costume worn by a crazy person with a death wish. The animal was real, and it was all its own thing. Kind of like a werewolf, humanoid and bestial, powerful shoulders and limbs, covered in a ragged fur, but the head was all wrong, too long and sleek, the snout came to a point like a beak. Suggested a picture he once saw of that beast from the Egyptian Myths, the one that hungered for the hearts of men unworthy of entry into the afterlife.

"*That's the spirit,*" the stranger said, ignorant of the rising shape. "Pardon the pun. You know your eyes are bugging out? Makes you look kind of creepy. Real freaky-deaky, you know what I'm saying?" He eased around Peter. "Manifesting for the non-sensitive types ain't easy, so don't worry too much about that. You can still move shit, though. All about heavy emotions. So, get real angry or horny or something. Let it all flow out through your fingers and pitch some quarters or maybe throw a dart at some dude's eyeball. Have some fun before midnight calls it quits for another year."

Even though Peter had not yet broken his gaze from the animal, he could still see what the stranger was doing. His senses were more acute, less reliant on direction. Awareness extended in a bubble around him, three-hundred-sixty-degrees. The stranger levered and yanked his corpse out of the car. The shape clambered up onto the stone it stood behind, rear leg claws hooking over the rounded top and securing its position. The stranger finally cajoled Peter's body free and assessed it: "Damn, you're a mess. But the blood is all that really matters—"

The animal growled, a low, yet ferocious, sound, stopping the stranger cold. He released the corpse and whipped around in time for the shape to leap from its position behind the stone. It bowled into Peter, first, passed right through him with a disturbing tickle and then slammed into the stranger behind him. That man howled curses and he tried to hold the spread wide jaws apart, but there was no stopping that toothy maw. It snapped shut first on the hands themselves, biting cleanly through meat and bone. Then, they wrenched open and caught the stranger in his midsection, carving out a morsel from his groin to his gullet. The chewing sounds following this were moist and terrible.

Peter stumbled forward. The ground felt spongy, insubstantial beneath his feet.

A deep voice grumbled a handful of unintelligible syllables behind him amidst the wet smacks, crunching bones, and greedy swallows.

Peter's moving legs froze. Had that terrible voice said, "Apologies?"

"It did," the voice said. It stopped chewing and the words became clearer. "Me manners is bad, yeah. I take you across. You want go early?"

The animal was staring into his back. Its jaws moved as though continuing to chew, but it made words instead. "Can use help, though."

"Help?" Peter snapped and wheeled on the thing. It was big and terrifying but, damn it, he was dead! What could it hope to do to him, now?

"Help, yeah." The appearance was animal. The eyes, however, twinkled with wicked intelligence. One paw patted the eviscerated stranger on the cheek. "Blackest witchcraft tonight."

"You caused the wreck."

The animal nodded. "Wish didn't." Its shoulders shifted in an approximation of a shrug. "Blood and meat is reliable lure." Again, the paw tapped the stranger on his cheek. There was nothing affectionate there. "Three more to tend to."

"A lure?" Peter took no solace from the animal's nod. "Why me?"

"They chose," the animal said. "First spells arranged for sacrifice. Me put you where needed for me."

Crazy talk. Crazy enough a talking animal. Crazy enough to be outside his own body. "Bring me back?"

"I guide to Other Place," the animal said. "Can't restore *here*." Now that terrible paw caressed his own corpse. "Too broke up."

The chorus from the Elvis tune, 'All Shook Up,' popped into his head. Wrong words, wrong attitude, but the brain is a mystery in how it leaps from one item to the next. Peter said, "It's not fair."

The animal nodded. Agreeable cannibal. "You help?"

"No!" The word was out before he had the chance to consider what all this meant. His backpack was laying upside down against one of the shattered headstones, ripped along the outermost pocket and spilling mechanical pencils and blue Bic pens into the dirt, but otherwise unharmed by the vehicle's passage off the highway, through the iron fence and into White Chapel cemetery.

"Wait," he pleaded with his bag. The animal did not stir, either.

Overhead, a sign announced this place's intent: WHERE MEMORY LIES IN BEAUTY. Peter was almost done with school. He was looking forward to the chance to get a little life and workplace experience under his belt before returning for a graduate program. Now, he was a ghost. Now, he was dead and gone and what the hell had he been working for? Coming here? He supposed he was on his way here all along, but... but you didn't think about it that way. You took one day at a time, made plans and followed them through until the unthinkable, yet inevitable, conclusion happened, and you left this life for whatever waited in the next.

That bag might not be the culmination of twelve years of public school and four years of university education, but it was the bag he used since freshman year at OU. It was the bag he carried three or five days a week, depending on how the class roster came together. It was the innocuous container that saw him through years of frustrating courses and cake walks, making friends, flirting with pretty people, maybe slipping into the library study room for a hand job from a boyfriend or girlfriend if he was lucky. It traveled from Ferndale to Rochester and back again. It had as many miles as its commuting owner. And yet, it was still functional in the world of cars and cemeteries and midterms and finals and spring breaks. "I can't handle this."

"Then wait. I come back when done." The animal lumbered off into the dark, leaving him with two corpses and his wrecked Yaris. Too many questions, not enough time to consider them. He sat down where he was, the spongy terrain felt even less substantial under his spectral rump.

"So, I'm dead," he said. At that moment his eyes shifted toward his own corpse, stretched out on the ground beside the savaged stranger. A witch, according to the animal. "I was killed by witchcraft."

Witchcraft? Such a goofy, dated thing. Who got killed by witchcraft, anymore? Peter dated a couple of Wiccans over the years, and they were just normal enough people who still believed trees and soil had mystic energy and nature was worth revering. It was like that old joke: What's the best thing about dating a Wiccan? They worship the ground you walk on.

That was, maybe, the hardest thing to wrap his head around. Not only was he dead, he was dead from a witch-craft-induced automobile accident. He realized there was one silver lining: "At least I'm not as dead as you," he said to the stranger's butchered carcass.

The laugh never manifested. The stranger's cocked head, and wide and terrified eyes were too much. Over-whelming Peter with shock. Worst of all, he decided, was not the chewed remnants spilled across the soil, but the way the man's lips had relaxed into a faint smile, a subtle promise of worse things to come for Peter.

Where was that man's ghost? Shouldn't he be sitting here, too? Waiting for the animal to come back. "Where are you, man? I didn't even get your name."

Maybe witches didn't make ghosts when they died. Went off to whatever reward or damnation awaited. Of course, the stranger got eaten by the animal, and maybe that meant it really was like that devouring beast from Egyptian lore—according to the myths he half-recalled, if that ancient eater got hold of a spirit, it was consumed whole, digested and, theoretically, shat on some spirit home's front lawn or sidewalk.

Elsewhere in the cemetery, Peter heard a commotion. A woman's scream. A man's shout. Pistol reports. Peter cocked his head to attention, and he turned a worried stare in the direction those sounds came from. Worry as habit, of course. What did he have to worry about now? He was dead.

It was just the remaining witch coven getting their come-uppance. It was just the animal tearing into them the way it ravaged the nude stranger. When it was done with them, it would come back here and... and guide him to the afterlife. Or, maybe, devour his soul, too.

Should I trust a thing that used me as a lure?

Well, what the hell else was he supposed to do? Somewhere farther in the massive bone yard, lights flickered to life. A fire, maybe. Small and controlled, not some wild blaze. Well, that was new, and it was not likely due to the animal. The thing had not struck Peter as a tool user. Did it even have opposable thumbs?

Crunching sounds, approaching footsteps. The animal on return vector? No, these were far too slow, cautious. Also, there were two sets moving just out of sync.

A man's deep voice broke the silence, asking, "What the hell is the car doing over there, Cerulean? You off your game?"

Not the animal.

"Magic's not a science, you bone head," a woman

replied. Cerulean was a color, but apparently it was also a name. She spoke with the strained annoyance of a teen valley girl. "It doesn't work with precision. We needed a car; we got a car. We needed a body, we get—"

Cerulean's voice cut off suddenly. Then, she said, "Milo? Shit. It's *Milo*, Dee."

Peter made out the two shapes, moving up on the scene from between some of the stones. He was not looking in their direction, per se, but he sensed and then saw them, nevertheless. More of that three-hundred-and-sixty-degree sight stuff.

The man was a few inches taller than six feet, and the woman just a few inches shorter. The man was black and maybe the dead stranger's younger brother. Similar noses, similar eyebrows. The woman was a pasty, pale thing, plain face framed by crooked white scars on either side, which ran from temple to jawline. They were both rangy sorts and, unlike the dead stranger, they were wearing dark ceremonial robes tied at the waist with gold cords. Witchcraft vestments, Peter supposed. Neither wore shoes.

The two made their way to the dead stranger. They walked right past Peter's ghost without acknowledging it. Did they see him? The dead stranger saw him.

"It's *Milo*, Dee," the woman repeated, aghast.

"Well, that's a thing, bra," the man called Dee said, low voice not quite drenched in mournful tones. The phrase was meaningless to Peter, but he sensed it carried no small weight for Dee. Something he and Milo said to one another with regularity. He looked around, his gaze sweeping past Peter without a pause. "You still here, bra? Watching over us?" He waited, and Peter remained silent. Dee muttered, "That spirit shit was always his turf."

Cerulean still stared at the corpse. "It *ate* him."

"Was going to eat us, too," Dee replied, sounding as aloof as a philosopher. "Would have, if Ginny didn't pop a cap in its ass and you..." He raised a hand and twiddled fingers in the universal sign of spellcasting.

The animal was dead, then. Or captured. Or otherwise removed from play. Peter wondered: *Now what am I supposed to do?*

"Want him for the ritual?" Dee asked.

"No way! He's our brother." The valley girl's inflections added a '*Duh!*' to this without one needing to be voiced.

"He's *my* brother, Cerulean," Dee corrected. "You a sista of the night, but you weren't blood to us. We need blood, yeah?"

"No way," she said. "We got the Devouring One. Better than any mortal blood sacrifice."

"Maybe some sweetbreads?" he teased. "Taste just like chitlins."

"Gah-*ross*."

"How about mister innocent bystander?"

"Don't need him anymore. Like I said."

Peter wanted to jump up. Scream at them to take his damned body. They killed him; they might as well use him instead of... instead of wasting... He sat on the spongy ground and gaped. His death was truly meaningless. These witches brought him here to use his blood. Now, they didn't even need him? "Mother*fuckers.*"

"Did you hear something?" Cerulean asked. She cocked her head at just the right moment, as though catching the curse.

Peter went suddenly silent. Could she hear him? If they did, what would they do? What could witches do with a ghost?

"I didn't hear anything."

"Maybe it was the wind."

"Sure. You head back, make sure Ginny got the fire how you need. I won't be long." He did not say he wanted a moment alone with his dead brother. She did not ask, just trudged back the way she came.

"You're a mess, bra."

Dee closed the driver's side door, but the damage prevented it from latching. The dome light inside extinguished until it yawed open far enough. When the light went, Peter realized he could still see as though it were dusk. When the light flickered back on, his vision cut down to just the light's radius. Weird.

He glared at the man's back, feeling a surge of hatred and anger and, most surprising of all, pity. Stones flicked up from the ground and pelted the man's back, butt and neck. He wheeled around, saw no one, and frowned. Then, he bared his teeth in a grin. "That you, Milo? Seems like something you'd do, wait for me to get all broke up and then mess with me."

Milo had said Peter could move things. Emotional overload resulted in kinetic force. "You killed me for nothing? I'm sorry your brother's dead," Peter growled, "but I'm really glad he's gone. You sickos all deserve the same thing!"

This rage was even more surprising in its power. Behind him, he saw something better than stones. Something more poetic. Dee did not see the backpack loaded with books until it slammed into his chest and propelled him back against the car, halfway into the upside-down driver's compartment. Rage gave way to a manic glee, intense enough to manifest as still more motion. Peter unleashed it and the door slammed against Dee once, twice, three times, first breaking the fingers that clutched the frame to stop from falling in, and then battering the man himself into unconsciousness. The man in robes slumped to the ground just in time for the door to close its fourth time, rebounding off Dee's head with a sick crunch.

Panic overwhelmed both the glee and the rage, and the car rocked up and then down again. Peter's emotions and the power that came with them was out of control. He wheeled around as the car turned enough while up on one side to come down atop the prone, unconscious Dee. If the door hadn't finished him, that would.

Terrified by his own violence, Peter ran into the graveyard. Running blind, he sometimes dodged headstones and other times passed right through them as easily as passing through the empty air. He was not aware of where he was going until he saw the fire's twinkling light and the two women around it. Pasty Cerulean and another, darker-complexioned woman in her early twenties. Ginny, he supposed that would be.

The witches had themselves a setup out of some antiquated painting. A small cauldron sitting over a small fire. The muck inside was thick as porridge, and it bubbled in a disgusting way. He realized now he could not smell anything —ghosts lost that ability, it seemed, when they lost their bodies—but he assumed it was disgusting. A quartet of skinned rabbits lay in a heap in the dirt, nearby.

The animal squatted on the earth, bleeding from a bullet wound on its forehead. A collar and chain bound it to a stake set in the earth, and that would have seemed humdrum impossible but for the shimmer. Each link in the chain and the collar and even the stake itself were translucent and a shimmering silver. Not solid at all. They were crafted from nothing more than moonlight, though where such light might have come from on a night as dark as this was anyone's guess.

"When will we feed it to the bowl?" Ginny asked. She sat cross-legged atop her robes. A large revolver rested on her nude thighs. She was a painfully thin woman, that pretty shade of black called redbone. Her eyes looked sunken in her skull.

"When Dee gets back," Cerulean said, craning her neck in the vague direction of the wreck. "We still have maybe thirty, thirty-five minutes before the witching hour is up." Looking pointedly at their prisoner, she added, "And then you get to help us raise up Hecate from her prison in Tartarus."

The animal's eyes rolled toward Peter. Tormented creature; pained and sad and embarrassed. It asked, "You came?"

"Shh!" Peter waved a finger before his lips to emphasize the need for silence.

"Deaf to the dead, these two. Other one was aware." The animal licked its chops. "He's in Tartarus, now."

Tartarus? That was from Greek myth, wasn't it? A part of the Underworld? Hecate, though, that was from *Macbeth*, right? Goddess or queen of the witches? So many myths jammed into one another, how was he supposed to understand any of this? Peter admitted, "I don't know what's happening."

"No need to," the animal replied. "Just give."

"Give? Give what?"

"Hand," snapped the animal. "Foot. Arm. Head. Not matter specifics. Just *give*."

The animal wanted to eat him. Or a part of him. What for? "I can move things," Peter said. "Maybe I can break your chains?"

The animal whimpered and the witches grinned at it. "Try, if must."

Peter decided he must. He focused on the chain. He tried to work up anger and found himself empty. The run from the wreck left more than a thin layer of slime on the tombstones behind him. It left his emotions. He could not even work up pity, just numbed exhaustion. "I hate this," he said without even a trace of Hatred's fire. "I can't . . . Can't do anything."

"These is magic, anyway," the animal said. "Not like throwing a rock."

"Do they need Dee's help? I think he's dead."

The animal considered this. "Don't think so. Me body is more sorcerous than expected. Harvesting me might crack the prison's walls like eggshells. Maybe let more than Hecate out."

Peter did not like the sound of that. "What can I do?"

"*Give.*"

Peter looked at his hands, his arms, his feet. They seemed substantial enough. Not the stuff of ghosts from the movies, nothing cartoonish or slimy. "Will it hurt?"

"Some might. Might need two limbs to get out. You fresh, remember pain. Memory sparks are easier for fresh ones to ignite. Still, dead ones got no nerves."

"I might hurt, if I expect it to?" Peter asked. Things hurt or they did not.

The animal nodded. "Got no nerves," it repeated, "and you're too fresh. Still possessed by life's notions."

He studied his hands in the flickering firelight, found the palms blank. All those little nicks and marks he accrued during his life were gone, not just the classic palmistry nonsense of life lines and love lines and whatnot, but the scars and the wrinkles. They were all gone.

"*Give.*"

This was his hand. The one he had been born with. Had spent his whole life with. Extending it seemed impossible.

"And if I... if I give you what you want? Will I... Will I get it back?"

"If I take you away," the animal said, "you won't need it."

Peter asked, "Heaven, you mean?"

"To some."

"Hell?"

Cerulean stood up, peered into the dark for her friend and saw something that made her smile. "About time!" Dee was tottering back like a reject from *The Walking Dead*. Not dead, Peter realized with both relief and a kernel of terror. She turned to Ginny. "You ready?"

The animal snarled. "*Give.*"

Peter stuck his left hand toward the animal's mouth before he could think twice. The beast leaned in with gaping jaws and chomped down, taking the offered limb all the way to the elbow.

Over the last ten minutes, he had grappled with the concept of his own death, almost accepting it, and then not. However, seeing the animal bite down on his arm up to the elbow? It brought him a few steps closer to acceptance, to resignation.

Peter wheeled aside, shrieking at the sight of his beautiful arm, gone, at the tatters on his shoulder which had been connective tissue for a limb. There was no blood, there was only terror, the fear of pain transformed into all too actual experience.

Pain flared up in his mind like a match and then it exploded like a stick of dynamite when the animal took a second bite all the way to his shoulder. It chewed, processed and then used whatever energy it claimed from Peter's offering. The chain split in two.

Ginny cursed and pointed her gun. Cerulean turned back, fingers curling and wreathed in burning black energy, mystical power.

Peter unleashed his emotional explosion toward the one called Ginny, and the effects were immediate. He possessed intensity but no fine controls. He lashed out with an ectoplasmic backhand, smacking the woman three steps backward. It also ripped the revolver from her grip and sent it flying aside. The weapon spun through the air like a shuriken for all of three seconds before rebounding off Cerulean's left ear. That blow was enough to distract her from using whatever sorcery had been close to hand. The dark energy massing around her curled fingers dissipated. Meanwhile, Ginny was stunned at the suddenness with which she was disarmed. She gaped at her empty hands even as her trigger finger squeezed and squeezed and squeezed on nothing.

The animal pounced, leaping over the cauldron and landing atop the distracted witch. Its terrible jaws encircled Cerulean's head before she could collect herself to mount a defense, and then snapped shut. The corpse's neck fountained blood when it wrenched its prize free, and her carcass tumbled back across a gravestone.

Ginny raced into the cemetery, shrieking. The animal bounded next toward the oncoming shape. Dee was bloody and dazed, but he had enough understanding to scream and throw his hands up in front of his face before the savage creature took them at the wrists as well as the nose just past them in a single bite. It then swatted the man aside with one mighty paw, opening his side, and bending him across the nearby headstone.

All that remained was Ginny. The animal turned its gory face her way.

"Let her go," Peter whispered. "Please. She's alone. Harmless. Frightened out of her mind."

"No," the animal snarled and bounded off after her. Its huffing breaths were loud, brutish, terrifying. Ginny made the mistake of looking back—a lesson Lot's wife could have shared—while keeping up her run. She hit a tombstone with her hip, fell out of her stride and crashed to the ground. Peter heard a solid impact of meat on a stone, though he could not say if it was shoulder or head. The animal leapt atop her, and she screamed as she clutched it by the chin, trying to keep those lethal jaws away.

The animal reared up and slammed both paws down on her. Several bones snapped, flesh pulped with a squelching sound, and the screams ceased in an instant.

The animal leaned in to worry and eat, and then it trotted back to Peter. "You show mercy," it said, mildly. "I do not."

"What crime did they commit?"

"Murdered you," it said. "Murdered more. Four rabbits. " It scuffed dirt over the flames, extinguishing them. "Also, kill two landlord women." It kicked dirt over the carcasses. "*And* tried to break Tartarus, released the dread imprisoned." It licked one claw clean as it considered, and then the other. "Also, Shot *me*."

The animal had not eaten him to the guts, but Peter suddenly felt hollowed out. Numb. Faint, if ghosts could experience such a sensation.

"I guide you, now." The animal trotted deeper into the cemetery. After a few steps, it stopped and grinned back at him. "You gave. I owe thanks."

"Glad I could lend a hand," Peter said without thinking. Then, he realized the implication and felt such horror. The animal laughed and led the way.

A dozen or more yards from the witches' cauldron, the animal stopped and turned to face Peter. "Your heart is large," it said. "I will not consume you."

"Thanks?" Peter said.

It raised a paw and swiped it through the air. Four slimy rents opened in the air itself, and through them Peter saw a brilliant white light. "Through this is the Other Place. Listen to heart. You will not see..." It struggled for a word and then decided on, "Hell."

"I can pass through this?"

"You are fresh dead, but dead."

Peter glanced back into the dark. Corpses waited there, witches and his own. His car. His life. "I really am dead," he said.

"Yes," the animal replied. "But you not yet know what that *means*. Go. *Learn*."

Learn. He knew a thing or two about that. What little life he lived had been dedicated to the topic. He turned back to the slimy rends, saw that they were shorter than they were a moment before. What the animal made, time unmade. If he lingered too long, they would close right up.

Peter put his remaining hand before his face to dull the light's intensity and stepped into the disappearing doorway the animal made. He was halfway through when he caught the smell of summer—lemonade and carnival popcorn and bubble gum and freshly mown lawn. He chuckled and took his hand down, to see all he could, smell all he could, savor all he could of this next, strange phase of existence.

PIECE BY PIECE

BY DANIEL WILLCOCKS

From stone to seed, all things feed.

er voice lingers, a gong struck inside an echo chamber the size of a thimble. Each syllable a dizzying pulse of pain and torture as the blood dries on my lips.

Ignore the wants, take what you need.

I laugh as I chew, great slathers of salty meat. Hands slick with grime, specked with sand. Still the endless dark swims by, unflinching, unknowing, even death must go on, it seems.

But she no longer will...

I CAN ONLY REMEMBER the feeling of prying my eyes open. That muscular flex you take for granted in life and beg for the ability to come back when you're bleeding on the floor, body nothing more than a hessian sack of tools dropped from a third story roof.

There was nothing there to greet me. A color deeper than black. A *not*-black. The not-black remained not-black no matter how many times I butterflied my eyelids, no matter how much I strained in the endless abyss for something to differentiate the nothing and create something. I was weightless. There was nothing beneath me. Nothing above, nothing to the sides, all was gone where only moments before had been everything. Ambulance flashes, wailing sirens, and crowds. For a precious few moments it had been oppressive, claustrophobic. Death felt like the correct end. A choice I had made.

No amount of CPR could bring back the unwilling.

Now I float on the other side of the spectrum—if "floating" you can call it. I'm cast out in an atmosphere of blank, spinning in a chamber of nought. Maybe not spinning. Spinning would imply movement, and that's something that I lack. I feel the presence of my arms and muster the strength to move, but there's no confirmation that such a signal has been received. The ghosts of my senses play with synapses that I'm not sure even exist anymore. Perhaps all that is left is a celestial aura of consciousness. Is this death? To float in a chasm of awareness, lost to everything that you once knew as life, as *you*?

At least it is painless, here. For a brief few moments I recall bone protruding from skin like brambles piercing wax paper. A searing bolt of pain, both ice-cold and scalding-hot, racing up my spine. The blackberry juices of blood seeping down my leg, knee in a place it shouldn't be, glass sprinkling the tarmac like freshly powdered snow in the throes of early winter.

I never believed that death could be so raw, so electric...
So beautiful.

MOTHER ONCE TOLD me of a place called Heaven. A place where the man who created the world sat on a throne made of cumulus, awaiting the hour of your passing to instill judgment upon you and decide your fate for all eternity.

I never believed in such a power, but Mum did, and so I played pretend. Even in her dying days, frail fingers laced together like vulture's talons, cheeks hollow and gaunt, skin an ashen-white, she choked out the words, a blessing that God would bestow upon her the grace to pass into his protection and live an afterlife of peace. Up there would be Grandpa. Up there would be Tommy, and Cupcake, and Julia, and Cyrill, and Mr Peaches. In the land where the sun didn't set, she would reunite with them all, hold their hands and skip into the great beyond. I wept by her bedside, inspired by her faith, saddened by her inevitable disappointment. By the time Mother died, I'd lived a life long enough to understand that God wasn't coming. My belief lay in biology, in the masterpieces of worms and flies. A decomposing body makes good fertilizer, as my rose bushes would confirm for you.

It hurt to know that Mother was about to enter a world for which she had never prepared. To face a reality that was far removed from her own making.

Not that I had prepared, either. Nothing could have prepared me for what came next.

THE FIRST WHITE spec of light was no larger than a pinhead, yet it blinded whatever vessel I was able to see through. A solitary star, breaking the infinite darkness, granting me a beacon of hope.

There is beauty in the simple things. When life and its worries are stripped away, it's easy to appreciate the minuscule. That one dot of light opened a world of possibility and hope. A baby's mouth yawning its first breath. I couldn't tear my gaze away. If I had retinas, the light would surely have burned its red mark inside my eyelids, irritated my vision as I tried to blink away the glowing stamp of annoyance, but in this eternity of non-black, the light became the one thing I could actually hold to. I watched it for hours, days, weeks, months—who knew how long. The light pulsed and danced, growing infinitesimally larger with each passing beat. When it was the size of a marble, another light shone, then a third, a fourth, until the non-black became black and everything around me was stars.

Corporeal tears fell down cheeks made of non-reality. Ghosts of emotion left over from my mortal body, the same way an amputee can still feel their missing limb on stormy nights. I marveled at the universe unfolding around me, the stars multiplying infinitum, galaxies blossoming like daffodils, swirling and hypnotic. Asteroids and meteors and comets streaking through the endless expanse of space. To be a single particle in this miraculous picture was a blessing, and one that I was humbled to accept. I wondered at the pieces of debris and dust passing by in eddies and waves, picturing each piece of grit as a former friend and loved one of mine. In that moment I understand the world, knew that existence was made of loops and cycles, that from these pieces of space dust came the world, and from the world came humans, and once the gift of life had been extinguished your particles were thrown back into the gumbo pot of life and creation, only to be mixed, tasted, and cast back into the universe again, ready to await whatever Mistress Universe bestowed upon the pieces that were once you.

I understood.

Until my feet crashed on solid ground. And then I didn't.

~

LANDING on that bed of sand was a softer experience than being front-loaded by the metallic grill of an eighteen-wheeler semi, but not by much.

The stars faded from sight as I screwed my eyes shut, clenched my teeth, and grunted, wallowing in the onslaught of pain that racked my body. I was me, though not as I knew myself. A quick glance showed the splinters in my shin, the lump where my rib had slipped its casing, an angry rash of shredded skin and dribbling blood from my skid across the blazing asphalt. The contrast to my moments before was stark. One minute floating in numb apathy, the next hurled headlong into a tunnel of emotion and torment.

It took some time to find a comfortable position to lie in. I must have tried about a thousand, but eventually the recovery position served me well enough. The pain was still present, a constant throb in the affected places of my body, but at least here I could breathe—if breathing is what you called this state of shallow inhalations and exhalations. The sand below me irritated my skin, found its way into my ear, but instead of the problems, I focused on the beauty that splattered the canvas above me.

The star-dappled cosmos was a welcome distraction as I closed my eyes and dared to sleep.

~

Wounds heal slowly.

Days lose meaning.

Time passes, as it always has.

An island.

There was no other word for it. A tiny island, surrounded by an endless sea. An island that stretched no larger in diameter than an open parachute, made entirely of dark sand that looked to have been made of onyx. When I was well enough to stand, I circled the island in moments, searching for anything substantial that I could hold onto. A tree. An animal. A shell.

There was nothing.

I filled my lungs with air, only a dull ache remaining from my busted rib. I kicked the sand and it fell where it lay. There was no wind with which to guide it. Above me, the universe stretched as far as I could see, reaching some form of horizon where it met the inky ocean that surrounded the island. Gentle waves impossibly lapped, providing a hushing lullaby to the world. It was nice. The first sound which I'd heard that hadn't been a grunt or cry of pain from trying to move and get comfortable again. Despite the fact that I was naked, the temperature was tepid, and I didn't suffer from the hot or cold.

Thank god for small favors.

I took my time to explore all angles of the island, searching out into the ocean for something that could give me any sense of direction. There was nothing. I wasn't surprised. There had been nothing for the longest time. If days should exist here—and I'm not sure they do—I'd be hard-pressed to determine the length of my inhabitance. At a push, I'd say three weeks.

Though, in truth, my heart told me it was years.

For the first time since I had arrived, my stomach growled.

LIKE THE CREATION of the stars in that infinite womb that followed death, the others sprang up across the ocean.

At first it was one, though with each blink of my eyes another would show. Dozens upon dozens of islands, each the size of my own, each with their own inhabitants.

Naked. The lot of them. Dazed and confused. Some were elderly, some were slender, others were obese, and all of them waved and shouted and ran and called and beat their fists and cried and laughed and jumped and kicked the sand until their voices were, presumably, hoarse.

I don't know if that was true. I couldn't hear them. They clearly couldn't hear me. My throat became a ream of sandpaper and each swallow was painful. I cast distrustful eyes at the black ocean, wondering whether drinking the liquid would hurt more than entering its fiery wrath.

The scars still stained my ankles. A few splashes on my shins and knees. When the first other appeared, my excitement had grown. I never pegged myself for one who craved the company of others, but to see another creature in a world you believed had isolated you in its foreverness, it brings out another side. She was in her sixties, skin starting to sag, but she kept in good shape. When she unfurled from her cocoon, she glanced in all directions. At first I believed she couldn't see me. Her eyes passed across my island without recognition, despite my enthusiastic waves and calls. I had all but given up, when hours later she waved back at me.

Sound didn't cross between islands, that soon became clear. We mimed, cupped hands behind ears and spelled words with our bodies. We beamed, smiles breaking our faces as we counted to three. She told me she was a swimmer. She would cross the void and unite us on my island. Though I felt a sudden hesitation at losing control of my own island, I welcomed the effort. Company in death, perhaps this might not be the exact route Mother had described, but if this woman could join me, who's to say the others wouldn't too? Mother and Father and all my loved ones united in the great beyond. No cumulus clouds. No man with a great white beard. Just me and the ones I loved most.

Wouldn't that be something?

The countdown went fast. Her smile unbroken as she confidently ran and dived headfirst into the water. Her body slipped from sight, not a splash to indicate where she'd gone. I marveled at the sight, impressed by her form, confirmed that her swimming training had allowed her to dive without much disturbance.

I don't know how long I waited for her to surface.

Dreams shattered like fallen glass as I narrowed my eyes at the charcoal sea, wondering if she would appear before me, launch herself from the ocean like a Baywatch actress and throw her arms around me. After some time, I ran to the water's edge, kicked at the ocean with striking conviction, as though my meager knock with my toes could in some way inflict damage on the body that had taken my only chance at company.

The heat was excruciating, swallowing every nerve ending in my foot. Every millimeter of skin touched by the ocean flared in white-hot pain that caused my skin to prick and my mouth to open into a colossal cavern of screams. Fireworks of white light exploded in my vision. I crumpled back onto the sand, retreating to the center of the island. Thousands upon thousands of needle-like teeth chomped into my flesh, tasted the skin, drew the blood. I could do nothing but wait and allow it to happen. It didn't make sense. The air wasn't warm, the ocean wasn't steaming, so what was this atrocious pain that ate at my senses?

Eventually the pain subsided. The ocean marked my legs. Great red splotches of fevered skin, painted like a Pollock.

Over the course of passing time I witnessed the other islanders experience the agony of submersion. Some with toe dips, others with dives. Tears glistened on cheeks of survivors. Mouths sprang open. Fists shook at the skies. We all had our own journeys to tread, I guess.

The woman never returned. I doubted she ever would.

When the sapling appeared, it was a welcome distraction.

With each passing second my hunger grew. The growling that had first pinched its dextrous fingers around my stomach swelled into a forceful belch. Until now I hadn't felt the need to excrete my bodily substances, but it became clear that was soon to change.

I slept intermittently, and not for long—though, in reality, I had no idea how long I slept for. Sand explored my crevices and found new homes. Skin chaffed and there was no means to clean myself as the cosmos whirled on by. On the neighboring islands, the residents crossed through a spectrum of behaviors: some of them running endlessly around their small patch of space, wearing circular tracks into the sand, others resigning themselves to mere pieces of frozen art to be studied by curious eyes, sat in trances, laying still.

I had been watching two of my neighbors with my own curious eyes for some time. At some point in the past I etched a groove into the sand with my toe, a safe distance from the water's edge. This was to act as my compass. To give me some state of solid direction. By returning to this point I could track the progress of those surrounding me and feel as if I had some semblance of control in this frustrating new reality.

A man and woman. It seemed they knew each other, though I couldn't ask how. The first thing I noticed was that the man had a tree on his island, a thick, knotted trunk stretching at least ten-feet into the air. Throngs of leaves and branches yielded fruit as white as snow. Unblemished. Virgin. The woman had a tree of her own, though half his size. Still, it bore its own fruit. Precious orbs, half the size of his.

My mouth salivated. My stomach yearned for the fruit— if fruit it was.

The second thing I noticed was that their islands were larger than mine and those around me. At least twice as large. Somehow they had each found a way to unlock a new level of this strange existence, and I longed to know how. I longed to understand. Until this point, my island had felt fine, a welcome embrace from the sea. But now, having seen the luxuries that others were living, I wanted more. *Needed more.*

I took a few steps backwards, searching for other islands that matched this impressive new standard. Trees had sprung up around me without my knowledge, each islander now tending to their new garden. I staggered backwards. Caught my heel. Fell on my ass.

Between my legs was a fresh, spring sapling. A single stalk with a crop of variegated leaves and several balls of white attached to the fragile stem. I tenderly held my hand beneath a leaf, unable to process what I was seeing. The leaf was crisp and delicate. One pinch too rough and it would snap. I stared at that sapling for some time, eyes wide and glassy. This was a wondrous thing, an indication that life could only improve. Maybe in death we learn from our mistakes, go through the process of discovering ourselves anew, and form a life one piece at a time. A rediscovery of the most important elements of existence. Joy in food. Wonder in drink. Ecstasy in love and sex.

Three fruits, each the size of a marble, reminding me of the pinhead of light back in the aeons past when I first arrived on this plane. Drool escaped my lips.

My stomach roared.

I plucked.

Juices exploded on my tongue.

Yum.

As DELICIOUS AS my feast of fruits had been, it was some time until the sapling bore fruit again.

I don't know how long I sat with the shrub between my legs, the fatty flesh of my body slowly withering away, but in the time that it took for more fruit to bear, my neighbors' trees had flourished.

Great towering monoliths pricked the sky, branches packed with an immense supply of fruit. Their islands doubling, then tripling in size as the gaps between them closed.

And there, alone, me and my plant. The note appeared before the fruit did. Scripted by an unseen hand. Scratched into the sand before me, the letters burning momentarily in shades of crimson and fire.

> *From stone to seed, all things feed.*
> *Ignore the wants, take what you need.*

The letters faded. The fruits appeared. I popped like them Xanax.

One. Two. Three.

Gulp.

Still, I felt empty.

~

I WONDER if it's possible to die twice. If maybe I'm being punished for something.

The other islands have grown. The trees have multiplied. Though my vision is limited from this distance, it seems they have tools. On the farthest reaches of sight, I was certain I saw fire. A number of the islands have connected, the ocean parting enough to create a causeway between them. I've witnessed hugs. Seen love-making. Heaven for some.

I find myself in Hell.

The sapling refuses to grow. While most islands foster towering trees as grand as oaks, my sapling's growth is stunted. I taste the fruit and yet my body shrinks before me. I can feel my ribs as though there is no skin there. My arms are stick thin, emulating the bracken that the sapling should mature to hold. My lips peel back and recede as my body drinks its own fluids and eats itself from the inside out. Those few seconds of respite are abysmal, those meager moments in which fruit juice zaps my tongue with citrus and my tastebuds come alive. The ultimate tease, to hold onto a second death and watch the world around you come alive while you wither from existence.

I'm so terribly alone.

Movement becomes painful. It's been days since I made an effort to move. Still, that legend burns in the sand, a strange scripture that teases me with a meaning I cannot grasp. For hours after it has faded, the words stain my retinas:

> *From stone to seed, all things feed.*
> *Ignore the wants, take what you need.*

I need food. Plain and simple. While my neighbors connect islands of four, five, ten people, I'm left out here alone like a chump. Lost to the void and forgotten. They used to look at me, wave encouragement my way.

Now I don't get a second glance.

Why should death be any different to life?

My stomach no longer growls. My appetite, too, has finally abandoned me.

I SLEEP for what feels like an eternity. Waking feels futile.

For the first time since arriving on the island, I feel rested, though it does little to my atrophied muscles. My skin is so thin I can see the inner workings of my body. Dark shapes of my organs pulsing and writhing on their final legs.

I marvel for some time at my beating heart. Its pace is slow, conserving the last of the energy it has. I feel I shall fade soon, and thank God for that. To die is to suffer a burden greater than life could bear.

I sit up, my bones protesting in a bristling language of their own. My eyes are dazzled with eruptions of white, sharp dots of light attacking my vision. I rapidly blink, I shield with my arm, the whites don't fade.

And why should they? The fruits are abundant, a great bushel of glorious white fruit, dozens upon dozens waiting to be picked and devoured. My parched mouth gasps a dry croak, my withered fingers, turned to thin, stick-like claws, shakily reach for the nearest yield. To pluck is an effort, but one I must make, and soon my mouth is bursting with juices.

My body responds in orgasmic delight. No longer needing to savor the budlings, I allow myself to indulge. After three juvenile fruits I feel sick, my stomach bulges, sticky residue paints my chin, but still I feast, dine and tuck into the impossible, laughing and almost choking with every bite. Tears don't come, for what liquid is there left in me? But now my jaw aches and I know I must keep on eating, indulging myself, losing myself in the erotic satiating efforts as the bush is stripped bare and my stomach is fed.

I purge. I eat. I vomit. I feast.

That is the way of *my* island.

By the time the fruit is gone, so is my mind. I lay on the rough sand, hands resting atop my stomach. I'm vaguely aware of my erection, my mind mostly lost to the bliss of digestion, eyes rolled into the back of my head, a drunken grin on my face.

I burp.

I chuckle.

Later on, I will have one of the most painful shits of my life.

But, for now, I am happy.

I am full.

Already I know it won't last long.

STRENGTH RETURNS TO MY BODY. For the first time since… sometime, I am able to walk the island.

It doesn't make sense. The hours I lost to lethargy have yielded growth. My island is larger, by several feet, in fact. The bushel rose from the sapling, and now I ponder the reasoning of it. Although my hips still protrude and my ribcage is on display, there is a thin veil of fleshy fat on my stomach, where before there was none. I am thankful there are no mirrors in the beyond. Even the ocean can't reflect my true form, not that I'd dare go near the Devil's water.

I am scarred by the other islanders. Their plots continue to grow at a rapid pace. Some have animals, creatures whose shape I cannot make out, but I can see their devilish forms pacing around excitedly as the occupants dance, drink, and be merry. Great orgies occur, their mouths pulled so wide open in pleasure it doesn't seem possible that I shouldn't hear their moans. Clusters of islands join into a natural raft that carries its residents across the ocean.

Yet there are still others like me.

They arrive every day. Some of them blink out within a short matter of time, others stay stationery in their progress, as do I. Sullen, miserable islanders with beards and frowns and saplings that barely stretch to the length of my cock.

At least I have my bushel.

Even if it is refusing to yield fruit again.

Stubborn bastard.

~

THREE TIMES the bush has given, and three times I have taken.

Fruit-drunk. That's what I give the name for my comatose state of satisfaction in the wake of my feast. It seems the fruits will only bloom when I'm on the cusp of my finality. When my thoughts linger on following in the steps of the woman and diving into the depths. When all I can think of is how the end should be better than this torturous state of monotony. In the final stages of will, the fruits appear as if they have always been there, and I, like the dutiful servant I am, chow down on its gifts.

I'm satisfied a little less each time. Maybe there's a lesson I'm missing here, I think, as those same words glow in the sand as though the onyx has turned to magma and some higher power is speaking to me.

I burp. I shit. I bleed. I sleep.

~

I'M LEFT with a lot of time to ponder, and so I do.

~

I WONDER if I've made the right choice. I question if there was another path. I replay the event over and over again, counting the steps I took into the road, listening to the screeching brakes of the semi careening down the highway, knowing that it had too much momentum to ever stop.

I taste metal on my tongue.

It's better than metal hitting my teeth.

My chapped lips are bleeding.

I SHOOK the bushel for hours before I eventually passed out.

I was desperate. My body throbbed for sustenance. All around me the other islanders raved and hollered in their silent bubbles, their own islands expanding into great expanses of territory, never getting closer to my own, but always growing, always stretching. Fires blazed and roasted meats cooked, tears pricked my eyes and I collapsed to my knees, holding my hands around the trunk of the bushel as though I could constrict its windpipe. I shoved leaves into my mouth, chewed on their sour crunch, but it wasn't enough. Compared to the fruits, the leaves tasted like dust. I fell onto my face, licked the sand, chewed the gritty particles until my teeth began to wear.

I couldn't swallow.

I could only cough.

Cough.

Splutter.

Slip into unconsciousness.

I feared I would sleep forever. As my eyes closed I became nothing more than the orb of conscious that had welcomed me into depth. The non-black returned, and I hung there, paralyzed. No body to move, no strength to try, no more thoughts to think. Wasted and turned into the same nothingness that surrounded me.

I believed that was it. That whatever crazed experiment surrounded the islands was over, and I could at last be free. I'd been stripped bare of all that I was, cast into eternal famine, tortured by the frivolities of strangers. The islands reflected the true needs of humanity, forsaking the wants of the mortal body and demanding an acceptance of the raw basics.

The bare necessities.

I chuckle, a faint image of a loin-clothed boy and a bear. I cough. But I don't. That cough isn't mine.

There's someone else here.

I STARE at her for hours, the latest yield of white fruit balancing in my shaking hands. Sat and hunched by the water's edge, arms folded about her knees as she stares into the infinite beyond. Long hair trailing to the crack between her cheeks.

I daren't approach her. Make a noise. I fear the slightest disturbance will cause her to vanish. A wisp in the forest. Immaterial. I knew I was starved for food, I didn't know I was famished for friendship, too.

I wait.

She'll notice me.

She'll come alive.

Surely?

"TELL ME YOUR NAME."

It feels strange to speak out loud. My throat, once raw from hollering, is now somewhat recovered, though the sensation of vibrations of sound are alien.

She sighs.

"Why are you here?" I ask.

She stares out at sea, unblinking. I trace her eye line,

wondering which island has her fixated. They're all entertaining, now. Life is buoyant. Life is vibrant. We sit on the couch, sedentary and sad.

"You stink." The first two words she utters to me. Disdain laced in each syllable. Her nose retracts into her face and an ugly snarl appears on her lips.

I nod. Why lie?

I extend a handful of fruit. "Here."

"No."

"Why?"

"Not hungry."

"How did you get here?"

She shrugs.

I ask more questions. She chooses to answer in silence. I bow my head and cry.

THE BUSH HAS BECOME an empty tree, and now I'm flanked by two wells that have run dry. On one side a tree that offers nothing to sate my hunger, on the other a woman who does nothing but sit and brood.

Life on the island is utter torture, and each passing moment stretches the limits of my patience. I wish for transport to the other islands, I get down on my knees and pray to Mother's God, and still the universe giveth nothing more.

My body withers once more.

So does hers.

Mine has greater effect, it seems. These skeletal arms shouldn't be mine.

Yet, here we are.

And there she is.

My mouth wastes water with salivation.

~

I AWAKE to the crunch of fruit and find her there, stretched on tiptoes as she picks the tree bare.

With wide eyes I examine what is left, only a few fruits the size of apples hanging from the branches. The sandy floor littered in husks of what has already been consumed. She turns from the tree, leaving a few morsels left as white-hot letters blaze into the sand.

> *From stone to seed, all things feed.*
> *Ignore the wants, take what you need.*

Anger coursing through my veins, my malnourished form in sudden shock at the few fruits remaining, my mouth casting highlight reels of my former gorging. My stomach remembers its distention and aches for the pain, but it will not come. There is too few left.

The woman laughs and the sound offends my ears. I shove her aside, surprised by her strength as she watches with malicious content. I can barely reach the fruit and it hurts to jump. My spine has curved as my body shrivels away, but after a few attempts I seize one, bite into the skin, and scream in agony.

Blood soaks the fruit, staining the virgin flesh crimson. Teeth stick to the fruit, pulled free from my gums and protruding from the skin like stubby wooden pegs, yellow-brown in their discoloration. I bring the fruit to my lips and suck, free the blood from the skin, use my remaining pegs to break off a piece and chew as though my life is depending on it. The sweet, citrus taste is tinged with the flavor of death and necrotic deterioration but at least it's something. I swallow my teeth whole because what else is there to do?

Tears paint my cheeks and all she can do is stand there, watching with head at an odd angle and those strange, unblinking eyes. In another life I'd have marveled at her body, feasted on her flesh with my gaze, wanted nothing more than to take her here and now, lose myself in the throes of sex and discard her like a wet rag later.

My penis stiffens.

I guess old habits die hard.

~

THE FRUIT DID nothing to restore my vitality.

I'm at the end, and yet still I don't die.

~

SHE'S asleep when I eventually open my eyes.

My hunger has returned with renewed fury. My stomach, so shrunken that the flesh caves below my ribs and almost touches the inside of my back, grumbles, rumbles, vibrates, rolls, yearns, longs...

They're eating hog roast—or, whatever passes for a hog in this land. The fire is blazing, two naked women rotating the creature on a spit. Plumes of smoke and heat rise into the air. An island, within easy swimming distance, yet a million miles away. The men are drinking from cups made of coconuts, and all I can do is lie here, on my side, dying...

Dying...

Dying...

I trace my tongue around wasp nest lips, no liquid to soften them. Sand has fallen into my mouth and I swallow it down, coughing as it trickles through my esophagus.

She's asleep. Snoozing by the island's edge, her chest

rising and falling. She is sideways, as am I. The cosmos above glitters its iridescent hues of bruises upon us, great galaxies and space dust and blazing suns at various stages of decomposition...

...all that once was must die.

Must die...

She must die.

Her form is silhouetted in the stunning glow of above. The islands beyond her are alive with activity, some as large as football pitches, one now holding at least fifty people on its banks, dancing, playing, sleeping, fucking. In the misty warble of my dying vision she morphs, two prongs appear and she is suspended by sticks. The fire blazes beneath her as she spins on its axis, the world spins on its axis, the universe spins in loops and cycles, the cycle continues...

I'm next to her before I'm aware that I've moved. She smells of sweat and hope. The sweat is salty and my body writhes with pleasure at the sensation of the smoothness of her skin on my tongue. Pin pricks like mountains mottle my skin.

She doesn't stir.

Light shines from behind.

Letters in the sand.

I ignore their message.

From stone to seed, all things feed.

"Please...No..."

"It's too late."

"No... The message... Heed the message!"

Her voice amplifies. Struggles against my grip. There's no going back.

"Stop!"

Words turn to screams.

Screams turn to weak protestations.

Then fade.

Silence in the overworld.

Chaos in the inner.

I can't shake it, but I can't stop. My body speaks for me, speaks with insatiable hunger, speaks with gurgling stomach and throbbing erection. Her voice lingers, a gong struck inside an echo chamber the size of a thimble, reverberating in my skull. Each syllable a dizzying pulse of pain and torture as the blood dries on my lips.

Ignore the wants, take what you need.

I laugh as I chew, great slathers of salty meat. I cry as I swallow. The laughter comes back in waves. Hands slick with grime, specked with sand. Still the endless dark swims by, unflinching, unknowing, even death must go on, it seems.

But *she* no longer will...

~

From stone to seed, all things feed.
Ignore the wants, take what you need.

THE WORDS WON'T LEAVE.

Stomach distended, fingers like brittle twigs, eyes clouded with tears, I ponder...

I think she was a test.

HER CORPSE VANISHES before I can pick the bones clean.

So much for simple pleasures.

I fucking hate this place.

MY DYING body sinks into the sand. It's been days since I've moved. Weeks since the tree has given. A lifetime since she appeared.

There isn't much of my body left to waste away. My organs are dried fruits inside a papier-mâché case, left outside in the rain for fair too long. They're dark like stones. My skin is grey and blue. It hurts to open my mouth. I've lost the ability to blink.

My last ounce of strength was spent on turning my head away from the other islands. Now, even that has gone. The nearest island is fixed in my gaze, a place where I have no choice but to watch as the crusted remains of blood finally lose their stink and become a part of me. The words are somewhere nearby, casting a faint luminescence of starlight that I can no longer read.

And still I ponder.

The other islanders are happy. Their bushels are full, their trees are heaving with fruit. Creatures of all sizes and shapes, though none of the world I once knew, dance and run and chase each other, dark tongues lolling out between moist lips. The people are happy. Their smiles are the scars of my world. In their frivolity I see my mother, the woman she had once been, beaming as she dazzled the dance floor and claimed her jive trophy way back in another lifetime, when '86 felt like mere days before. They laugh, yet still the sound evades me as I am cast into this eternal cocoon of muteness. I have no liquid with which to cry. They have it all where they are. Even the ocean can't save me. It never could.

In the center of the throng of islanders sits a woman, crouched on a log, arms wrapped tightly around her as though in hugging herself she has gifted herself the world. She hasn't moved in some time, and while the others cast dreary distraction around her, she seems settled. Happy.

Familiar.

I look at the form of my mother, a woman whose years have rolled back like tides peeling from the shore, dark hair trailing down her back where once it was grey. There's a peaceful expression on her face, one that I haven't seen in all of my lifetime. One that I only knew existed in monochrome polaroids and nostalgic storytelling.

It is then that I read the truth in her face. A truth I knew all along, but refused to accept.

I killed my mother.

Maybe it hadn't been a direct transaction, I never once traded blood for coin or violence, but the years weathered her from the moment I was born. A restless child with an insatiable appetite for destruction, chaos, and greed. I can see it, then. Life flashing before me in pulses. A mother losing her patience and reaching the end of her tether long before I found the needle. Her conditions exacerbated by worry, love, and heartache. Cancer may have claimed her, but I was the judge, jury, and executioner, and that was the truth that had evaded my former life. The one thing the island has given me is time. Time to play out the tapes, rewind them, analyze them with excruciating keenness. I was selfish, I'll admit. Mother was an enemy, even though she wasn't. I tore her apart, piece-by-piece, day-by-day, and, in kind, the afterlife has sunken me into a pit of my own creation.

> *From stone to seed, all things feed.*
> *Ignore the wants, take what you need.*

The island knew. So, now, do I. My greed was my largest downfall. My life was made of wants, and never by needs. In consuming everything, I was left with nothing.

Nothing.

Nothing.

Nothing is all I had once she passed. Emptiness is what I returned home to every night. Each night I crawled up inside my sleeping bag, windows smashed, floor littered with other users, shivering, fighting their own battles, staining the tiled floors with melted-butter urine. Wallpaper peeling, stained from nicotine as the sun rose and stung eyes that wouldn't close and still I wanted more, more, more, needed more, because all that I had known was gone, all that was good was vanished, and life was less worth living than in the nothing it had been for so long, and I cried for days, weeks, more days, until I was a river run dry and my pain had eroded the banks of what was left to be human, until my reflection in the shower of broken glass on the floor showed me a man who was not a man but a husk and in that husk was only damnation and anything had to be better than this because she was gone, buried in my rose garden, and I was now gone, too...

I killed my mother.

I had hoped the highway would kill me, too.

Ah well. At least it gave it a damn good try.

~

My bones break with years unnumbered.
    They look like stones.
    The ocean claims the island.
    Bones to stones.
    Stones to sand.
    An existence made of loops and cycles.
    Mum waves.
    Piece by piece.
    All turns black.

SECRET PLACES

BY HARVEY CLICK

Carey's apartment wasn't in a nice part of town, and Denise was glad Greg was in the car watching her as she climbed the steps. She knocked because the doorbell didn't work, and after a minute she started banging with her fist.

"All right, you don't have to knock the whole damn building down," Carey said when he finally opened the door. He sniffled and wiped his nose with a blue bandanna. "Come in."

"I don't want to come in," she said.

"Then you better go wait in your car." He glanced at the wristwatch she had given him five years ago as an anniversary present and said, "It's only 8:45, and Tommy's mine until 9:00."

Denise gritted her teeth and went in. The living room looked tidy and bare as always—Carey had never liked to own a lot of things. Some quiet piano music was playing on the stereo upstairs, a tune she thought she recognized but couldn't place.

"Where's Tommy?" she asked.

"Upstairs playing with my keyboard," Carey said. "Can't you hear him?"

Denise felt a sharp pang of resentment. She had never known that Tommy could play a note. Maybe he wasn't really her son any longer.

Carey grinned and wiped his nose again. "I've been teaching him a few licks," he said. "He's catching on pretty well, don't you think? Sit down and get comfortable."

"I don't want to sit down, I don't have all night."

"Well, he's mine for twelve more minutes, so you may as well get comfortable. I'd offer you a drink, but all I have is that sugary soda pop he likes."

Denise sat down and said, "Bullshit. You always have an extra bottle of bourbon stashed away somewhere. You're just saving it to guzzle after he leaves."

"No bottles up my sleeve and no track marks either," he said. "I told you, I quit all that junk twelve months ago."

"Sure you did. You told me you quit snorting coke too, but every time I see you you're wiping your nose."

"I've got a sinus infection," he said. "I've been clean for a year, now." He sat down and stared at her with that sweet, annoying smile.

She tried to find something else to look at, but there wasn't much in the small living room—a futon, the two chairs they were sitting on, a coffee table and, on the walls, half a dozen paintings that Carey had painted himself. She stared at her watch for a while and then glanced at his face.

It didn't look healthy, and she felt something stirring that she didn't want to feel. Eighteen years ago, when she met him, he had looked like a blue-eyed, golden-haired angel. Three years ago, when she left him, he had looked like a sunken-eyed, fallen angel, his golden hair greasy and his face ravaged by drugs. Now, he looked like someone who just needed a good deep grave and a mound of dirt to cover him.

"Listen, I've got to get up and go to work tomorrow," she said. "I'm sure you don't remember what that's like."

"I remember a lot of things," he said. "I remember that night in the old house when we ate psilocybin mushrooms and made love all night long with the tape recorder recording our moans and sighs, and the next day we ran them through my synthesizer to make a symphony of love. Remember that one, babe? That's probably the night Tommy was conceived. He was our greatest creation, but I'm sure we could still make some nice music together."

Denise stood up and brushed her skirt down past her knees. "Get real," she said. "You haven't made anything like music since you turned your brains into jelly. You're a drug addict, and you're killing yourself a little faster every week. You don't deserve any custody rights."

She was beginning to shout, and the music upstairs stopped. Carey grabbed her arm and pulled her outside onto the little front porch.

"Tommy heard you," Carey said. "I don't want you talking like that around my son, do you hear? I told you I've given up drugs and, even if I hadn't, you know damn well I'd never use them around Tommy. He loves me, he thinks I'm the greatest dad in the world. That's the only thing you can't steal from me."

"I didn't steal anything," she said.

"You stole my house," he said. "You stole my dreams. You steal my paycheck every month, but you're not gonna steal my son."

"I paid for that house," she said. "As far as child support goes, the kind of money you pay isn't even worth taking to the bank."

Carey smiled his sweet smile, and his ruined angel-face told her she was lying. In fact, he had paid a sizable down payment and several years of mortgage for the house and the ten acres of land she lived on. That was back when his arty rock band had made a couple of albums on a major label. Then, the bass player had died of a heroin overdose, the guitar player had become a born-again Christian, and now the drummer was selling insurance in an office on High Street. The only band member still playing music was Carey, and the music he played now was the kind he hated most, light piano jazz four nights a week at a pretentious cocktail lounge. The money he made didn't add up to much child-support.

His smile faded when he glanced at her car. "Did you have to bring *him*?" he asked. "Does he have to follow you everywhere? Does he follow you into the bathroom?"

"We're probably going to get married," she said. "Get used to it."

"He's living in my house. He doesn't need to come here and gawk at my crummy little apartment too."

"Greg doesn't live with me," Denise said. "Not yet."

"No, he just sleeps there seven nights a week. Tommy tells me everything. He can even hear you fucking—you better be more careful with the grunts and moans."

"I think your time's up," she said.

Carey looked at his watch and said, "No, I've got three more minutes. Three more minutes to look at that bastard sitting in your car. You know what he is? He's a big square box with nothing inside."

"You don't even know him," she said.

"Yeah, I do. He eats Cheerios every morning and his favorite dinner is hamburgers with Velveeta cheese. He thinks sushi's for sissies and David Lynch movies are for lunatics. Mr. Squarebox. Tommy hates him, you know."

"Tommy hates him because you tell him to," she said. "Now Tommy's starting to hate me too."

"Tommy hates him because he knows there's only one man for him and there's only one man for you, and you know that, too. Someday we're going to be together again, babe, just the three of us."

"Don't hold your breath," she said.

"You know we're joined at the hip," he said. "We got the *link*, babe. All those acid trips we did together, we learned to read each other's minds. Tell me something, can Mr. Squarebox read your mind and know what you really want? I'll bet he can't even read a book unless it has a lot of pictures."

"Your time's up," Denise said. She opened the door and yelled, "Come on, Tommy, we're leaving."

Carey grabbed her arm and pulled her close. "You know I'm right, babe," he whispered in her ear. "We're like twins. We've got our special memories and we've got our secret places. We've got the link."

Greg started honking, and Tommy came down the stairs, saying, "All right, all right, I'm coming," but Denise could see that he didn't want to.

TOMMY SULKED in the back seat without speaking and, when they got home, he ran up to his room. The next evening, he played with his food without eating it. When he started putting his French fries in his milk glass, Denise yelled, "Stop that!" But he kept doing it, and the milk overflowed onto the table.

"If you're not going to eat, go to your room," she said, and he did.

The next night he was hungry enough to behave at the table, though he wouldn't speak except to grunt whenever Denise asked him a question. After dinner, she and Greg sat on the sofa watching his favorite show, a stupid sitcom. He wanted to cuddle and kiss, but she wasn't in the mood. She was disentangling herself from his embrace when she saw Tommy standing there staring at them with a hateful expression.

"What are you doing?" she said. "Why are you making that ugly face?"

"'Cause this show sucks," he said. It was probably the first full sentence he'd said to her since leaving his father's apartment.

"Okay, put something else on," she said.

Tommy aimed the remote control at her and Greg and started pushing the buttons. "The same stupid show's on every channel," he said. He threw the control on the floor and ran up to his room.

Denise felt like crying but didn't. Greg held her and said, "It's okay, Denny. He's a good kid, he just acts weird after he sees his father. We'll get this worked out."

Greg was a nice man, even if he was a square box, and pretty soon his soft words and hard muscles made her feel better. He led her upstairs, but when they got in bed, she rolled away from him and clutched her pillow.

"What's wrong?" Greg asked.

"Tommy can hear us when we have sex," she said. "That's what Carey told me. He's probably in his room listening right now."

The week went downhill from there, Tommy growing more sullen each day and Greg acting hurt because Denise wouldn't have sex with him. Saturday, he was sitting in the dining room staring at his laptop, and she knew he was either reading sports news or gawking at photos of hot cheerleaders in skimpy outfits, since that's what he did every Saturday morning. Maybe Carey's right, she thought—maybe Greg really is a square box with nothing inside.

"Where are those keys to the cabin?" she asked. "I can't find them in the kitchen drawer."

"I moved them to that drawer in the bookcase," he said without looking up, and she felt another stab of annoyance. It was her house—what right did he have moving things without telling her?

"What do you want with them?" he asked. "Are we going to the lake today?"

"Carey is. He called and said he lost his key."

Greg looked up from his screen and frowned. "I don't like him using our cabin," he said. "He probably takes drugs there."

"What do you mean *our* cabin? If it belonged to me it wouldn't be *ours*, it would be *mine*, but, in fact, it isn't mine, it's Carey's. It's one of the few things he got in the settlement. He just lets us use it as a courtesy. I'm sure I've told you that."

"Oh." Greg sipped his coffee and frowned some more. "Well then, I think we should buy our own cabin. I don't like having Carey in our lives like this, all the time Carey wanting this and Carey wanting that."

"I have a great idea," she said. "You're paying money for a nice apartment, but you never use it. Why don't you go spend your day there and leave me the fuck alone. You can gawk at your bimbo cheerleaders there just as well as here."

Greg's frown crumpled into something more painful, but he shut his laptop without speaking and went to the bathroom to collect his shaving gear. Denise stood with her arms crossed, already regretting her temper tantrum, but at the same time looking forward to some time to herself. But, not really to herself, since Tommy would still be around.

As soon as Greg's car pulled out of the driveway, she called Carey. "Are you planning to take drugs at the cabin?" she asked.

"I told you, I'm clean. I've been clean for twelve months now."

"Do you swear that on a Bible or whatever else you happen to believe in?"

"Yes."

"Would you like to take Tommy with you?"

His "yes" was quiet, but she could hear joy ringing in it like faint bells. According to the custody agreement, he was allowed to have Tommy only one weekend per month, and this was the first time she'd given him an extra weekend.

"I'll swing by in an hour," he said. "Make sure he packs his fishing gear, a warm blanket, a flashlight, and a good book. We'll read it together around the fireplace tonight."

As she helped Tommy pack, his excitement was almost more painful to her than his usual resentment. Why didn't he love her the way he loved his father? Every day he looked more like Carey, same angel-blue eyes, same delicate face, same long, golden hair, and every day he seemed less like her own child.

He was looking through his Harry Potter collection, trying to decide which volume to pack, when she heard Carey's old, red Volkswagen chugging into the driveway. She hurried downstairs and met him in the yard, not wanting him to come in.

He stood there, staring at the house. "I always hated that vinyl siding, I wanted wood," he said. "But I like the color.

The slate blue was your idea, remember? I wanted something darker."

He stepped past the corner of the attached garage and stared at the woods behind it. The old farmhouse was half-hidden back there in the autumn trees, its siding black with rot and the collapsing slate roof bowed in the center like the back of a crippled nag. It was already falling into ruin when they bought the land and built the new house, but Carey had turned it into his music and painting studio. He always liked ruins.

"I see my old friend still stands," he said. "I'm surprised Mr. Squarebox hasn't torn it down yet."

"It's not his to tear down."

"No, it will always be ours, won't it? That's one of our special places, the place where our son was conceived." He smiled his sweet smile and said, "Maybe we'll be there again someday, making love with our tape recorder on."

"Maybe in your dreams."

"Why don't you leave Mr. Squarebox to his Cheerios and come camping with us?" he said. "Just Tommy and me and babe makes three."

She started to say, "You're such an asshole," but Tommy came running out of the house with his fishing rod and duffle bag, and Carey yelled, "There's my boy!"

She had gotten so used to having Greg and Tommy around that she wasn't sure what to do by herself. She mopped the kitchen, stared at her computer for a while, watched some TV and ate a sandwich. She regretted snapping at Greg. He was a kind man, even if he was square. She wanted to marry him so she could forget about Carey's ruined smile, but there was an angry boy standing between them.

The sun was going down when she called her friend, Ginger. "Got any plans tonight?" she asked.

"Nope. Let's go out and boogie. If you get too fucked up to drive, you can spend the night here."

Ginger's house was just ten miles away, but it was in a foreign world because it was in the city. Buying land in the country had been Carey's idea and, at first, Denise had hated the isolation. Then, the silence started to sound good, and she gave up a better job in town to keep accounts for a tractor dealership not far from the house. Now, country silence was in her blood, and she couldn't imagine living in the city again. She wondered how Carey could stand it.

He hates cities even more than I do, she thought as she parked in front of Ginger's little two-story house. He lives in a place he hates and makes his living playing the kind of music he hates. It's like he's punishing himself.

No, it's like I'm punishing him. I took it all away from him.

As she rang Ginger's doorbell, she glimpsed Carey's pale face for a moment in the porch light and saw the sadness in his smile. A sharp, damp breeze blew up her coat and made her shiver.

"You look all ragged," Ginger said. "What's wrong, you and Greg been fighting?"

"No, it's more like me and Tommy," Denise said. "He's been a real pain in the butt. He doesn't like Greg very much."

"Kids," Ginger said. "Only time I have a life is when mine are with their dad. Want some reefer?"

The marijuana was powerful and, after a couple hits, Denise began to feel paranoid. She thought she heard

Carey's voice, but it was just a thin ambulance siren receding in the distance. Then she heard his voice again. "We've got our secret places," he seemed to be saying. "We've got the link."

"What's wrong, Denny?" Ginger asked.

"Nothing. This dope's too strong for me."

"Yeah, it's some righteous shit okay. Wanna do a couple lines to clear your head?"

Denise snorted some coke through a straw, and her head rang like a tuning fork. She heard the siren again, somewhere in the distance, but coming closer.

"My nerves are shot," she said. "I let Tommy go camping with Carey, and now I'm not sure it was a good idea."

"Nothing involving that asshole is a good idea, in my opinion," Ginger said. "Madam Alex says he's going to cause some bad trouble pretty soon." She relit the joint and took a deep hit.

"Who's Madam Alex?"

"You know, that spiritualist medium I've been seeing. She's the real thing, Denny, you have to meet her."

"She said something about Carey?"

"She said I know some drug addict sicko who's going to cause some bad trouble pretty soon, and Carey's the only drug addict sicko I know."

"He says he's quit."

"Yep, and the bear says he quit shitting in the woods. He's not straight and sober like you and me." Ginger choked on her weed and began to giggle.

The siren kept coming closer. The ambulance seemed to be prowling all the streets around the house, looking for some sort of misery. The thin wail reminded Denise of one of Carey's old songs, but she couldn't remember the words —something about hate and death.

"You remember one of Carey's songs that goes, 'They say you can't take it with you, but I'm gonna try'?" she asked. "I think it's on his first album."

"I never could stand his music," Ginger said. "Too morbid. His songs all sound like suicide notes to me."

"There's something about a book and a flashlight," Denise said. "Something like 'Better bring a bright flashlight, 'cause it's dark down below.' You remember that line?"

"Nope," Ginger said. "You're getting weird, Denny. Maybe you need another hit."

"Flashlight, blanket, better pack a novel," Denise said. "That's what he wanted Tommy to pack today, just like in the song. It's weird."

"Nope, *you're* weird, Denny. You're getting freaky on me."

"I guess I am. Sorry, Ginger, but it's been a rough week and I'm not feeling so hot. I think I better go home and go to bed."

"Damn, girl, you just got here!"

On the way home she called Tommy to make sure he was all right. "I caught three great, big bass," he said. "Daddy cooked them on the hibachi, and he said they was the best fishes he ever ate in his whole life. Now we're reading Harry Potter out loud."

It was obvious Tommy was eager to get off the phone, so she told him she loved him and hung up. When she got home, she drank a glass of wine and went straight to bed. She felt exhausted, maybe because of the weed, and soon she was dreaming she was lying on the bed Carey used to keep in the old house. Carey was lying next to her, flat on his back and deathly still with his eyes open. He was naked and so was she, and she felt uneasy because she didn't think she was supposed to be lying in bed naked with him. She was trying to explain to him that they shouldn't be in bed together like this when suddenly, without moving, Carey let out a high-pitched shriek.

Denise sat up, terrified. It was the same siren she'd heard at Ginger's house, but it wasn't somewhere outside—it was right in the room, in fact, right inside her head, and she realized it was Carey's voice shrieking.

She grabbed her cellphone from the nightstand and called Tommy's number, but he didn't answer. No wonder—it was after two in the morning and he'd be fast asleep—but she let it ring until it went to voicemail and then tried calling again. Carey didn't own a cellphone because he thought they caused brain tumors—like he'd notice.

She told herself there was nothing to worry about, but she threw on her clothes anyway, and a few minutes later she was driving fast in the direction of the cabin. October drizzle painted the highway dark, and the siren seemed to be following her car, warbling in the wind like lyrics of an old song she couldn't quite remember. Headlights glared on her wet windshield, and she saw Carey's sweet ruined smile in the smear of the wiper blade. Then, she thought she heard his voice.

> *Babe, I have seen the other side,*
> *and I've found a secret place where I can hide...*

The drizzle turned into a hard rain as she turned off the highway onto a narrow back road that twisted through the hills. A cold wind was trying to blow her car off the wet asphalt, and soon she had no idea which direction she was going. Some months had passed since she had traveled these roads and, back then, it was Greg who had always done the driving.

But she felt that Carey was the one steering her wheel

now. She slowed down and turned into a muddy gravel lane. Yes, this was the place. She remembered a warm glow of long-ago nights, the smell of marijuana smoke and wood crackling in the fireplace, Carey's face young and handsome in the flickering firelight and still filled with hope. Those were good days while they lasted.

The pitted gravel lane ended at the cabin, and his red Volkswagen was parked beside it. She got out and knocked on the door, but no one answered. She knocked again.

There was a rustling behind her. She turned and saw Carey emerging from the dark woods. He was stark naked, his long hair plastered against his thin shoulders in the cold rain. He stared at her with a look of utter confusion.

"Jesus Christ, you asshole!" she yelled. "You're stoned out of your fucking mind. Where's Tommy?"

He staggered closer, still staring at her as if he had no idea who she was or even what country he was in. He stopped a few feet away from her and tottered on his feet like a thin, drenched weed swaying in the wind.

"Where is he?" she yelled. "He better not be out here in this rain. I swear to God, I'll press charges."

Carey opened his mouth to answer, but only a gargling noise came out. Suddenly, a red gash opened in his throat and blood poured out. He clutched at it with an agonized expression, and blood trickled between his fingers, turning the rain on his naked chest red.

Denise stepped back, confused and terrified. She opened the cabin door and groped her way inside. The only light came from a few embers in the fireplace, but it was enough for her to dimly make out a flashlight on the table. She switched it on, aimed it around the room, and yelled Tommy's name several times.

The front room was a small living room with a tiny

kitchenette attached. The doors to the two bedrooms were shut. She opened the nearer one and saw Tommy lying in the bed, but as she moved the flashlight beam to his face, she saw that it wasn't Tommy after all. It was Carey, covered with blood. His throat was slashed and, though his eyes were wide open, she knew he was dead.

But she had just seen him outside.

She screamed and fell against the doorframe, barely able to stand. When she was able to stop screaming, she went to the other bedroom door and opened it. Tommy lay crumpled on the floor with the side of his head bashed open.

CAREY LINDEN, Caucasion male, thirty-six years old, killed his son, Tommy Linden, age ten, by beating him to death with a ball bat. He then killed himself by severing his left carotid artery and partially severing his larynx with a box cutter. The violence of the homicide suggested it was an unpremeditated crime of passion.

So said the police report, but Denise didn't believe the act was unpremeditated. "I think he was planning this for years," she told Greg. "Somewhere in the back of his mind, anyway. Maybe not killing Tommy, but killing himself, at least."

"Quit thinking about it, Denny," Greg said. "This isn't helping you."

Today was day thirteen, and it felt just as horrible as the other twelve days. Her throat was so sore from crying that she didn't think she could do it anymore, but every few minutes the painful, racking noise would emerge again from her throat like a vomit of razor blades. Tommy's funeral had been Saturday, a full week after his death because the police had kept his body for several days. Though funerals are supposed to comfort the grieving, she could imagine nothing worse. Greg had practically needed to carry her to her chair at the graveside, and then he'd needed to hold her shoulder tightly to keep her from falling out of it.

"Listen to this," she said.

Carey's first album was already on the CD player because she'd been listening to it much of the afternoon while Greg was away at work. She put on the third track, and the long instrumental opening filled the living room, muted drums beating slowly, a thin shriek of a guitar somewhere in the distance like an ambulance far away, coming closer, and Carey's keyboard following behind it, weaving together a sad, sweet hymn that built relentlessly into a thundering, drug-demented funeral dirge.

"What is this?" Greg asked.

She handed him the CD case and watched him stare at the cover, a cemetery scene painted by Carey. The name of the band, The Messengers, was scrawled in red letters in the brooding night sky like graffiti finger-painted in blood. The name of the album, "Telegram from the Tomb," was carved in the stone marking an open grave. She remembered when he had painted it, and the blood-red letters were her own idea.

The instruments suddenly hushed. They drew their breath and started again, like quiet, dark figures rustling in the misty distance, and Carey's small, hollow voice tiptoed between them like a mournful ghost.

> *Babe, I have seen the other side,*
> *and I've found a secret place where I can hide*
> *in the darkness, waiting there beyond the gate,*

safe from ugliness and pain and beastly hate.

She hit the pause button and said, "You see what I mean? It's like he thought of death as some kind of secret hiding place. I think he killed Tommy so he could keep him all to himself in his secret place, like, in death, Tommy would belong to him."

"I don't think that's what the words mean," Greg said. "I think it's just some kind of drug message."

The coroner had found no trace of drugs in his body, and the police had interviewed two of his close friends who said he'd been clean for twelve months, but she didn't believe it.

"Even if he was clean, it didn't make any difference," she said, though Greg had already heard this argument several times before. "He did so many drugs for so long that he made himself permanently crazy. Do you think a ghost can be insane, too? I mean, is he just as demented now as he was before?"

She hit the play button, and Carey sang:

> *Babe, you have thrust me in the hole,*
> *you stole my heart, stole my house, stole my soul,*
> *guess our secrets are all that I can keep—*
> *I've hid them safe beneath the ground, six feet*
>   *deep.*

"It's so weird," she said. "He wrote those words long before we split up, like he already knew I was going to leave him."

"Please, sweetheart, let go of it."

"Listen to this one," she said, and kicked the player up to track seven. This song was faster and louder, drums pounding deep and a furious guitar clashing like steel against the angry keyboard. Carey's voice sounded lean and hard.

> *They say you can't take it with you,*
> *but I'm gonna try,*
> *gonna pack some equipment*
> *before I die.*
> *Gonna bring a heavy blanket,*
> *'cause it's cold in the ground,*
> *gonna bring my radio,*
> *'cause worms make no sound!*

The keyboard and guitar clashed together like swords. "Can you please turn it down?" Greg yelled.

The instruments screamed louder, and Carey's voice screamed over them.

> *Better bring a bright flashlight,*
> *'cause it's dark down below.*
> *Better pack a good long novel,*
> *'cause forever goes by slow!*

Denise shut off the stereo, and the sudden silence made the room seem huge and empty. "Blanket, flashlight, novel," she said. "Those are exactly the things Carey told Tommy to bring."

"That doesn't mean anything. People bring flashlights and blankets when they go camping."

"It's like he was planning this years ago," she said.

"Denny, you're just making things harder for yourself."

"Carey's mind was complicated," she said. "You wouldn't understand."

She heard the tone of contempt in her voice, but right now Greg's feelings didn't seem very important. What was important was her intuition, and it was telling her that Carey had planned this for a long time—and his dirty work wasn't finished.

"He's going to kill me next," she said quietly. "If he can."

"What?"

"Carey's ghost wants to kill me. He killed Tommy to keep him for himself, and he wants me all for himself, too."

Greg held her and said, "Denny, please, you have to stop thinking like this. There's no such thing as a ghost and nobody's going to kill you."

"I told you a hundred times, I saw his ghost outside the cabin."

"No, you didn't. You need to let go of these horrible thoughts, sweetheart. They're just making things worse. You were in a state of shock that night, and you thought you saw something that wasn't there. There wasn't any ghost, and nobody's going to hurt you."

He was patting her back awkwardly, as if he were burping a baby, and she didn't feel soothed. She was thinking of the final words Carey had spoken to her: "Just Tommy and me and babe makes three."

"You think you'll be able to sleep tonight?" Greg asked.

"Yeah, I'm halfway there, now," Denise said. "I'll be all the way in a few more minutes."

It was a lie, but Greg sounded so tired that she didn't want to keep him awake again. It was already past midnight, and his usual bedtime was right after the eleven o'clock news. She'd kept him awake many nights now with her talk and tears, but she intended to face the rest of this night alone.

"You promise you'll see the doctor Monday?" he asked.

"I promise."

"You need to ask her for some kind of sedative to soothe your nerves."

"I will."

"I love you," he said.

"Love you, too."

She kissed his forehead and watched his eyes fall shut. He was a good man, but she wondered if he had fallen in love with the wrong person. He had no idea that she still took drugs occasionally and sometimes even slept with other men. And he'd surely be shocked if he knew some of the things she and Carey had done years ago, long after the eleven o'clock news was over.

Though he loved her, she knew he would never understand her, just as he would never believe in intuition or premonitions or ghosts or the link she and Carey shared. Her link to a dead murderer.

Her mind was racing, and when she was sure he was fast asleep she eased out of bed and put her robe on. Downstairs, she poured a glass of wine and sat at the kitchen table in the dark. She felt something pulling at her thoughts, and she believed it was her link with Carey. He was trying to influence her in some way, trying to draw her into his darkness, and she waited to hear what words he would say, but no words came.

It occurred to her that, by slashing his own throat, maybe he'd rendered even his ghost speechless; in front of the cabin he'd tried to speak, but then the gash had appeared and only a gargling noise had come out.

She was sipping her wine when a terrible thought suddenly came to her: *This isn't the first time he has killed!*

The thought startled her. Had she been married to a serial killer without knowing it? Had Carey murdered others while they were living together and raising their son? It seemed hard to believe, but the thought was lodged in her head and refused to go away. Certainly, Carey had always been a deeply private person, with his dark songs, his secret places, his unknowable mysteries.

She had no doubt he wanted to kill her so the three of them could be together. Surely ghosts couldn't kill, since they had no substance, but she believed he was trying to use their link to drive her to suicide. It wouldn't be difficult; suicide had been on her mind every day since she'd found Tommy's body.

She felt him pulling at her, trying to draw her outside into the night. She told herself she wasn't afraid of Carey's ghost and didn't fear death. Life was what frightened her. She wanted to confront him, scream at him, call him a bastard and a murderer, shout him away into whatever deep circle of hell he belonged in, and, most of all, get him out of her head.

She put on shoes, slipped a warm coat over her robe, and stepped out the back door. The late October breeze was chilly. The woods were dark and deep, gnarled trees still clutching some of their leaves, unwilling to let go of the dead. The old farmhouse was a blot of deeper darkness but, as she approached it, she thought she saw a dim light in one of the downstairs windows. Impossible—the electric had been shut off three years ago, right after Carey moved out.

But something pale and luminous kept flitting across the window of the big front room that Carey had turned into his music studio. Then she heard him singing, if singing was the right word. It was the kind of mournful wailing that he used to call his "elemental music," but this sounded gargled and strangled, as if it was coming out of a slashed throat.

A sudden gust swept a confetti of dead leaves down from the trees, and she pulled her coat tighter. Pale ghost-light flitted across the dirty glass, and when she was a few feet away from it she saw him.

He was stark naked, his thin white body glistening like a luminous eel in the front room lit by no light other than his skin. He was dancing slowly, with his slender arms stretched above his head, but as she came closer and stared through the dirty glass she saw that his feet weren't quite touching the floor. His arms seemed to be suspended by ropes from the sagging ceiling, but there weren't any ropes.

He spun slowly in the ruined room, blood leaking from his throat whenever he sang too loudly. His penis was erect, and it looked longer and thicker than she remembered. His sad, elemental wailing turned into the semblance of a tune she recognized and, though he apparently wasn't able to utter the lyrics, her mind filled them in:

> *Tommy, we have reached the other side,*
> *and I've found a secret place where we can hide*
> *in the darkness, waiting here beyond the gate,*
> *safe from ugliness and pain and beastly hate.*

She must have let out a sound, because he suddenly spun around and spotted her with bloodshot, staring eyes of death. He tried to speak, but the wound in his throat opened wide and an ugly gurgling noise came out. His face contorted with horror, and he clutched the wound and tried again to speak, but there was just the wet wheezing sound of bloody air blowing between his fingers.

Denise wanted to scream curses at him, but she wasn't able to speak much more clearly than he was. Her words came out in a hoarse, dry rasp: "You bastard, you fucking bastard! You killed my son."

His naked, white body swept toward her, and his head and shoulders came crashing through the window, the glass shredding his face as it broke.

Denise had fallen to the ground, and Carey's wounded throat bled onto her face while he stared down at her. His trunk was hanging out of the window, his bare chest cut and pierced with broken glass. He was trying to reach down and grab her, but the window ledge was too high, and his arms were shaking spasmodically, as if he could control them no better than his voice.

She tasted his blood dripping onto her lips. She tried to get up but couldn't. Her body was paralyzed; it felt like part of the dirt. She was sprawled in an awkward position with her legs wide apart, and she didn't want to be exposed to him like that, but she couldn't close them. As he stared down at her, a cold gust of wind blew a dead leaf up her robe, and she felt it inching up her bare thigh like a dry, withered hand.

Carey's shaky hands were inscribing a figure like a jagged circle in the air. At first, she thought he was trying to cast some sort of magical spell that only the dead knew, but then she realized he was drawing a picture of his secret place, the place where he wanted her to be. *Just Tommy and me and babe makes three, in our own special circle of hell.*

It was an invitation.

The dead leaf felt its way up her thigh with its dry little fingers and discovered that she wasn't wearing underwear. She tried to shut her legs as it began scratching against her most secret place, but her muscles were made of gelatin.

Carey gazed down at her, still drawing a jagged circle in the air, and at last she found her voice. "You sick fucking bastard!" she shouted. "Go back to hell, where you belong!"

She was still shouting when she heard the back door open and Greg shouted, "Denny, what's wrong?" As he helped her up from the dead leaves and broken glass, she saw that Carey was no longer hanging out the window. But now he seemed to be everywhere, in the rustling trees, in the chill night air, and in the folds of her brain.

"GHOSTS *CAN* KILL YOU," Ginger said. "I just got off the phone with Madame Alex, and she says it's not even unusual."

"But they don't have any substance," Denise said.

"Didn't you tell me he broke the window in that old house? Isn't that exactly what you said? Madame Alex says poltergeists can throw objects around a room and knock over heavy tables. She's seen it happen many times. So, why can't they grab up a butcher knife and stab you with it? She says they have some kind of ectoplasmic body, and it can kill you just as dead as Ted Bundy."

Carey obviously did have some sort of body. After Greg had led her into the house last night, Denise looked in the bathroom mirror and found wet blood on her face. But she wasn't cut anywhere—it was Carey's blood, dead man's blood. She had scrubbed her face with soap three times, but she could still feel it there like a permanent mark.

"You got to do something about this, right away," Ginger said. "Madame Alex says a lot of times what you think are ghosts are really demons, though, in Carey's case, there's probably not much difference. She can help you, she knows how to clear out ghosts and demons. She's done it many times, cleared out houses that were so haunted you wouldn't even want to set foot in them. You need to get her out there right away, Denny. She's not cheap, but she knows what she's doing."

Denise's heart felt funny, as if somebody were pressing a cold hand against it, and she held the phone away from her ear. She doubted Madame Alex could eradicate this horror from her life, and she wasn't sure she wanted her to. Carey's ghost felt like some tenuous connection to Tommy, or maybe just a connection to death, and maybe that was what she really wanted.

"Denny, are you there?" Ginger asked.

"I don't think I want some kind of ghost hunter out here. I'll try to deal with it myself."

"Denny, you *can't* deal with it by yourself. You're gonna end up dead."

"I gotta hang up now. Greg's calling for me."

It wasn't true; through the kitchen window she saw Greg raking leaves in the backyard. When she got up that morning, she was surprised to find he wasn't at work, and it took her a moment to realize it was Saturday. She had taken a month of unpaid leave from her job and, without a schedule, time had become a confusing blur. She was glad she wouldn't be spending the day alone but, at the same time, it seemed a chore to be with him or anyone else. If he were at work, she could lie in bed and wallow in her misery, which was all she really wanted to do. Now she needed to act like a normal human being.

She put on a jacket and stepped outside. Greg stopped raking and smiled at her.

"How are you feeling?" he asked.

"Pretty good."

"Nice day," he said.

"Yeah."

Though the air was cool, and clouds were gathering in the north, the sky overhead was bright with early afternoon sun.

"It's going to rain later," he said. "But tomorrow's supposed to be beautiful, seventy-eight degrees and sunny. Let's have a picnic and go hiking."

"I don't think I'm up for that."

"Sunshine, fresh air, exercise, that would be the best thing for you. Get you out of this house."

She nestled her face against his shoulder. His denim jacket smelled like him, masculine, simple, and comforting, the smell of sanity and good common sense, the kind of common sense that believed sunshine, fresh air, and exercise could cure anything. But she knew it couldn't.

"I don't think I want to," she said.

"Well, you can't just sit around every day feeling miserable. I'll buy some sandwich meat after dinner and pack us a nice picnic lunch."

"Where do you want to go?"

"How about Ash Cave?"

Ash Cave was in Hocking Hills State Park just a few miles from Lake Logan, where Tommy had been killed.

"That's too close to the..." She couldn't quite get the word *cabin* out of her mouth.

"Look, Denny, you need to reclaim your life, and this is one way to do it. We hike around in the beautiful hills on a nice sunny day, and then that part of the state will no longer be tainted by what happened there. It's a way to make things good again."

He let his rake fall so he could hold her. He felt big and muscular and sensible and... blind.

"I don't know," she said.

She noticed he was staring at the old house, and she hoped he wouldn't ask any more questions about what had happened there. Last night she'd told him she had stepped out for some air and had fallen when a raccoon startled her by scuttling out of the broken window. She didn't think he'd believed her, but he hadn't pressed the matter.

"I've been thinking," he said. "Let's have that old house torn down before it falls down. The roof is caving in. Why don't I call around and get some estimates? You know what would be nice on that spot? A tennis court."

She pulled away, suddenly angry. What the hell was he talking about? A fucking tennis court. It wasn't his house, it was hers, hers and Carey's. It was a sacred place, the place where Tommy had been conceived.

"What makes you think this is your land anyway?" she said. "Last time I looked at the deed, it belonged to me."

"Sorry." Greg picked up his rake and started raking.

"You don't understand anything," she said. There was a hard edge in her voice, and she felt the words weren't her own. They were Carey's words; she believed he was somehow speaking through her. "You've never made music or painted a painting," she said, "and you've never tried to see what's on the other side of the canvas. You've never really lived, and you don't know anything about life or death."

Greg leaned on his rake and stared at her. "You're right, I guess I don't know much about art and music," he said. "I guess I'm stupid that way. But I know I love you, and I know I want both of us to be happy."

"Happy," she said. "Baby, I've seen the other side, and that word doesn't mean anything to me anymore."

She hurried back into the house and hid in the bedroom, trying to make sense out of her feelings. Greg was trying to help her become well again, but she wasn't sure she wanted to be well. His kindness was useless because he wasn't able to bring Tommy back, and he wasn't able to understand the dark power that was luring her away from his world of sunshine and sanity. She hated Carey but, at the same time, was drawn to him. Or maybe she was just drawn to death, because Tommy was there somewhere on the other side.

> *Guess our secrets are all that I can keep—*
> *I've hid them safe beneath the ground, six feet*
>   *deep.*

It was getting dark when Greg tapped on the bedroom door and said, "Dinner's ready."

"I'm not hungry," she said.

"I'm sorry for what I said about tearing down the old house. I apologize."

"I'm not mad at you, I'm just not feeling good."

"Denny, you've got to eat."

She came downstairs, reluctantly. Greg had grilled two ribeye steaks in the backyard, steamed some little redskin potatoes, and fixed a salad. They ate without speaking. The meat was tender and juicy, but she found it hard to chew and left most of it on her plate.

"I should go pick up some picnic food for tomorrow," he said after clearing away their dishes. "Want to come with me?"

"No, I think I'll watch a little TV. Thanks for fixing dinner."

She put on her coat as soon as his taillights disappeared out of the driveway. She thought of returning to the old house, but something told her that wasn't the place Carey had reserved for their date tonight. She got in her car and drove south, not sure where she was going.

"Where will it be tonight?" she asked out loud.

She remembered a little fishing park with a few dilapidated picnic tables beside the river. She and Carey used to go there some nights. She remembered one soft summer night when they dropped some mescaline there and then drifted down the river in a rubber raft watching the stars throb and blaze like great pulsing hearts.

She drove to the riverbank, sat on the grass and watched the still water. She felt oddly peaceful, her mind nearly blank and her muscles comfortable and relaxed. She felt no fear or apprehension, only a calm eagerness. The air smelled like rain, and she felt a few drops.

Then she saw him in the distance on the other side of the river walking toward her on the water. His naked body glowed silver-white like a thin sliver of moon glistening in the night air. He was staggering, or maybe slipping on the still water, smooth as ice. He stopped a few feet away from the bank and gazed at her. He looked emaciated, his clammy white skin clinging to frail bones, and she wondered if dead people could waste away with illness like the living.

"I want you to take me to Tommy," she said. "I want to be with him again."

Carey tried to speak, and the bloody gash appeared in his throat. He clamped his hand over it and when he tried again an ugly squawking sound emerged. "Squaw! Squaw!" he seemed to be saying.

"I'm not afraid of death," she said. "I no longer have anything to live for. You've taken everything away from me, so, now, take me to my son."

Carey's face contorted in a terrible grimace, maybe a malevolent grin or maybe something else, and he again inscribed a jagged circle in the air with his spasmodically jerking hands.

Thunder cracked overhead, and suddenly a cold, hard rain was falling, beating the surface of the river into an angry froth. The pale apparition seemed to melt in the rain until there was nothing left but a glowing puddle on the river, and then it, too, disappeared.

"You bastard!" she shouted. "Where did you go?"

She stood there in the rain for a long time, but he didn't return. Finally, she pulled her wet coat tighter and went to her car, feeling jilted, as if death had stood her up.

LAST NIGHT's rain left the air clean and pure. The sky was a perfect blue and the sun shone warm and bright through the bare branches. After eating a picnic lunch, they climbed down steep steps carved into cool, ancient rock and eventually came to a large, open cave beneath a massive overhanging ledge. A waterfall ran from the top of the ledge to a small, clear pool in a rock basin beneath them. The cool cave air and the water's echoing roar soothed her pain like an icepack placed on a sore muscle.

They stood inside the cave for several minutes without speaking and then descended into a valley green with fern. Despite the nice weather, there'd been few cars in the parking lot and, so far, they'd seen nobody else. The place seemed to belong to them and, as they began to climb out of the valley, she reached for Greg's hand and held it tightly, as if he were guiding her up into a happier world.

He was pointing out birds and plants and other colorful details, obviously trying to cheer her up and keep her focused on the here and now, but she wasn't paying any attention to his words. She was wondering why she was able to see Carey's ghost but not Tommy's. She'd never been religious and had never believed in Heaven or Hell, but, now that she had proof of some sort of afterlife, she was rethinking her beliefs. If souls survived, then there probably was some sort of heaven and hell, maybe nothing like what churchgoers believed in with angels and demons and all that, but surely murderers and fiends wouldn't enjoy the same afterlife as kind and loving people?

Carey's ghost was a hellish thing. Maybe his soul would always have to wander about on Earth, tormented and confused, because of the evil deed he'd done. Maybe his throat would always gape open with his own self-inflicted wound, rendering him speechless and isolated. Maybe his hands would always convulse and shake, so he couldn't even communicate with them. Maybe, by killing himself and his son, he had removed himself for all eternity from the fellowship of others.

But Tommy had been cut down in his innocence, and it wouldn't be his fate to roam about Earth helplessly, like his killer. That's why she hadn't seen his ghost. Surely, there must be a sunny and joyful place for the innocent, a place much better than Earth.

"Look, there's a blue jay," Greg said, and he went on cheerfully talking about how even though blue jays were beautiful birds they sometimes stole other birds' nests and destroyed their eggs.

But Denise wasn't thinking about birds. She was thinking that her desire to die was selfish and wrong. Tommy was in a better place—he had to be—and the terrible pain she was feeling was self-pity rather than pity for him. Surely, Tommy was feeling no pain now, and she was doing him no good by wallowing in her own.

For a long while they'd been ascending a steep, narrow path and, at last, they reached the pinnacle of a high ledge. They stopped to gaze down into the deep gorge in front of them. Greg stopped chattering, maybe because he couldn't find words for what they were looking at. He slung his denim jacket over his shoulder and held her hand tightly.

The view here was magnificent, and the depth of the gorge caused Denise's stomach to tighten. She made a silent promise to the natural beauty down there far below her feet. She would no longer seek out Carey or his dark ticket to death. She would devote every effort to becoming well again. She knew the pain of Tommy's loss would always be with her, like a hollow place in her heart, but she would make the hurt a little smaller each day until it became a manageable ache, a distant throb.

But then she saw him. He was on the other side of the gorge, perched in the top of a stunted pine like a demonic angel on top of a Christmas tree.

She took a step back and let out a sound. "What?" Greg asked.

She pointed and said, "Can you see him?"

"I don't see anyone," he said. "We seem to have the place all to ourselves."

"It's Carey."

"No, it's not. Carey's dead. It's just your nerves, sweetheart." Greg put his arm around her waist and held her tightly. "Look at something else, and the image will disappear. Look at those goldfinches."

She tried to look at something else, but Carey had stepped out of the tree and was walking toward her on the air above the gorge. He seemed to be having trouble keeping his balance, and his thin arms were stretched out at his sides like a tightrope walker's bar.

He stopped, maybe, twenty feet in front of her, still standing on air, so close now she could see the pale blue of his eyes. He looked out of place in this sunshine, naked and skinny and white with the pallor of death, a phantom of the night, far out of his element. He no longer looked frightening, but clownish, and even ridiculous, as he struggled to stay upright in the slippery air.

He stared at her and started making the same squawking noise he'd made last night. "Squaw! Squaw!" he screamed while clutching his hands against the bleeding wound on his throat.

"Go away," she said quietly. "You don't have any link with me anymore."

"What did you say?" Greg asked.

"I'm telling Carey to get the fuck away from me. I won't allow him to haunt me anymore."

Carey looked desperate, his face contorted with some kind of agony. He pulled his bloody hands away from his throat and began drawing the same jagged circle in the air—but his hands weren't jerking quite so badly today, and Denise suddenly realized it wasn't a circle after all.

It was a box. A square box.

A terrible chill ran down her back. She pulled away from Greg's embrace and said, "You."

"Huh?" Greg said.

"Squaw! Squaw!" Carey was shrieking. And then the words came out: "Squaw-box! Squarebox killed us!"

She backed farther away from Greg and said, "You did it. You killed my son."

"Are you crazy?" Greg said.

"No, you are. You had a spare key to the cabin. You drove down there and sneaked in and killed them." She pulled her cellphone from her shirt pocket and said, "I'm calling the police."

Carey was squawking and shrieking, his throat gurgling with blood. "He'll kill you!" he shrieked. "Run!"

Greg grabbed her wrist. He wrenched the phone from her hand and tossed it into the gorge. He got ahold of her other wrist and pulled her close. She tried to put her knee in his groin, but he had her pressed too close against his body.

"Calm down," he said. He shoved her to the ground and fell on top of her, pinning her there with two hundred pounds of hard muscle. When she started screaming, he reached for his denim jacket, which had fallen to the ground, and shoved one of the sleeves into her mouth.

His expression was calm and bland. "I didn't mean to kill Tommy," he said. "You have to believe me. I didn't know he was there, nobody told me, and I'm sorry, I had to do it. But I think you can understand why I had to get rid of Carey. He was always going to be standing between us, ruining our relationship. You were too connected to him. You even admitted the two of you had some kind of link. And all that trouble we were having with Tommy, you know perfectly well it was Carey's fault. Tommy was never going to accept me as a father because he was too wrapped up with that degenerate drug addict. And that's all he was, Denny, a damn degenerate."

She heard Carey shrieking somewhere nearby, and suddenly his naked body fell onto Greg's back. Denise felt the cold bones beneath his icy skin whenever his hands brushed against her face, but Greg didn't seem to notice anything. There was no *link*, nothing for Carey to grab onto, and he tugged desperately at Greg's shoulders with no effect.

"But you have to understand, I didn't want to kill

Tommy. You have to believe that. I took care of Carey and was getting ready to leave when Tommy woke up and came wandering out of the other bedroom. I didn't even know he was there but, after he saw me, I didn't have any choice, and I did what I had to do."

Denise was struggling desperately and choking on the jacket sleeve, but Greg was calm. His expression was blandly pleasant, and his voice sounded even-tempered and reasonable, as if he were explaining some everyday matter.

"You have to understand, Denny, I did this for you. I did it for us. I wanted us to have a happy life together, and we'd never have that with Carey standing between us. People sometimes have to kill, sweetheart. They do it for war and they do it for love. I've had to do it before, myself. I had to kill my own brother when I was just sixteen. He had some dirt on me and was going to get me in a lot of trouble, so I had to throw him in front of a freight train. I didn't want to, but I had no choice."

Greg raised his head and looked carefully around in all directions. "Don't think badly of me, Denny," he said. "I have a good heart, and I love you, and I wish I didn't have to do this."

Before she knew what was happening, he wrenched her to her feet and hurled her over the ledge. Time slowed and nearly stopped. She saw him gazing down at her from the ledge, and his face was pleasantly bland with a faint smile that seemed to say, "Job well done."

The jacket sleeve was no longer in her mouth, and her scream pierced the sunny air and echoed off the stone walls of the abyss. She looked down at her feet and saw they were pumping up and down as if she were peddling a bicycle, and far beneath them she saw the rocky bottom of the gorge. It was coming closer, but slowly, slowly, as if it had all the time in the world and was in no hurry to extinguish her life.

And then she saw them standing together down there, looking up at her, and they looked so much alike, Carey and Tommy, both of them pale and skinny with long, golden hair and pale, blue eyes. They were watching her expectantly and, as she drew closer, they both raised their arms as if intending to catch her. In the last moment, just before she reached them, she heard Carey's voice in her mind:

Just Tommy and me and babe makes three.

SHEOL

BY PAUL STANSFIELD

The end came quickly for Keith Moody, and relatively painlessly. In fact, it was precisely the sort of death that most people, given their choice, would pick; dying while asleep.

It was a brain embolism in Keith's case. He was even dreaming when it happened. Like other outside stimuli, such as alarm clocks going off, or conversation, the slight pain and confusion of dying was actually briefly incorporated into Keith's dream. One minute, he was having anal sex with Brooke Shields; the next, he was sniffing cocaine with the members of Mötley Crüe. The coke, when inhaled, caused some irritation, and weird images to go through his mind. Keith had never actually done cocaine, so he was unsure of how it felt or what it did, exactly. So, his mind threw in an approximate cause for his real-life trauma. But then his brain shut down and he died, all without waking up.

The next thing Keith was aware of was standing in a strange place. The sky was purplish-black, with no sun, although a dim sort of light nevertheless could still be seen.

All around him were many, many people, more than he'd seen at one time ever, including at a rock concert in a stadium. Thousands and thousands, perhaps millions. All naked, too. Here and there, Keith noticed huge piles of worms. Two kinds; white tiny maggots and larger, brown-reddish earthworms. The ground—or, more properly, the floor—was a dingy light gray, and it felt like concrete. That was all.

He turned around, several times, to see if he could find anything more. He couldn't. The same people, worms, and sky in all directions. Keith looked closely at himself. Aside from his also being naked, he looked basically the same. Same body hair, same height and weight, same moles, same scars. Well, he did look extremely pale, even by his light Irish ancestry standards. But maybe that was because of the light.

He looked around some more, and grinned. *What a strange dream!* This observation always cheered him. Whenever he realized in a dream that he was dreaming, he usually chose to change it, make it more fun. Keith tried to do this now. Thought of float-flying, but nothing happened. Pictured himself in a zoot suit, standing in a garish Monte Carlo casino; again, nothing. Imagined himself hitting the World Series-winning home run for the San Diego Padres, without success. *Oh well, might as well make the most of it.*

Keith wandered over to his nearest neighbors (a short trip) and started talking. First, he addressed a man in his sixties who was sitting and staring off into space. "Hi, where are we?"

The man didn't even look up.

Keith tried again on a fortyish woman with a pot belly. Again, no response.

He asked, perhaps, thirty people this question before a

teenaged girl finally answered. "Sheol," she said in a quiet monotone.

"Where's Sheol located?" he asked his helpful informant.

"I don't know."

"Well, what's your name? I'm Keith. Keith Moody."

"I don't know."

"You don't know your name?"

"No." Keith shook his head bemusedly at this and, after it was apparent she had nothing more to say, walked away. He stared some more at his comrades. He noticed that although all the various human races were represented, they all looked pale somehow. White, Black, Asian, Indian—all paler colors of whatever shade they were. *Strange.* As he studied the crowd, he abruptly saw a woman blink into existence. She resembled all the others. After a moment, she sat down on the hard floor next to some other people. There was complete silence. Probably millions of people together, none talking. He shook his head again.

A few minutes later, a boy popped into being. He was Asian, probably nine or ten years old. This time Keith ran up to this newcomer. "Who are you?" he asked.

The boy looked back at him. A first, here. "I'm Randy Wilson."

"Where are you from?"

"Fort Wayne, Indiana."

It went on like this for several minutes. Keith learned Randy's address, phone number, what grade he was in, how many siblings Randy had, what TV shows he liked, what his father did for a living. Finally, he paused, having run out of immediate questions. Randy took this opportunity to ask one of his own.

"Where's my family? We were driving to Gary to see my Nana. Then I was here. Where are they?"

Now it was Keith's turn to say he didn't know. Just as he did, a very old, tall woman interrupted. "If they died like you, they're here somewhere. If not, they're still alive. You can look, but you probably won't find them, even if they are here."

Randy took this news calmly. Before Keith could scold her for her insensitivity, she said, "You're quite curious, aren't you? So was I. I got here hours before you did. I managed to learn some."

At last! He forgot all about Randy. "Okay, where are we? One person called it 'Sheol', but where is it?"

"That person was right. This place is called Sheol. As to where, I don't know. But I do know this is the afterlife. You died and were sent here, like everybody. And there's no escape from here."

Keith smiled at this. He still thought it was a dream, but he didn't feel like arguing that point. "So, is this Heaven, or Hell?"

"Neither. They don't exist. The dead come here. Although, as you can see, and as you'll experience, it's closer to Hell than Heaven."

"All right, then. How come more people don't talk? They just sit there."

"Because this is The Land of Forgetfulness. Once you're here for a while, you forget who you were, and other personal details. Then, after that, you forget how to talk. It happens to everyone."

"What's the deal with these worms?"

She sighed. "I don't know why they're here, but they are. In great numbers. We all use them to sleep on, and to cover us at night."

Keith shivered and laughed. "Yeah, right! Some bedding! I'd sooner lay on the ground."

"No, you won't. The ground's hard. And it gets cold. The worms and maggots provide some warmth. You'll see."

"So, there's day and night here, huh? And we need to sleep?"

"Yes. Apparently, night lasts about nine hours. The total 'day' lasts about as long as on Earth. And you do get tired."

"What about food and water? Do we also eat the worms?"

"No. We don't need food or drink. You'll see. You won't remember what it feels like to be hungry or thirsty."

"Who's in charge here at Sheol?"

"No one. I guess whoever or whatever runs the universe put us here, but no one rules. There's nothing to rule, really."

"No one dies and leaves?"

"Nope. We can't die again. We're here forever." As she finished this sentence, Keith noticed a change in the large crowds. All those who had been sitting now stood up, and everyone trudged over to the nearest mound of worms. Each person scattered an inch-thick pile of maggots on the ground, lay down, and scooped piles of earthworms on top until they were covered. Then, they closed their eyes and went to sleep. Keith stared, both fascinated and revolted as, one by one, the millions of visible people did this. He noticed, too, as the old woman had said, it was getting distinctly darker and colder. Even his informant finally went over, gathered up a worm bed, and fell asleep.

Keith was fairly tired now, too, but couldn't stomach the thought of putting worms on himself. He peered around in the semidarkness for other objects. Nothing. He lay down on the hard, cold ground and tried to sleep.

It quickly became unbearable. Resignedly, he stumbled over to a large, still pile of worms and threw some maggots down. After a minute of revulsion, he lay down. They weren't as bad as he thought. Like the people, they seemed subdued. Only slightly squirmy. He gave in entirely and tossed earthworms on himself, keeping them away from his face. After what seemed an eternity, he fell asleep, thinking just before he did, *I'm gonna be working out this dream in therapy for years.*

~

DAY BROKE, albeit in a subtle way. Keith awakened to find the temperature had risen back to the original 60–65 degrees, and the lighting had gone from utter black to dim but visible. This also caused Keith to think perhaps he wasn't dreaming, maybe they were right, and that he'd died and gone to the afterlife. He thought of this grim prospect for a good fifteen minutes or so. Finally, he sighed and joined his fellows in gathering up his wormy bedding and shoving it into rough piles. With great disgust, he picked out several maggots and worms that had crawled into his ears and his ass. A maggot had even gone into the tip of his urethra. He managed to get it out and threw it on the pile, shivering with revulsion as he did. Keith tried to put the incident out of his mind by finding the old woman he'd talked to the previous day. It wasn't difficult. She was standing twenty feet from him.

He quickly approached her. "Remember me?"

She smiled slightly. "Yes. We were talking about this place yesterday."

He returned her grin. "Exactly. And I have many more questions. Most of them philosophical and religious."

"I don't know as much about that. But I know someone who did. Maybe he still does. Come with me." She led him away from their area. They walked perhaps a hundred yards away, his hostess looking carefully at each face. Eventually she pointed to a Latino-looking man in his fifties. "Father Swan might be able to help you."

At this, the man looked up. His eyes, unlike his neighbors, weren't blank. He motioned Keith to sit down. "How can I help you, son?"

Keith sat down and got right to the point. "Why is God punishing all of us by putting us here?"

"Is it punishment?" Swan's green eyes glittered.

"I'd say so. I don't see any angels playing flutes or people basking in loving bliss. I see zombie-like, mute people doing nothing, forced to put worms on themselves to warm up at night."

"When you forget everything, you won't be so unhappy. You'll just be. And I wouldn't call it punishment. Every person comes here. Good and bad people. I saw a vicious, unrepentant serial killer, whose name escapes me, here along with several people I know to be nearly saints. Or, take me. I was a pretty decent fellow on Earth, yet I'm here."

"So was I! What is this? I was taught that good people go to Heaven, and bad to Hell. Why didn't we?"

"I share your confusion, in part. I do remember reading of this place in the Old Testament, in the early parts. They just changed the discussion of the afterlife gradually until they got the Heaven and Hell bit. Apparently, they were right the first time."

"So, was being a good Christian a waste of time? Should I have just been a hedonist, had fun?"

"My gut feeling is no; you did the right thing. But, at the same time, it wouldn't make a difference in where you went after death. Whether you were Christian or not doesn't either. I've met members of all the major religions. Buddhists, Muslims, Jews, Hindus, etc. Some good and some bad. All here, just the same."

"This doesn't bother you?" screamed Keith. This apathy was driving him nuts.

Swan's tone stayed mild and calm. "It did at first. But I've come to accept it. Besides, I'll forget everything soon enough."

"Well, fuck that! I'm not going to accept it. I don't want to forget."

"It won't matter. You will."

That was it for Keith. He stalked off angrily, leaving Swan and the old woman without another word. He walked for about ten minutes, until he was in the midst of a different set of people. He had some serious thinking to do.

DAWN BROKE, and Keith leapt up out of his pile of vermin. It was his fifth day here, and he had a busy day planned. It was nice to have a plan that involved action, for a change. He'd spent the last three days praying feverishly. On the second day, to God. Then, when nothing changed, even his internal feelings, he'd prayed the next day to an amorphous, non-Christian Creator being. The fourth day—which, again was identical to the others—prompted Keith to pray to Evil, and to Satan in general, out of desperation. Again, no change.

So, today he was an atheist. No more praying to anyone. He was his own deity, free to do what he wished. And he had certain questions he wanted answered. The foremost being, what happens when you tried to kill someone here?

And so, imbued with his zeal, he looked at the faces of

his immediate comrades, studying them. After a few minutes he found a guy who resembled someone he'd hated back home in Jersey. That guy had been a bully who'd picked on Keith. This one was close enough. He walked up to his intended victim, who sat there unmoving, looking arguably like Rodin's 'The Thinker.' The man's hair was a sickly yellow color.

Keith reared back, and hit the man with a haymaker, using all his strength. The man flew backward, landing flat on his back, his nose trickling blood. Even this was slow, though. Keith waited to see what the guy would do.

The man resumed his sitting position and made no sound. Didn't even take notice of the slight wound. Didn't even look up at Keith, who was standing right in front of him.

That was the most infuriating thing of all. Keith knocked him over again, jumped on the man's torso, and started pummeling the man's face. Punch after punch, letting all the anger and frustration of the past few days pour out of him. The man's face broke and bled some more under the attack, but, as always, not as dramatically as on Earth. The man made no effort to defend himself, however, and still made no sound. Finally, Keith gave in completely to his rage. He grabbed the man's throat with both hands and slammed his head against the hard ground eight times until the skull was broken thoroughly, and his victim's brains and blood lay strewn in a big mess over his body. Keith paused for a second, unsure of what he'd done. Ashamed, he looked up and around. No change. All the people were in the exact same positions as before. Only one woman raised her head slowly, casually took in the kill scene, then lowered it again without changing expression. This renewed Keith's fury. He gave the corpse's head a few more slams for good measure.

Then he stared into the man's eyes (or what he could see of them through the cuts and bruises). No movement. No sign of life.

Keith crowed triumphantly, "I killed someone! He's dead! I killed an already dead person!" He let loose some curses, too, daring any gods or goddesses to punish him for his crime. Again, nothing happened. He thought some more and smiled. He'd always wondered what human flesh tasted like. Here was his chance.

He tore a chunk of flesh from his victim's ruined face and popped it in his mouth. Forced himself to chew. It was awful. Not bad tasting, exactly, just a complete lack of taste. Spitefully, he kept going and forced himself to swallow. His esophagus didn't help much, either. It took him several minutes to actually get the flesh down. Disappointed, he turned back to the corpse. Grabbed a handful of slimy, wet brains. Keith put these in his mouth, too, and gagged. No taste! Worse than plain rice cakes. Resignedly, he spat out the brains and walked away. Spent the rest of the day alternately feeling guilty and victorious, and ultimately, just hollow.

THE FOLLOWING DAY, he woke up somewhat happily as another idea struck him. Sex! He'd try to have sex. Why not? He wasn't concerned about being punished, anymore. Might as well.

Thus invigorated, he removed the worms and maggots from himself (and, as always, from within himself, although he'd gotten used to this) and walked around, searching for a prospective mate. Keith tried to ignore the nagging doubt he had with this idea: he had no lust here. He was naked, and everyone else was, including many young attractive women, but he'd yet to be turned on. He remembered what it was like to want someone sexually, but he didn't feel it. Really, the only reason he was enthusiastic at all was the idea of doing something different.

But these thoughts he managed to suppress. Then he had a revelation. As he watched, dumbstruck, a woman popped into existence. A very familiar woman. An ex-lover, in fact. An astounding coincidence, considering he'd only bedded seven women in his life. But, sure enough, it looked exactly like his college girlfriend, Sheila. And the new people had better memories! He wasted no time in approaching her.

"Sheila, is that you?" He already knew the answer. Could see the characteristic largish mole right below her belly button.

"Yes," she said.

"It's me, Keith Moody," he said, and waited to see if she said anything else. She didn't. He was afraid of this; roughly half of the newcomers seemed as dull and sedated as the veterans, right away. Of the others, most of them forgot everything within hours.

But, maybe in this case, it didn't matter. "You want to have sex?" he asked.

She shrugged and just stared at him. Thus encouraged (or more properly, not discouraged) he set about making love to her.

It was a disaster. Completely disappointing. Kissing her, caressing her, was like kissing or touching a warm, fleshy robot. He felt nothing, and it was obvious she didn't either. He kept at it, though, angrily trying to get some pleasure, any pleasure, or at least something new. She didn't seem to care one way or the other. Keith tried to warm her up, using both finger and tongue, to no avail. She seemed disinterested and dry. Quite a contrast to the excitement this had caused her back in college. He did have a moment of joy when, with her willing (if jaded) help, he achieved an erection. Even that was wrong, somehow, though. He was happy only because he did get it up, not in the act itself. But he had to see it through. Keith entered her, pumping away madly.

And madly. And madly. It must have been forty or fifty minutes. Still no indications that he would come, or that she would, or anything. Ironic, really. There had been times in his life when women had said he'd come too fast; now he wasn't at all, but no one was benefiting from it. This was so pointless, and joyless. Had he ever really enjoyed this? It was hard to believe. And Sheila looked like she was reading tax forms. Completely dead. Well, they both were, but animated. At least he was. Finally, he stopped. Withdrew. He started to apologize but stopped as Sheila simply sat up and stared off into space. Didn't appear to notice him. Probably, she didn't. It was a familiar sight to Keith. Just especially depressing this time.

Without another word, he stood up and walked off. Before he'd gone fifty feet, he stopped in shock and horror. The murder victim of the previous day sat in front of him, wounds healed, 'living' again. Even this unfortunate action had failed.

~

KEITH WAS UP and about at first light, walking around briskly. It was one of the few fun things left. Not all that stimulating, but much better than sitting or standing around, as his comrades did constantly. It was also one of the few new or different activities he'd tried that worked properly. He had tried. He always gave himself credit for that. In the three days since the ill-fated sexual encounter with Sheila, he'd tried to buck the trends and learn things about Sheol at every turn. One night, Keith had attempted to stay awake at night. He'd managed to hold out for two or three hours before the cold had driven him back into the familiar cocoon of invertebrates. The lack of light, even dim lighting, hadn't helped either. Walking around had been pretty futile as he'd kept running into worm-covered people. As he'd stood there, shivering violently, he hadn't felt all that rebellious, or innovative, just foolish. So, that experiment had failed, too.

The next day, he'd studied the worms more. He was very curious about them, and why they were here. They clearly didn't eat either, yet still survived, if in the same subdued manner as the humans. Out of boredom and cathartic cruelty he'd dispatched several, wondering if they, too, would appear, unharmed, the next day, à la his blonde murder victim. Of course, how would he tell? All worms pretty much looked the same. Keith had eaten a few as well. Which had caused him some measure of mirth, remembering the old kid's song, 'Nobody loves me. Everybody hates me. I'm going to eat worms and die.' Alas, the worms were as unflavorful as the human flesh. In addition, their slight squirming did nothing for their charms. He'd choked down a few, then quit.

For his next attempt at distraction, he'd tried self-mutilation. He'd systematically sat down and destroyed his left pinky toe. Had banged it against the floor until it was shattered, then continued damaging it until he could actually tear it off. It hadn't been very difficult. His sensitivity to pain was significantly less than on Earth. The pain was more annoying than agonizing. And this act was also as useless.

The next morning, he had been miraculously restored. Keith figured even if he found a way to 'kill' himself it would also be temporary. No escape.

The only good thing about this place was he had plenty of time to think, especially about himself. He remembered hearing stories that portrayed ghosts as being overpoweringly envious of the living. He could strongly identify with that. If he was given the opportunity to be on Earth, haunting someplace, he knew he would be. It'd be tough to refrain from abusing the living, incredibly tough, knowing what he did now. Kevin's regret was acute. All the opportunities he'd missed haunted him. Every night he'd stayed in because he was slightly tired, all the hours wasted watching moronic TV shows, all the bullies he'd avoided, all the women he'd been afraid to ask out. Or, shit... there was much worse. All the general moralizing he'd done, every hedonistic pleasure he'd left undone, because it was 'wrong' or 'sinful'—and for what? It had made no difference. It was funny, blackly funny, but he couldn't laugh at it; it was too fresh and real. Although it could have been worse. He could have been a priest, or a complacently poor person. Wasting his life for a later eternal reward that—*surprise!*—hadn't been granted.

Yeah, life had been more precious than he'd dreamed. There'd been crappy times, true, but more good times to balance it out. Even pathetic, miserable lives sounded better than this. And altruism was bunk, he'd decided. Let anyone see what waited for them after death, and then see if they ever sacrificed their health or life for someone else. Not likely. Even for their own kid. Sure, you loved them, they were cute, but so what, when you'd all be in Sheol eventually, mute, mindless drones for eternity?

Thoughts like these disturbed him. Keith was still

capable of feeling guilt, feeling that he was being too pessimistic, too selfish. Then, existing even an hour or two in Sheol crushed these optimistic, selfless thoughts. Shit, this place would turn Norman Vincent Peale to despair. Was he dead? Keith didn't know. Oh well, it was only a matter of time. 'Course old Norm most likely wouldn't be depressed for long. He'd be without memory just like all the others, soon enough.

That was the root of Keith's problem; memory. Obviously, his was unusually good for this place. No one he'd met (and the number of people he'd met here was well into five digits so far) had retained memories as well as he had for so long. Randy Wilson, the old lady, and even Father Swan had all lost even the ability to speak days ago. As far as he could tell, his mind was pretty intact; his memory seemed about as sharp as when alive. Mind you, it hadn't been particularly great then, but now, comparatively, it was astounding. Was this a blessing or a curse? Sometimes he thought joining the herd might be a relief, other times not. One of his few satisfactions left was feeling special, feeling superior to the loathsome zombies. But knowledge undeniably caused him so much pain at the same time.

Not that, ultimately, his opinion mattered. He could yearn for stupid numbness, but he wouldn't necessarily get it. Or he might dread it and forget everything all the same. No choice. No power, no control whatsoever. Why he alone had this memory was also puzzling. The answer to this was similarly unknown to him, frustratingly so.

This thought was on the periphery of his mind now as he strode about. It was his new calling of the moment. Keith was curious about the borders of Sheol, if any. He planned to walk and walk, and see if there were rivers or walls, or a fiery moat to keep people in. Or, if this was a planet, see how long it took to circumnavigate it. It was something to do. It was a casual stroll. He stopped often to observe people. Another hobby of his was seeing if he could recognize famous dead people. This was problematic too, though. Anyone who died before the advent of photography might stay anonymous since they looked different from paintings. Also, the people themselves usually didn't recall their identities, of course. Still, it passed the time. Keith told himself he'd seen Einstein, Lindbergh, Teddy Roosevelt, and a recently deceased supermodel whose name he (and she) didn't remember. Whether they really were these people was beside the point.

As he bedded down that night, probably twenty miles from his previous home, Keith hatched another possible scheme. Maybe he could convince some vegetables to lay atop one another in a large stack, like in *Yertle the Turtle*. Maybe he could enjoy a better view, or amuse himself by high diving off them into a large pile of worms. Might be —*gasp!*—diverting, even fun. Worth a shot. He drifted off in a slightly more pleasant mood.

Around him, Sheol continued.

THE COLD DARK FOREVER
BY C.W. BLACKWELL

Central California, August 1924

The two men staggered up the coyote trail, one tall and steady, the other leaning into the first with sweat at his temples and an oily stain at the belly of his shirt. Where they stepped, the trail darkened with blood, flies dancing over the mottled dirt. When they reached the top of the ridge they rested and waited for the cover of darkness.

"It's cold, Billy," said Calum. He lay against the trunk of a fallen oak with his arms folded. *Trembling.*

Billy sat with a leather knapsack in his lap, the hasps undone, and the main pocket flapped open. In his hands lay a pearl necklace with a large opal pendant. He tilted his head to the sky. "Gotta give it another hour before we build a fire," said Billy. "They'll know it's us if they see the smoke."

"I feel cold is all," Calum said. Blood lacquered the oak stump beside him. "Feels like the more I bleed the colder I get."

Billy let the necklace slip into the knapsack. It made a small chime as it settled atop the rest of the jewelry in the bag. "You'll be fine, brother," said Billy. He said it as though he really believed it. "It went straight through. Remember when you popped me with Pa's twenty-two? Bullet went in and out. I was up in the truck shovelin' oat hay the very next week. Just a skeeter bite on either side."

Calum had a faraway look. "I was thinkin' maybe I'd die out here," he said. "Maybe I bled too much."

"Horseshit," said Billy. "All you need is rest." He cupped his ear and turned to the canyon. "You hear that sound, little brother?"

Calum lifted his head but didn't say whether he heard it or not.

"They're runnin' bloodhounds out in the redwoods," said Billy. "The sheriff, maybe. But I guess it could be Grady's men. It was wise of us to coast down the river a ways."

"They won't find us up here, will they?"

"No sir. They'll quit when it gets dark."

They lay on their backs and listened to the distant howls haunting the valley. Stars now freckled the eastern sky and Orion's bow drifted from behind the bald peak of Loma Prieta.

"Hey Billy," said Calum. "You remember when Uncle Vic died and Ma and Pa had themselves a quarrel?"

Billy took a long time to answer. The bloodhounds had quieted and the sounds of frogs and night insects had taken over. "Yeah I remember. They was drunk is all."

"Not that drunk. I remember what they was quarrelin' about."

"Ma was mad 'cause Pa drank all the hooch at the funeral."

"That weren't it."

"I know you gonna tell me, so just get it outta your craw, little brother."

"It was about Uncle Vic. Ma said he was in a better place and Pa said it weren't so. Said there ain't such a thing as a better place after you die and all that's left is the box they put you in."

Billy watched Calum in the dark. He looked small and slight. Like a shadow someone tore off and left behind. A slack-shouldered figure with eyes full of starlight. "You ain't gonna die. Not now."

"Maybe not. Just that I'm hearin' Pa's words in my head. He had a name for it, you know."

"A name for what?"

"For after you die. He called it *the cold dark forever*."

"Well, that ain't what Ma called it and that ain't what Reverend Peters called it, neither. Pa was a mean old man with funny ideas. Especially when that corn liquor got a hold of him."

"Just that the more I think on it, the colder I get."

"Well, stop thinkin' on it." There was contempt in Billy's voice. He stood in the darkness and raked his hair with his fingers in exasperation. Billy thought he could hear Calum crying. "Guess it's safe to build us a fire. Wouldn't that do you some good, little brother?"

"That's all I been hopin' for."

BILLY WOKE at first light and stirred the contents of the knapsack. A telluric scent of dust and metal filled the air. He rose and tapped Calum with the toe of his boot.

"Let's get on, little brother," he said.

Calum didn't respond.

Billy watched him for a moment, ravens croaking in the redwood boughs. He knelt and patted his cheek.

Calum blinked and gasped.

"Hell, Calum," said Billy. He spat in the dirt. "I was just plannin' your funeral. Can't you get up?"

Calum lay there, blinking. Thin, white ash tumbled from the firepit and he watched it drift through the campsite. "I was havin' a nightmare, Billy." His face pressed to the back of his hand and it made his speech sloppy. "We gotta turn back. Ain't nothin' good ahead of us."

"Back where? We got enough fancy gold and silver chains to make the pope jealous. You know something I don't?"

"It was about Pa. The nightmare. He was dancin' by a big roarin' fire with one of them necklaces we stole swingin' around his belly. Jar of whiskey in his hand. We were someplace I never been before. Someplace deep in the woods."

"Well, that don't sound wrong except for Pa bein' alive."

"You were there too, Billy. But there were bites all over your body and you were bleedin' like a stuck pig. All torn up. Like a bear got to you. Then you took to laughin' and waggin' your finger at the moon. When I looked up, the moon was carved into one of them devil stars we saw in Uncle Vic's book. You know what I'm talkin' about? He called it a *pentygram*."

"Damn if that ain't some kinda nightmare."

"You were in a world of hurt, brother."

They sat for a moment, their thoughts wandering. The mist was thinning in the trees. Paper wasps with their long and draping bodies floated between the branches. Billy hoisted the knapsack over his shoulder and was about to speak when Calum put a finger to his lips.

Billy froze.

They heard a scream farther down the ridge.

Dogs barking and whining.

A shriek of utter agony.

"Are them screams the way we're headed?"

"I reckon so," said Billy.

"Well then," whispered Calum. He pushed himself halfway up, one foot on the ground and the other bent as if in prayer. He turned his head and winked. "Ain't I a mighty fine prognosticator?"

IT WAS mid-morning before Calum could walk the trail. He complained that his legs felt numb, and his eyes fluttered as if on the very edge of consciousness. Tiny fingerlets of blood dangled from the hem of his shirt.

"We got to get you cleaned up," said Billy. "Get you some fresh clothes."

"Maybe there's a good store in Monterey. Like them department stores back in Memphis."

"They'd fix you up good, little brother."

"Barter me a fancy hat with all them jewels."

"That'd be just fine."

"Wish they could see us all dressed up. You know, back home. Think we'll ever see home again?"

"Shit. We been run out of damn near every state in the union. Ain't no such thing as home."

Calum stopped and squinted into the distance.

"You see that?"

It took Billy a moment to see it. The trail dipped around a thicket of coyote brush and, where it picked back up, he saw a figure lying in the dirt. They walked slowly, Billy with his arm hooked under Calum's shoulder.

"Is he sleepin' or is he dead?" said Calum.

Billy looked for movement. After a moment, he said: "If he was the fella doin' all the screamin', then I'd wager he's dead." From inside the leather bag he slid a lead pipe about the length of his forearm.

Calum swayed in his boots, watching him.

Billy inched forward, pipe held aloft like some slow-motion assailant. When he cleared the coyote brush he recoiled and coughed into his hand. Flies spun through the air. He dropped the lead pipe into the dirt, and he doubled over and retched.

"What is it, Billy?" Calum shuffled closer.

Billy caught his breath and looked again.

Sprawled over the trail lay a torn and twisted figure. The hair on the body signaled it was male, although the face was indiscernible. The flesh had been chewed completely from the skull. Only the blue eyes remained. The torso was exposed, and from the stomach a pink mass of viscera unspooled like stanchion rope onto the trail.

Insects everywhere.

"Just like my dream," said Calum. "Only it was you that was all chewed up."

Billy took a step closer and peered over the body, rocking to his tiptoes. "Is that an ear of corn in his mouth?" he said.

"Looks like it," said Calum. He came up beside the body and looked it over. "Stalk, roots and all. Looks like someone damn near kicked it down his throat."

Billy knelt in the dirt and reached for the corpse.

"Don't touch it, Billy."

"Why not?"

"Looks like somebody put the curse on it."

"I keep tellin' you there ain't such a thing." Billy searched around the body. When he stood again, he was holding a silver revolver. He opened the cylinder and inspected the chambers. "It's full of brass. Old boy never squeezed one off. Not a single shot."

"Think he was lookin' for us?"

"Maybe. Maybe he forgot to feed them bloodhounds."

"Wouldn't that be somethin'," said Calum. "Turned on him like a pack of wolves. His own doggies. Bet he tried to reason with 'em and that's why he didn't shoot."

Billy went for the cornstalk, as if to yank it from the corpse's mouth but, before he could reach it, Calum made a pitiful whimper.

"What now?" Billy said.

Calum pointed down the hill.

Sitting on the trail sat a lone bloodhound, its snout filthy with blood and gore. The knobs of its eyes jerked back and forth. Another hound appeared from behind and trotted into the tanoak scrub and lay with its paws outstretched, ears pert and watching the two men. The animals passed their tongues over their bloody mouths, a reddish drool falling over the trail.

Billy thumbed the revolver and leveled it in the air.

The dogs watched him warily. Sad eyes with a weeping crust at the eye corners. "Get!" Billy yelled. "Go on, if you ain't stupid enough to get shot."

The animals took an interest in Billy's threats. They wagged their tails and perked their ears, as if some backyard game was to commence. Billy stomped and kicked up a cloud of dust, but the dogs only watched him with a sort of joyous amusement.

"I think they like you, brother," said Calum.

"They won't like me when I shoot their peckers off."

"You couldn't hit an elephant pecker if it was pokin' you in the eye."

"Like hell I couldn't."

The dogs suddenly stood and pointed their snouts toward the deep forest, tails still and jaws slightly parted. They cocked their heads, listening. A girl's voice beckoned from somewhere beyond the trees, her tiny call carrying through the labyrinth of redwoods.

The voice grew louder, calling the dogs by name.

"*Andromalius, Andrealphus.*"

Billy could just make her out in the shadows, a small figure with black hair and a gray cotton dress.

The animals trotted off the trail and disappeared.

"Well, I'll be," said Billy. "Who do you suppose that was?"

Calum didn't answer.

Billy turned and found him on his hands and knees, breathing hard. He donned the knapsack and ran to him, pulling him up so his head lay in the crook of his elbow.

"What happened, brother?" Billy said. "Talk to me."

Calum heaved and shuddered. Eyes swimming. A trickle of pink saliva traversed his cheek.

Billy lifted him into the air as one might cradle a child. He looked up the trail and back down again. "Dammit all," he said. His voice had taken a desperate tone. Panic brewing. "You ain't gonna make it much further, are you?" He stepped off the trail into the tree shadows, calling to the girl, searching for the sound of her voice.

~

THE PATH WAS CROWDED with young tanoaks and blackberry brambles. The immense crowns of redwood trees loomed overhead. He called to the girl, stopping every few minutes to search for signs of her passing. He stumbled into a tiny stream, looking to the far bank to see where the path picked up again. Calum went into a spasm, head jerking and eyes fluttering. Hair damp with sweat. A rocky sand bar stretched down the middle of the stream, and here Billy laid his brother down.

"Ain't gonna let you die," said Billy. He cupped his hands into the water and washed the blood from Calum's face. "There's a house close by and I'm gonna find it. Get you some help."

Calum blinked his eyes, pupils contracting slightly.

"Where are we?" he said.

"In the woods. Headed to Monterey."

"Them dogs is g-gone?"

"Yes, sir. Ran off to their master."

Calum swallowed hard. "They ain't dogs, theys d-devils."

"That's just the fever talkin'."

"No, no it ain't. I saw them standin' up like m-men."

"Standin' up? No sir. They ran off on all fours like dogs is supposed to."

Calum clutched his gut and moaned. He caught his breath and looked hard into Billy's eyes. "I saw it, Bill. Just when they reached that little g-girl. They stood up on two legs and she greeted them with some kind of salute. One of them turned and l-looked at me with them evil black devil eyes. That's when I fell over. Like it pulled somethin' out of m-me." Billy tried to shush him, but Calum only spoke louder. "Leave me, brother. Bury me in the w-woods. Ain't nothin out here but the worst kinds of evil."

~

CALUM HAD LOST CONSCIOUSNESS AGAIN. Billy rinsed the bloody shirt in the stream and cleaned the wound the best he could. The bullet had hit him just under the final rib and there was now a sickly green flare around the wound and a constant gelid substance that welled from the hole. Billy dressed Calum and carried him to the path beyond the stream.

The light began to change as the trail curved into a narrow valley. Beyond the treeline was a large cornfield, the summer light smoldering in the golden anthers. Green blades hissing in the breeze. Billy elbowed through the cornfield and, when he finally crossed the length of it, he found a small barn and a farmhouse built against a grassy bluff.

He called out, but there was no answer.

He lumbered onto a dirt driveway and made a circle as he went, looking for signs of inhabitants. He called out a second time. A pair of crows gawked from the roof of the barn. Bumblebees meandered in the blue houndstongue. Beside the barn sat an old stable, but no horses. No carriage or wagon. It was as if the property had been abandoned for the season, if not for the entire year.

Or perhaps longer.

Billy went to the barn and toed the door open. It was dark and cool inside. Thin sheets of sunlight filtering between the clapboards. There were two small stables in back and the rusted chassis of an old, steel plough. He found a pen full of loose hay in the corner and he kicked open the pen gate and set Calum in the straw. He patted Calum's chest and kissed him on the forehead and he went back up the driveway toward the farmhouse.

The house was old and weather-worn. The paint had mostly peeled from the wood, revealing the gray woodgrain beneath. The door had rotted off the hinges and it lay slanted in the threshold. He stood in the doorway with one hand on his hip and the other holding the wood grip of the revolver. Bloodstains on his hands. On his clothes. He looked like an outlaw from some dime-store paperback.

He peered into the darkness of the front room.

A cool breeze.

The dry rustling of leaves.

He turned. The girl from the woods stood in the driveway, the bloodhounds sitting on either side. Her messy black curls fell over her shoulders, skin pale as the moon. She stared coolly, eyes unblinking. If there was an expression on her face, Billy couldn't make it out.

"Hello, miss," he said. He tried a polite smile, but it was short-lived. He eyed the hounds and they eyed him back. "Your ma and pa around?"

"They're away," she said.

"They comin' back? My little brother's hurt bad. I set him in the barn 'til I could find somebody."

"They'll return tonight for the festival."

Billy glanced around the property. "Don't look like you're settin' up for a festival."

"Tonight, the full moon will pass completely through the Earth's shadow. It won't happen for another three years."

"Is that so?" Billy wiped the sweat from his forehead with the back of his hand. He came down the porch steps and stood in the driveway. "There's a fella out in the woods," he said. "Looked like he got chewed up pretty bad. You wouldn't know what happened to him, would you?"

The hounds licked their snouts and their ears perked.

"Could've been a mountain lion," she said.

"Someone jammed a whole ear of corn in his mouth."

"Maybe he was having a picnic." She turned her head slowly to the barn and watched it a long while, as if she had heard a sound there. When she turned back, she said: "Your brother is about to die."

Billy stiffened. "Why'd you say that?"

"I can help him, you know."

"How?"

"I have medicine."

"What kind of medicine?"

"The kind that will bring him to his feet again."

Billy hurried to the barn. When he kicked the door open, he found Calum sprawled in the straw with his eyes hammered in their lids and his mouth slanted open. Billy knelt beside him and cupped his face with both hands. The pupils were dilated, red veins spidering through the sclera. His skin hung pale and loose against the jawbone. He lifted Calum and pressed his forehead to the young man's temple.

"I'm sorry, brother," said Billy. "We'll get you fixed up. This little girl here says she got medicine. I told you I ain't gonna let you die."

A shadow passed through the barn and the girl appeared in the doorway. She was dragging a canvas tarp piled with cornstalks, the dark green ears still attached, cornsilk spilling from the husks.

"Lay him there," she said, pointing to the center of the barn.

Billy did as she asked, gently settling Calum's head and wicking the sweat from his hair with his fingers. A stain darkened the young man's trousers and the smell of urine folded into the air. "You brought the medicine?" he asked.

"Yes. Now, remove his clothes."

Billy unbuttoned Calum's shirt. "Just the shirt?"

"Every stitch. Put it in a pile."

Billy worked the clothes off. The body smelled of profound sickness. When he finished, he set the clothes in a pile and backed away slowly. "What's next?"

"Take the clothes and set them outside," she said. She'd stripped the leaves from the cornstalks and was fashioning the bare stalks into tightly wound braids. "There are two pails outside. Bring them to me."

Billy went to fetch the pails. Along the outside wall sat two crude buckets hollowed from oak rounds with handles made of braided reeds. One of the buckets contained water, in the other was a thick white substance like wall paint. Billy set the pails by Calum's feet. The girl had spread Calum's arms out and moved his legs apart like da Vinci's 'Vitruvian Man.' She gathered a large handful of cornsilk and dipped it in the water, wringing it over the lightly breathing body.

The bloodhounds had slipped into the barn and were panting in the shadows. They pressed their bellies to the ground and watched with a peculiar interest.

"He ain't breathin' too well," said Billy.

The hounds growled when he spoke.

"The medicine will help," she said, pointing to the second bucket. "Hand it to me." She dipped the cornsilk in the second bucket and began pasting Calum with the white substance. It clung to his skin like grease. She worked slowly, starting at the bullet wound and circling outward. She lifted his limbs to cover the undersides and rocked the body on its side to paint his back. When she moved him, she did so with the strength of someone of a much larger stature. Within minutes, Calum had become a pure white figure that nearly glowed as if by some inner luminescence.

"How fast will it work?" Billy asked. "He still don't look good."

The girl shushed him and arranged the cornstalk braids around Calum's body in careful geometries. A line from his head to his left foot. Another to his right. She lifted the head and placed a cornstalk along the length of his outstretched arms. She crossed another pair from hands to feet so that he was now laying atop a precisely fashioned pentagram.

"I've seen that symbol before," said Billy. "Calum dreamt of it last night." He took a step toward Calum, searching for signs of movement.

The body was still.

The breathing had stopped completely.

"He better start breathin' again," said Billy, moving closer. He called his brother's name, then turned to the girl and said, "I don't know what you done here, but it sure as hell ain't natural."

The dogs rose, showing their fangs.

"Stay back," the girl hissed. Her voice was harsh, her eyes like tiny dark fruits. "You must not disturb the body."

"The body? You told me you could help him. He sure don't look helped." Billy squared off with the girl and she took a step back. As if by some silent command, the hounds leapt at Billy, jaws clamping his wrists. They dragged him toward the open doorway. Billy shook them off and shouldered against the door. He pulled the revolver from the back of his pants, but before he could shoot, the dogs attacked a second time.

The gun fired and a round hit the dirt.

The animals tore at Billy's arm until the gun fell away, and one of them leaped onto his chest and tackled him to the ground. He fell hard, the air knocked from his lungs.

Gasping.

He slapped the ground, searching for the revolver.

"I told you to stay back," the girl said.

The bloodhounds now stood over him, towering on their hind legs. Nightmarish beasts with jet black eyes. From their heads had grown slick obsidian horns. One held a long wooden spade, claws curled around the handle.

The spade came down on Billy's head.

A flash of white followed by darkness.

THE FULL MOON was up when Billy awoke, sprawled in the dirt with his left eye swollen shut. He pushed himself slowly to his feet, a sharp pain at his temples. His mauled arm still bleeding. He saw a flicker of light in the barn. Calum was gone, but the cornstalk pentagram was still intact. There were candles sputtering at the five points of the star and a ghostly white impression where Calum had lain.

He searched for the leather knapsack, but couldn't find it anywhere.

The revolver was also gone.

He turned to the driveway.

"Calum," he called.

He staggered to the farmhouse but found it dark and empty. Coyotes yipped from some faraway den and Billy thought he could hear a steady drumbeat echoing through the valley. He climbed the old porch steps, the wood creaking as he went. At the top of the steps, he turned and looked over the cornfield. He saw a flutter of light at the far end of the field as if a bonfire was raging there. He could almost smell the smoke.

The beat continued.

Da-dum da-dum da-dum.

Movement at the field line.

Someone stepping from the cornstalks.

A nude male, painted white, an ear of corn in his mouth.

"Calum?"

It was him, no doubt. Calum waved in an exaggerated arc with his palm sweeping the air and he turned and disappeared into the cornfield.

Billy followed, calling after him. The corn was white where Calum had passed through, and he followed the stained leaves deep into the field. He could hear him walking just ahead, the lashing and whipping of leaves and husks as he pressed ever deeper.

"Calum. Wait up, little brother."

The beat grew louder, the smoke thicker.

The glow of a fire.

The crackle of firewood.

He emerged at a circular plot in the field where a large fire raged and figures danced to the beat of a deerskin drum. Men and women circled the fire, their nude forms painted a ghostly white. All of them with their jaws hammered open and corn stalks dangling from their mouths. At the outer rim of the circle, animals danced on their hind legs, stomping like drunkards. From their necks hung the stolen necklaces. Silver and gold. Opals and pearls. Some with large pendants swinging at their hairy stomachs, sparkling in the fireglow.

Billy stood in a sort of mute wonder.

At the edge of the circle, the black-haired girl sat atop a brambling woodpile in a nest made of straw and cornsilk. Her beetle black eyes locked on Billy, face distorted in the roiling heat. On her head sat a crown made of yellow corn cobs.

Calum circled by, and Billy grabbed his arm.

The skin was cold and yielding.

"Calum, let's go."

Calum stomped to the beat in a mechanical lumber.

From the eyes wept a sickly rheum.

The smell of rot and woodsmoke.

The girl rose atop her strange nest and pointed at Billy. She drifted higher still, so that she hung suspended in the smoke-thick air, a bewitched form pressed against the full moon.

The dancing stopped.

The revelers turned to Billy.

He gave Calum another glance and released his arm.

"I'm sorry little brother," he said, tears building in his eyes. "I'm sorry for all of it."

Billy turned and ran

He ran without any notion of which direction he was headed. The cornstalks rose above his head, occulting the landscape. All he could see of the world beyond the cornfield was the full moon, and it was now dimming in a bloody gradient.

The night grew dark and the stars returned.

He heard a sound behind him.

Something careening through the cornfield.

Billy looked. A bloodhound scrabbled at his heels. It bit his calf and sent him tumbling into the furrows. He flipped on his back and the hound crawled atop his chest, biting his face. He bent a cornstalk around the hound's throat and pulled tight. The hound thrashed its head with its tongue lolling from side to side and soon the cornstalk tore from the soil, roots breaking from their rootbeds.

He got to his feet and ran.

This time, he didn't get far.

He cleared the cornfield, but the hound leapt and brought him to the ground again, biting and tearing every limb. Billy batted it with his fists but it wouldn't quit. Other animals appeared at the field line, and they skittered toward him with their lips snarling. Some catlike and some caprine. All with horns and eyes black as coal.

Billy couldn't hold them off.

The animals pinned his legs to the ground and he felt their hot mouths nudging at his chin, trying for the soft of his throat. He punched and bucked his body, but they were too strong, *too many*.

The painted figures arrived, swaying in the dark.

Dead eyes wandering in their lids.

Calum stood over him and slid the ear of corn from his mouth.

Shattered teeth, black gums.

"*Pa was right, brother.*" His voice popped and hissed like pulled roots. "*It's cold and dark, just like he said.*"

Billy screamed.

The animals tore his stomach and clawed at the wound.

The smell of blood and redwood needles.

Calum pointed to the sky. The moon had turned completely red, ragged lines tearing across the surface like claw marks. The lines ran to the very rim of the sphere in five points, forming a crude pentagram. An evil eye blearing from the cosmos.

"*It's cold, Billy,*" he said. He stood hunched and crooked like a tangled marionette. Jaw working as if by some hidden lever. "*Cold and dark.*"

The beat returned.

Da-dum da-dum da-dum.

Billy's vision waned, a vignette of bloody snouts and fangs.

A chill welled from deep within his body.

"*Come, brother,*" Calum said. "*It's just like Pa said. Come see, brother. It's so very cold and dark.*"

THE FORK IN THE ROAD

BY J. THORN

The boy stares at you through the flames crawling through his hair. He's screaming. You can't hear his words, but you can read his lips before they burn off.

"Help me!"

You could be in a room. Or a cavern. You don't know. What you do know is that you've never experienced heat like this, a nauseous feeling in your stomach like sour milk and rotten eggs. The air shimmers as paint bubbles and rolls down the wall like giant tears.

"I can't!" you scream, but the raging inferno steals your words. You can't hear yourself and so you know the boy can't hear you.

Something falls, fire devouring the board or beam. You want to take a deep breath, but you can't—every inhalation is filled with shards of glass.

The boy turns around and you can now see that he's standing in front of a window. The flames dance before the opening, passing in front of the night sky like demonic clouds.

Is the boy going to jump?

Should he jump?

These questions roll through your head. You try to take a step forward, but nothing happens. You feel paralyzed despite the fact that you're standing upright.

"I'll come for you," you say, although you don't know what that means. You don't know where the boy is going or how you'll get there. You can't imagine standing in a world not drowned in fire.

And then the fire fades, the smell of burnt plastic lingering on your tongue as darkness closes in from all sides.

∽

You lean back into the leather bucket seats, the glow from the gauges casting a golden haze across the dashboard of the 1977 Corvette.

You reach for the gearshift, the FM radio crackling with static. No songs, no talk. A dry, cool wind whistles past your ear as you rest your arm on top of the door. The sky stretches above the open T-top, a black curtain of silk punctuated by a handful of glimmering stars. The air smells like fresh asphalt, but you can see weeds sprouting through cracks in the highway, the painted yellow lines faded to a ghostly luminescence.

When you turn your head to the right, you see her for the first time.

"Shift."

"What did you say? Where did you come from?"

The woman laughs, her eyes wet and ancient. She has pulled her hair back into a tight ponytail, filaments of gray dancing through jet-black locks. The woman smiles at you, her teeth as white as a spring swan.

"You need to shift. Can you drive a stick?"

You look down and notice your left foot on the clutch. Your right hand is on the gearshift. You realize you can.

"Yes. But why should I shift? The RPMs aren't even in the red."

She nods but does not respond.

You glance in the rearview mirror and see nothing but a black void. Through the windshield and beyond fenders flared like the curve of a woman's hips, you see the road sliding beneath the Corvette. You're driving somewhere. With someone. In some time.

"Who are you? What are you doing here?"

"So many questions..." she trails off without answering any of yours.

"Where are we going?"

This time, she answers. "East. To Canal."

You nod as if the answer makes complete sense. It makes none.

"Are you coming with me?"

"It depends on how far you're going."

An answer. The first. Something to build on. You try harder.

"Do you have a name?"

"Yes."

Another terse answer, a frustrating itch originating beneath the skin—impossible to scratch.

"Then, what should I call you?"

"Noe."

You glance in the mirror perched near the driver-side door where you see, what you think is, a flash of light. But when you blink, the mirror is back to reflecting the enormity of the darkness.

"Am I being punished or rewarded? This is my favorite car of all time."

"Well, then," Noe responds. But she doesn't.

You feel a queasiness in your stomach, a sour, roiling mash of nerves and anxiety. You want to vomit, and in the next moment, it passes.

Noe notices. "It's coming."

"What is coming?"

"You'll see."

An artist of evasion, a mistress of ambiguity.

"What will happen if I try crashing this thing? I could drive it off the road and right into a big rock, or a guardrail, or a tractor trailer, or something."

"No, you can't."

You don't understand what she means. You are the one driving. Noe is in the passenger seat. Her life is in your hands.

"Try it."

You yank the leather-wrapped steering wheel to the right. The headlights cut across the unfolding highway and into the vast stretch of desert—but only for a split second. The highway returns beneath the Corvette. You veer to the other side. It happens again.

"See."

Her smugness weighs on you as heavily as the dark night.

"I guess I can't slam on the brakes either. Should I try that and see what happens?"

Noe smiles and shakes her head as if it doesn't matter. You know it won't, but you do it anyway. The Corvette doesn't stop, doesn't even slow down.

"How much do you remember?"

A boy? A fire? The thoughts dissipate before you can

grab at them.

Now she is asking you questions. You want to ignore her, to punish her for not being direct with you. But you can't withhold. You answer her.

"Nothing."

Your father owned a 1977 Corvette when you were a teenager. He'd let you drive it sometimes. He'd sold the Corvette. He'd died. Maybe your response isn't entirely true.

"You won't remember circumstances. Only snippets of images, fragments of conversations, fractals of dreams."

Now she is answering questions that you are not asking.

"Why?"

Noe chuckles—the sound of crushed gravel inside a glass jar. "Why what?"

"Why is that all I can remember? I know I had a father. I know he's passed, but I can't see his face. Why can't I see his face?"

"Because you're not looking at it."

You finally shift the 350, 180-horsepower engine into fifth gear. The car rumbles, the wind now whipping through and yet, Noe's hair remains perfectly bound by her hair wrap.

"You're going to have to decide."

"Decide what?" you ask, your mouth turning dry and your palms sweating. "What do I have to decide?"

"You'll see."

Fighting her won't enlighten you. You don't think acquiescing will either. She's been in this car before, driving down this highway many times. You don't know how you know that, but you do.

"I'm tired." You yawn, your eyes burning. "Can I stop to rest?"

"Not possible."

"Why not?"

Another smile. Another shrug. Another avoided question.

"Are we related?"

"Yes, of course."

"How?"

"The universe."

Her answer makes sense, and, it doesn't. You gratefully accept it because you know Noe doesn't often offer answers.

"How will I know?"

"Know what?"

You scoff, tiring of the verbal jousting. "How far I must drive? How will I know when to stop?"

"The fork."

"When will I see the fork?"

"When you arrive at it."

A rumble begins beneath your feet, on the floorboard. The energy moves up through the soles of your shoes, into your ankles, and it is vibrating up your leg. You shiver. Your hands shake.

"Ah, yes," Noe says. "Here it comes."

"Here comes what? What are you expecting to happen?"

Noe reaches over and twists the knob on the radio. The station locks onto a song—a long-forgotten guitar solo from a tune you barely remember in a time you can't recall.

"I don't like that song. I don't know what it is, but I don't like it."

"It's not for you."

Noe turns up the volume.

"What do you mean? Music belongs to everyone. It's not yours."

"The song is mine."

With that, Noe leans back into her seat, stretches her

legs, and closes her eyes. She's smiling and mouthing the lyrics to a song without vocals.

"You won't be able to choose nothing. Nope. You're being forced to the fork and you'll have to decide which way to go."

"How do you know all this? How do you know what's happening?"

"East. To Canal." She says it again as if she's said it a billion times. Maybe she has. You have no way of knowing.

"And I'm looking for the fork?"

"The fork will find you, provided you can outrun it."

Outrun what? This time, you swallow your question because you know Noe's answer won't possibly satisfy you.

YOU FEEL the car's engine straining. The pop-up headlights illuminate a rust-colored haze settling on the dark highway. You smell dry dirt or sand, ancient earth. When Noe looks at you, you instinctively look in the mirror and that's when you see it.

"What is that? What's behind us?"

"Firestorm."

Now you smell burning wood, charred and black and strong enough to make your eyes water. It's all so surreal—Biblical. Flames. Hellfire. Burning. You decide not to ask the obvious because you don't want to hear the answer.

"Where is it coming from?"

Noe chuckles. "The question you should be asking is where is it taking you."

The physics don't make sense. It's night, black as deep space. And yet, you can see the smoke rising in the west and chasing you east toward the horizon. Flames and heat—utter destruction.

"I can outrun it. This car is fast."

"Confidence."

You wonder if each word causes Noe pain and that's why she chooses to use so few of them.

"I don't hear anything."

You move your ear closer to the open window, but you still hear nothing but the wind whipping by as you push the needle of the speedometer past 125 mph. You're in fifth gear, but the Corvette's accelerator still has plenty of cushion. Your foot is applying slight pressure and yet, you're barreling down the highway faster than you've ever driven before.

But the fire is getting closer. Somehow, the storm is moving faster.

"Okay. I can't outrun it, can I? You knew that, but you had to let me figure it out on my own."

"We all figure everything out on our own."

"How far do I have to get before we're safe? Will we be safe?"

"It needs you to get to the fork."

You nod and put a bit more pressure on the gas pedal. Noe hasn't explained what the fork is or why the firestorm needs you to get there. Even so, you feel pressured to drive faster. There's something about the flames that unnerves Noe. You've seen her glance into the side mirror several times since the firestorm appeared. She doesn't want you to notice her watching it. But you do.

"What if I just stop? Take my foot off the gas, kill the engine, let the car drift onto the shoulder."

Noe pauses and for the first time you can see her confidence is shaken—for just a moment. She grins widely, tucking a loose strand of hair behind her ear. The wind hadn't touched her ponytail until now. Until the smell of burning came closer.

"You don't want to do that."

"Why not? Why can't I pull over and let the firestorm go past? We can roll up the windows and wait for it to blow by."

"It doesn't work like that. We are below, at the root of the flames and we cannot outrun or outwit it."

"What? I don't know what you mean. Please explain it to me."

"We've made this run before. You and I."

You nod, feeling as though Noe is going to have to tell you more. You've seen a chink in her armor, a crack in her granite façade that means she's either worried or in unchartered territory—dealing with a situation she hasn't seen before.

You push the pedal down harder, the Corvette now approaching 150 mph. When you look in the rearview mirror, it appears as though the firestorm is gaining on you. The faster you drive, the faster it moves, unfurling tongues of orange and red flames into the sky like a demonic version of the aurora borealis.

"Yes. You should do that."

Noe seems relieved by your decision to drive faster, not frightened by it. She's concerned about the firestorm. She doesn't want to make this drive again, although you have no memory of making it with her before.

"How much longer until we make it to the fork? Five miles? Ten miles?"

She squints as if she's doing the calculations in her head. But she knows exactly how far it is. You know she knows that.

"It's not far. But we can't drive inside of the firestorm. It'll melt the tires, stall the engine."

"So, I have to stay ahead of it."

"Yes."

And then it hits you. A glimmer of memory. Not much more than a tickle in your stomach, a tingle at the base of your spine. You feel heat. The smell of smoke intensifies so much that you start coughing and you can't stop. You hear crying. And yet, it is just you, the highway, Noe, and the firestorm on your trail.

"What's burning? What's on fire?"

"Just stay ahead of the firestorm."

Noe leans back and closes her eyes. For the first time, she appears tired and worn. She's made this drive hundreds, possibly thousands of times. You know this, even though she won't disclose it.

"Was I in the fire?" You don't know why you ask the question, but it feels right, so you wait for Noe's reply.

"Yes."

"Why?"

"Because."

She must be stalling, hoping you'll make it to the fork before she has to answer your question. Noe uses her right hand to rub her forehead. She turns and looks at you, holding your gaze for an uncomfortably long time.

"Because you chose to enter it."

"I chose to enter the fire? Why? What does that mean?"

"It means you were willing to make a sacrifice."

"Like, to a god or something? A sacrifice to appease a supreme being?"

Noe's smile is wide, warm, genuine. "No, not like that."

"Then like what? Tell me."

The firestorm is now two or three car lengths behind

you. You can't see the sky any longer, the headlights turning the air in front of the Corvette into an orange soup. You don't think you're in the flames but they're close. The burning stench makes your eyes water.

She stares out the windshield and you think she's in a trance. You need answers.

"Like what? I need you to explain or I'm stopping."

Noe raises one hand and lets it fall to her lap. She shakes her head before continuing.

"You sacrificed yourself, so you get to drive the highway again. Some don't ever get behind the wheel, let alone multiple times."

Another jolt. You look out your window across the barren landscape and, this time, you see a child standing among flames. It's a boy. *That* boy. He's yelling for his mother. The fire has singed his clothes and burned the hair from his head. He's moments from death. You know this. You feel it.

"What have I done?"

"Your actions are not things to regret, but to cherish."

Pain. It sears the left side of your body and blinds your left eye. You can feel your skin bubbling, burning off your bones. You look down and you see nothing out of the ordinary, but the pain is eviscerating, stealing the air from your lungs.

"There isn't much time. You need to get to the fork before the firestorm overtakes us or you'll be forced to drive again."

Now you're outside of the Corvette, standing inside a building on a shaking platform that is so hot that it's melting the tips of your boots. You can no longer see out of your left eye and you've lost control of your left hand. The boy— nothing more than a child—wails. He's shouting at you, waving his arms and yet you're stuck, unable to retreat or approach. You see the open window framed by flames and you want to walk toward it, but you can't. You're stuck. And so is the boy. You try to ask Noe another question, but the pain paralyzes your mouth and steals your words before they can escape from your lips.

"Faster. We're almost to the fork."

Back inside the Corvette.

You don't reply. You can't nod. Instead, you use every ounce of strength you have to slam the accelerator to the floor. The fire seeps into the car and you can hear the pistons misfiring underneath the hood.

"There!"

You lift your head as high as you can, and through the open window, which is hovering just beyond the wind-shield, you see it. There's a fork in the road. You'll have to go left or right, and you won't have much time to decide.

You feel the fire licking at the car's undercarriage. Even in the dark you can see waves of heat coming off the highway. It's getting hotter the closer you get to the fork. You're certain of it.

"Why am I getting so hot? Why is the temperature going up?"

"There's something you need to do before you decide at the fork."

"What?"

Noe drops her voice to almost a whisper. "Reversion."

"Reversion? What is that? What does that mean? It sounds odd."

"It's not good or bad. It just is."

You nod as if you understand. You don't.

"I'm here to facilitate the reversion."

"Okay." You want to ask more questions, but you're not even sure of what you don't know.

"Do you remember the flames and the boy?"

It's an odd question and you start to ask her what she means when the intensity of the visualization increases. You can see it in your head, like a lucid dream. Someone stands near a window, their back to you. All around the person a fire rages. An inferno.

"What does this mean? Is this reversion some kind of message or something?"

"No. It's more like an intentional recollection but untainted by the imperfections of memory."

It's getting too hot for you to focus on the esoteric and nebulous words spoken by Noe. Instead, you nod and allow her to continue.

"Do you recognize him?"

"No," you respond before you can see his face. Somehow, you doubt you'll recognize him even if he turns around, which he doesn't.

"That's okay. I didn't think you would. You would have had no reason to."

Noe pauses, then continues, "Do you know why you're there?"

"It's a fire. Why would I be at a fire? What am I doing there?"

"I can't say for certain. But I know that you made your own decision. You were not forced to walk into the flames."

"But I did? I walked into something that was burning?"

"Yes." Noe winces. "Yes, you did so completely voluntarily."

"Who is the person at the window?"

"A boy. Someone you don't know."

"Does he need help?"

"Yes. If he isn't rescued, he'll die. There's a good chance he'll die even if he is rescued. And you know this."

Your head hurts. You can't imagine how Noe can possibly know what you were thinking inside of a memory you can't quite recall. A reversion, as she calls it.

"I have to save him. I don't know why, but I do."

"Yes. That is true."

You glance down at the speedometer and notice that you're driving faster. The heat is so intense that some of the plastic on the dashboard is beginning to melt. It wilts and droops like warm taffy.

Noe is waiting for something from you, but you don't know what.

"Okay. So..."

"Allow the reversion to unfold the way it is meant to."

You don't know what a reversion is, let alone how it's supposed to unfold, but what choice do you have? You'll wait for Noe to tell you what to do because there isn't anything else you can do.

"Allow yourself to go to him."

You do. You walk—in your vision—up to the boy. You put a hand on his shoulder. A hand with an enormous glove, the other wrapped around an ax. You can hear your own breathing inside of a helmet with a face shield.

"I'm a fireman."

"Yes."

"I'm on a call and I've found a boy. He's trapped by the fire."

"Yes."

You turn the boy around and his eyes are wide but watery. Tears streak clean lines down his ash-covered face.

He's trying to say something, but you hear nothing except the roar of the fire.

"I must save him. He's just a kid."

"Let the reversion unfold."

You're now aware of Noe's presence but only on the periphery of your vision. The Corvette tears down the highway with you behind the wheel, but your mind is somewhere else—in a reversion, fighting a fire, and attempting to rescue an innocent child.

"The building. It's about to collapse. I can tell."

"Right."

Your altered mind, your brain in the reversion, calculates the options. There is only time for you to toss the boy from the window before the roof collapses. It is his life or yours.

"I don't know what to do."

"You do. You've already done it."

You hesitate for a moment, allowing the reversion to pull you along in the swift, burning current.

Noe is crying.

You toss the ax to the side. You grab the boy beneath the arms and hurl him through the open window where, below, the men from your company wait to catch him. You stick your head out of the window and you see him land in the arms of a fireman. They both tumble to the ground, injured but alive. You pull back as you hear the burning timbers in their death throes.

"I'm going to die."

The thought in the reversion echoes past your lips as you speak the same words. The flames flare up and blind you with their brilliance and then you're back in the driver's seat of the Corvette.

"The reversion. Is it over?"

"It is over, yes. And it never gets easier."

It's an odd comment from Noe and something you tell yourself you'll need to think about when you get to wherever it is you're supposed to be. But you don't know where that is, or when that'll happen, or why you can't remember the reversion in the way that Noe does.

"So, now what?"

"Now that we're through the reversion, we come to your choice."

"What choice?"

"The fork. You need to decide which road to take."

You shake your head, pounding your fists on the steering wheel.

"But I don't understand. This isn't fair. You're asking me to do things and I have no clue what's going on."

"I'm not asking you to do anything. You are driving. Not me."

You decide not to say anything else to Noe until you reach the fork. What else is there to say? She knows what to expect and you don't. So, you drive. Hands on the wheel, pedal to the floor. You drive.

~

"Left or right."

"Why do I have to choose?"

"Because this is how it works. It's how it's always been and how it'll always be."

You see the fork coming up fast. The Corvette shimmies and you downshift before you realize what you're doing. The chrome side pipes breathe fire and the air has turned into nothing but an orange haze underlit by the flickering headlights.

"Where do the roads go?"

"Left loops you back around. Right takes you through to Canal."

"Canal Street? I don't even know what city that's in."

"It's irrelevant." Noe pinches the top of her nose, the words coming with a practiced staccato. "Just pick."

"Right."

"Are you sure?"

"No. You won't tell me what will happen when I choose or where we're headed. How could I possibly be sure? I'm going with my gut."

Noe straightens up in her seat. She turns and faces you, leaning forward and leveling a solid gaze at you.

"You are?"

"Yes."

"Well, that's unusual." She sighs and then continues, "Not something I recall."

The fork is now less than 20 feet away and you start turning the wheel to the right. You've made your decision and, even if Noe protests, it's too late to turn left now.

"Here we go."

The Corvette fishtails and you can feel the tires spinning on the gravel. The engine coughs but doesn't stall. The rear end of the car comes back around and you're now through the turn. The firestorm that's been chasing you from behind has disappeared. The night sky returns but, on the horizon, you can see the bleeding edge of day where purple ink is spilling up into the black canvas.

"You did it."

Noe says it as if she never thought you would.

You smile, raising an eyebrow at her like a proud child. "Yep."

She sits up straight, a small grin upon her face. "Punch it."

You slam the pedal down and feel the horsepower pinning your shoulders to the back of the seat. The sun must be rising on the eastern horizon as the night sky begins to fade. The Corvette accelerates, only now it feels as though the tires have come off the ground, the suspension holding you like an egg in a carton.

"We're going faster. Why is that happening?"

"It's because we're getting closer. That's how it always works. The closer you get, the faster you go."

You see the light on the horizon as it seeps up into what's left of the night. Almost instantly, the smoke dissipates, revealing the crystal-clear zenith you saw earlier.

"Do I keep going?"

"You've made the choice already. There's no decision left to make." Noe smiles at you and it lights up your chest like a shot of whisky.

You smile back. Something has shifted in her. You sense a different dynamic now. Kinder, more open.

"Look."

You turn away from Noe and stare through the windshield to see the tip of the sun cresting the eastern horizon. The first beams warm your face. Tears stream from your eyes. You don't wipe them away.

"This is emotional for everyone involved."

Things may have shifted between you and Noe, but you don't understand what she means. You're getting tired despite getting closer and so you decide you're done asking her questions. Whatever happens now will happen.

"The road will widen and then it will constrict to a single lane. Drive through the tunnel."

You sense a renewed spirit in Noe, a nostalgic wave as if she hasn't been here in a long time. You forget the name of the street. You don't bother asking about the name of the city. When you come out the other side of the tunnel, you'll be there. Somewhere. A place she thinks you belong and that will have to satisfy you.

"We're almost there."

The sun is now hovering over the horizon, illuminating the entrance to a single-lane tunnel. It's built of rock with a single traffic light hanging over the entrance. The light is green.

"Get ready."

You take one more look at Noe before realizing your hands are no longer on the wheel. Your feet are no longer pushing the pedals. The Corvette is driving you.

"Thank you," you say to Noe as the tears continue to flow.

"You're welcome." She's crying, too, both of you laughing at each other.

At the moment the front end of the Corvette enters the tunnel, you feel a weightlessness. The car fades away as does the feeling of Noe's presence. Everything is black inside of the tunnel. You hear muffled sounds and feel warm water surrounding your body.

And then, a faint light appears at the end of the tunnel. You can tell because you're going in that direction, headfirst. You bring your hands up to wipe your eyes, but you miss. They won't do what you're telling them to do.

The light grows and now you must close your eyes because it hurts them. There are voices, ones you recognize but cannot understand. Your body pauses for a moment and, for the briefest of seconds, you think you might be stuck in the tunnel, until a force propels you forward.

The world explodes. You scream, you cry, you squeeze your eyes tight from the blinding light. You don't understand where the sounds are coming from or what they mean.

More words reach your ears, but they're impossible to decipher. But you can feel the love inside them all the same.

"Oh, Mary. It's a boy. I love you so much."

THE BUS

BY M.B.VUJACIC

Alright, so this is the situation:

My name is Steve Capstone, and today is... Damn, I actually have no idea. My watch and my phone are gone, and there's no sun here, so I can't even figure out what time it is. The sky hasn't changed in the past... twenty-four hours? God, why am I even wasting time writing in this notebook? Might as well use it as toilet paper.

Fuck it.

Okay, sorry, let me try again.

My name is Steve, and it's Friday. Yeah, sure, why not? Friday's good. Anyway, I'm trapped on a bus. It's one of those ugly public-transportation six-wheelers with metal hand-holds and plastic seats that make your ass itch. And, man, has it seen better days. The paint is chipped and crumbling, the doors and the handholds brown with rust. The seats cracked and many of them missing, and the windows are nearly opaque with grime. There's dust and dirt every-where, as if the bus has been dragged out of a junkyard.

I woke up on its floor with no clue how I got there. The last thing I remember is stopping by some chick's place on our way downtown. Jordan lowered the passenger-side window and gave her pizza, and then I put the car in gear and drove on. Next thing I know, I'm here and my pockets are empty.

Jordan's here, too. He's my best friend. I've known him since high school. We played basketball, went to parties, picked up chicks, all that good stuff. The first thing I saw after waking up was him on his knees, his head in his hands, his eyes shut tight. Like me, he's been robbed of everything he had in his pockets. I'm glad he's here. I mean, I'm not *glad*, I'm just relieved I don't have to go through this alone.

Not that I could be *alone* here if I tried. There are four-teen other passengers on the bus. They're the most diverse group ever seen outside of a Hollywood blockbuster. We have a skinhead, a hillbilly, a stewardess, a tattooed house-wife, a Latino gangsta type, a young nurse, a black yuppie, a Mexican construction worker, a hulkish bouncer, an effemi-nate teenager, a woman in orange prison overalls, and two Indian guys who look like brothers. There's also a twelve-year-old kid. He just sits there, watching people with this curious expression on his face, like we're all actors in a movie. I keep expecting him to start crying, but he's pretty chill. Jordan thinks maybe the kid's retarded.

The bus is moving. We can hear the engine grinding and feel the wheels turning, but... but that's crazy because there's no ground here. We're sailing—yes, the bus is sailing, like a ship—on a sea of tar. Of course, I can't confirm it's really tar, but it's viscous and smelly and it bubbles, just like hot tar. It's all around us, reaching to the horizon and beyond. Sometimes I glimpse giant shapes in the distance, but there's no land and the air is too murky to see clearly. I can't find the sun but I guess it has to be there somewhere, because the sky is as bright as, say, on a stormy day. Speaking of the sky, it's blood-red and strewn with brown clouds that Jordan says look like giant turds. Or scabs.

The bus doesn't have a driver, but that's okay because it doesn't have gas pedals, or a dashboard, or even a goddamn steering wheel, either. Jordan thinks it's controlled remotely via satellite. My theory is the wheels are just for show—the bus is actually attached to a track, like a monorail. We just can't see it because it's under the tar.

I lied when I said I don't know why I'm writing this. The truth is, I hate being around people. Don't take me wrong, I'm not a loner or a jerk or anything, I got lots of friends. I just need my space. A few hours alone, so I can lean back and watch TV, or whatever. But I can't do that here, because I'm stuck with all these people, and we have no TV, no internet, no video games, not even a John where I could be alone for a minute.

I found this notebook, the pen already tucked in it, under one of the seats. Its front cover is blackened as if by fire and someone has burned out the first thirty pages or so, but the rest are fine. It really helps. Puts me in my own little bubble. I used to keep a diary as a kid, so it reminds me of that. Now, if only all these people could stop bawling and panicking and fucking *talking* for one second, I'd be golden.

Jesus Christ, I have to get out of here.

THE LATINO SMASHED the skinhead's nose.

Jordan and I were breaking off one of the rusted handhold poles to use as a dipstick to test the tar's depth, when the Latino roared at the skinhead to get the hell out of his face. The skinhead told him to take it easy, and the Latino clocked him. I've no idea what happened. I think the skinhead stepped on his foot while they were trying to pry the doors open, or something.

Later, his nose still gushing, the skinhead approached us and asked if we needed help with the pole. Jordan called him Nazi scum and told him to step away if he didn't want us to use *him* as a dipstick. The housewife then told us we should all treat each other well because we were being watched and judged and bickering among ourselves would only make our cases harder to defend. She spoke quietly, like we were conspiring, and she had these facial tics that made her nose and mouth twitch every time she finished a thought. Her tattoos all depicted saints and crucifixes, pale and blue. Jordan told her to hit the road, too.

At the time, I thought he'd done the right thing. Why would we hang out with racists and weirdos, right? But now, the Latino, the yuppie, the construction worker, and the woman in prison overalls are all sitting together, talking quietly. Makes me wonder if we might have a little crew forming here.

Anyway, we broke off the pole and forced open the middle doors. Holding onto the doorway, Jordan leaned out and stuck the pole into the tar. It made no ripples and left no trail in the blackness. It merely stretched it a little. Like a needle puncturing skin.

Jordan howled and lurched forward; the pole ripped from his hand. I grabbed his shoulder and yanked him back at the last moment. We fell on the floor and watched the pole get sucked into the tar. He looked at me then, his face chalky, and screamed: "Something *grabbed* it, man! *Something grabbed the pole!*"

Something in the tar.

JORDAN THINKS we've been abducted by aliens.

He says they must've shot us with tranquilizer darts, thrown us in the bus, and beamed us into space with a big-ass magnet. We're on another planet, one made entirely of liquid—a *gross giant*, he calls it, claiming he saw a documentary about it on TV—and the aliens are experimenting on us. When I asked him why the bus doesn't just sink, what with it being on a water planet and all, he shrugged and told me the aliens must've outfitted it with propellers.

Alien or not, I hope whoever put us here will shake things up soon because this place is getting toxic. Ever since the pole fiasco, I've felt this tension in the air, with people almost coming to blows over dumb stuff like accidentally brushing one another's shoulder or looking at someone for too long. It's like watching a bunch of dogs sniffing each other, tails taut, just itching for an opportunity to go for the throat. Even the yuppie and the girly teenager, neither of whom I'd bet have ever actually thrown a punch, remind me of angry little rats eager to snap at someone's ankle.

It doesn't help that Juan, the Latino, has indeed formed his own crew. The yuppie, the construction worker, and the prisoner woman are at his side at all times now, and they seem to be well on their way to convincing the Indian brothers to join them. The hillbilly, the skinhead, and the bouncer have joined forces too. The rest of the passengers keep to themselves, staring into the distance like those creepy 'realistic' mannequins every clothing store has in its window nowadays. Only the twelve year old, Kevin, gets along with everyone.

Also, there's another, bigger problem. I've been on this bus for three days now, but I haven't taken a single piss, or felt the need to. I don't sleep, either. Or eat. Or drink. Nobody else does, yet we aren't getting any thinner. Jordan thinks the aliens feed us and flush our bowels every day, then wipe our memories. It's the only explanation that makes sense, he says.

He wishes they washed our clothes too, while they were at it.

WE WERE WRONG. Jesus Christ, we were so wrong.

Jordan and I assumed there was some animal in the tar, an alien octopus or something. But it's the tar itself. It's alive. It's *fucking alive*. Christ Almighty. My hands are shaking. I've been sitting on them for half an hour, but they still won't keep steady. Shit. This is what happened.

Juan has drawn more people to his side. Yeah, there are racially divided sides now, like in a goddamn prison. Juan's group numbers six people—one woman and five guys, and they control the front of the bus. Richie, the hillbilly, owns the back. He has three men under his command, and they no longer go anywhere near Juan's 'territory.'

Lakisha, the woman in prison overalls, has regular sex with Juan and gives him massages. They do it right there, in front of everyone. The housewife complains to no end, ranting how this kind of sin will doom us all. Others complain as well, but nobody dares actually confront Juan about it, no matter how often Lakisha goes down on him or how loud she moans.

The shit finally hit the fan today. Lakisha was on her knees, her head bobbing up and down between Juan's legs, when Kevin, the kid, walked up to them. Normally, Juan and his cronies didn't let him near, or one of the other women kept the boy occupied, while Juan was getting it on with Lakisha. This must've sparked Kevin's curiosity because, this time, he sneaked in for a closer look. Juan saw him standing next to them, watching the proceedings with the same empty expression he always wore, and Juan *laughed*.

The skinhead exploded. He stomped to the front of the bus, calling Juan a "degenerate spik" and threatening to break his skull. Richie shouted at him to back down, but the skinhead didn't give a damn. He barreled through the Indian brothers and slammed his fist into Juan's face. Somehow, despite his pants being crumpled around his ankles, Juan sprung up. He roared incoherently and grabbed the skinhead by the neck. The Indian brothers tried to separate them, but then Richie charged in and punched one of the brothers in the back of the head. All hell broke loose.

I don't know if it was an accident, or if Juan did it on purpose. One moment fists were flying left and right, the next the skinhead was flung, arms flailing, through the open doors. At the last instant, he clamped his hand on the rusted doorway and I saw his goddamn fingernails break, baring red flesh, and then he splashed into the tar.

Jaws, claws, and tentacles sprung out all around him, devouring his arms, legs, face. Pitch black, they came directly from the tar. Hell, they *were* tar. And there was this sound. A deep, visceral gurgle, like the groan of an empty stomach. It came from all around us and lingered long after the skinhead had disappeared on the horizon.

Jesus Christ, *what is this place*?

~

WE THREW our lot in with Richie the hillbilly, and I hate myself for it.

He's been pestering us to join him for days, now. He and his huge bouncer buddy would stroll to the middle of the bus and sit behind Jordan and me. Then Richie would look at where Juan and his crew were lying around with their shirts off and their feet up and tell us how it was only a matter of time before *they* threw us whiteys out of the bus so *they* could have all the women to themselves. Richie and his guys lacked the manpower to prevent this, but with us on their side the odds would be equal.

Every time they gave us that speech, I felt the urge to tell them to stuff their bigotry up their asses. And, every time, I'd think of the way Juan watched us—his bloodshot eyes sliding from one face to another, lingering just long enough to make you feel like you were being challenged—and instead of blowing Richie off, I'd tell him we'd let him know if we changed our mind. I kept expecting Jordan to interfere, but he just sat there, nodding his head at whatever I said, the conviction with which he'd told the skinhead to fuck off gone.

But today we gave in and joined Richie and his crew at the back of the bus. Richie and the bouncer took that as a green light to do whatever they want, because now they're dropping racial slurs every other sentence and boasting about serving time at Crim's Cove. The effeminate teenager giggles like a girl at everything they say. Christ. I have to keep reminding myself that, as much as I want to kick their teeth in, at least Richie and his pals didn't rape anyone.

Yeah, Juan raped the housewife. That's what made us join Richie. Juan and the Indian brothers approached her seat and began talking to her quietly. She shook her head, then waved her hands in a go-away gesture. Juan grabbed a fistful of her hair and dragged her to the front of the bus where they ripped off her clothes and took her, one by one. She shrieked about judgment and the bus being our last chance and how they'd never be able to explain themselves if they went on with this, but then Juan gave her face the speed bag treatment and she quieted. The yuppie and the construction worker looked terrified, but didn't dare interfere. Kevin saw everything, and nobody cared enough to so much as cover his eyes. Not that they needed to.

The fucking kid was grinning the entire time.

JORDAN HAS ABANDONED the alien abduction theory.

Now he thinks we're trapped in the Matrix. In reality, we're all lying in some top-secret underground base with our brains connected to a supercomputer. Some government organization—CIA, NASA, the Men in Black, you name it—is using us as guinea pigs to test their new virtual reality tech. Or deliberately running a nightmare simulation to see how people would behave in a situation like this.

If that's the case, they must be pretty disappointed. We've been in this bus for, maybe, two weeks and it's already a jungle. Richie has even armed us. With shanks. He and the bouncer gathered pieces of splintered seats, then tore the teenager's shirt to strips and wrapped them around the shards of plastic to form makeshift handles. They claim they could turn one of the handhold poles into a spear, but they don't want to attract Juan's attention just yet.

Jordan tells me not to worry. Since this is a computer-generated simulation, dying will probably cause us to wake up in the real world. Worst case scenario, we'd feel some "artificial pain," whatever that means. Of course, when I suggested he test that theory by sticking his shank into his throat, he told me to shut up.

So much for scientific research.

THE ENTIRE BUS smells like Juan's innards.

That's the good news. The bad news is... Christ, I don't even know how to say it...

He was raping the housewife again when Richie got up and started walking. The bouncer followed, then the effeminate teenager, and, lastly, Jordan and me. Juan saw us coming and, without the slightest hesitation, looked at his crew and screamed that "the hour of *revolución* has come." Yes, he used those exact words.

The only ones who came to stand at his side were the Indian brothers. The yuppie and the construction worker stayed in their seats, their eyes hopping rapidly between him and Richie. I don't know if they chickened out or if they, too, thought him a madman, but God, I was so relieved. I really thought Juan would back down.

Instead, he drew out a shank of his own and howled like an animal. The Indians didn't look as insane as him, but they must've seen something in Richie's eyes before I did, because they produced their own shanks and took position at Juan's sides, like movie bad guys making a last stand.

And a last stand it was. Spitting and growling, Juan kept swinging at Richie and the bouncer until they shoved him against the back of a seat and buried his own shank handle-deep in his belly. Despite being outnumbered, the Indian brothers managed to cut Jordan's arm and almost push me out of the bus. We slashed them all over their faces and necks and kicked them out like bloody sacks. The tar ate them just like it had eaten the skinhead. I leaned against a window afterward, deafened by the pounding in my temples. I was so glad the rapists had been dealt with.

Only, it wasn't enough for Richie. He charged into the front and drove his shank into Lakisha's neck, turning her scream into a wet gurgle. The bouncer ran in and bashed the yuppie's head against the wall. The construction worker threw a punch but slipped and stumbled and then Richie and the bouncer were all over him. Afterward, they dragged their victims—still kicking and groaning and begging for mercy—to the doors and threw them out. That deep intestinal growl returned, growing louder with each body they dropped into the tar.

They left Juan for last. I thought they just wanted to taunt him but, instead, they cut up his pants and used the strips to tie his wrists to a pole. Then Richie grabbed the shank protruding from Juan's belly, and *twisted*. The smell of shit filled the bus. Jordan and I turned and vomited, and so did almost everyone else. Even the bouncer couldn't keep from clamping a hand over his nose. Only Richie laughed.

It went on and on. I expected Juan to die or lose consciousness, but no, he kept writhing and shrieking like a pig being butchered.

Now, I'm not a doctor or anything, and I know people don't just die instantly like in the movies, and that adrenaline can keep you going when you should be cold... But this still makes no sense because, you see, it's been a fucking long time—days, at least—since they tied him to that pole and *Juan's still alive.*

I'm looking at him as I write this. His midsection resembles mashed tomatoes and there's more blood on the floor than he could possibly have in his body. Not only is he alive and awake, they have to keep tightening his bonds because he keeps trying to free himself. Richie says he has no intention of throwing Juan out. He gets his kicks out of teaching Kevin how to best cut Juan up, an activity Kevin enjoys even more than Richie. The kid even gave Juan a nickname.

Punchbag.

THE HOUSEWIFE STEPPED off the bus.

She'd been awfully quiet since Juan and the Indian brothers raped her and, come to think of it, I guess I should've seen it coming. She simply stood up and went to the open doors, her slippers squishing through Juan's blood. She lingered in the doorway for a while, staring at the red sky. Jordan asked her what she was doing, and she looked at us, broken nose twitching, and said, "It's the end in the tar. It's kinder than what they'll do to us." Then she took another step and was consumed.

What must've tipped her over the edge was the sight of the bouncer raping the stewardess. Yeah, rape is back. In retrospect, I feel like a moron for ever thinking it'd go away. The stewardess followed the housewife's example soon after. Richie realized what she was about to do an instant too late. He tried to tackle her, but her naked body was slick with sweat and blood, and she slipped past him. That made the nurse the last woman on the bus. They tied her to one of the seats to keep her from getting away. Then they did the same to the effeminate teenager.

Richie and the bouncer don't bother putting their clothes on anymore. They just stroll around with their dicks swaying, rambling about God and judgment and how they're the kings of this bus. They tell the nurse and the teenager they'll end up like Juan if they don't behave, and then laugh as if amused by their own wit. Kevin giggles at all this like it's a cartoon he's watching. They haven't turned on Jordan and me yet, but we both know it's only a matter of time. I'm pretty sure they do, too.

Jordan's convinced the bus can't keep going forever. Sooner or later, it has to arrive at a station. He has no idea—not even a theory—what this station might be like, but he knows for a fact he doesn't want to share it with Richie and the bouncer. He says we have to do something.

We have to bury those motherfuckers.

JESUS, there's blood all over this notebook.

It's my fault. I forgot to wipe my hands. Not that there's much clean cloth left to wipe them with. Even my shirt is torn and soaked with spit and sweat and blood and other stuff I don't want to think about. Damn. Now half the pages are soaked and some of them are stuck together. Damn, damn, damn.

As of an hour ago, Jordan and I are officially murderers. The bouncer was taking the teenager from behind, their naked bodies glistening with perspiration, when Jordan walked up to him and drove a shank into the bouncer's kidney. The bouncer actually kept thrusting for a few moments before his moans became screams. Richie rushed to his aid, shank raised, bellowing so hard spittle flew from his mouth.

I ran in and swung my own sharp piece of bus seat—Richie's own handiwork—and I don't know if I got lucky or if Richie didn't see me coming, but the next thing I know my shank's sticking out of his throat and his face is right next to mine and his eyeballs are fucking huge and he's vomiting red all over me. I fell, and he fell on top of me, and I swear to God he would've strangled me if Jordan wasn't there to pull him off.

The two of them were both very much alive, struggling even, as we dragged them to the doors and kicked them out. Juan was, too. His mouth—what was left of it, anyway—kept opening and closing as we cut him loose and rolled his ravaged body into the tar. I don't think he was trying to thank us. Can't say I blame him. The nurse and the teenager didn't thank us after we freed them, and I can't say I blame them either. Only Kevin acts like none of this bothers him.

The bus sails on.

Jordan was right. There really is a station.

It appeared on the horizon about an hour ago, straight ahead. It flickers there, a fiery speck, its light so sharp I can't look at it for more than a few seconds at a time. The nurse wailed the moment she saw it, and so did the teenager. They ran to the back of the bus and crawled under the seats, their naked bodies curling on the floor like oversized fetuses. Kevin didn't scream or try to flee, but he has paled visibly. He just stands at the front of the bus now, staring at the distant glow, unfazed by its brightness.

Jordan looks sick. His face is pasty and his teeth chatter. His skin glistens with a layer of sweat thick enough to drink. He thinks we're on our way to Hell. That that's where the things waiting for us at that station will send us. When I told him that sailing across a tar-sea could hardly be compared to roasting eternally in a lake of fire, he looked at me and said we deserve to be here. Because of all the pizzas we sold. And because of what we did to Bobby Nickelsen.

I told him to go fuck himself.

~

No.

This can't be happening.

Jesus Christ, get me out of here.

Shit.

Shit.

SHIT.

~

Everything is shit.

Christ Almighty, maybe Jordan was right. Not about us going to Hell, because fuck that, but about us deserving to be here. You see, we used to sell *pizzas*. That's what we called the merchandise so that we could safely take orders, in case the cops were listening. *Vegetariana* was weed, *capricciosa* was junk, *margherita* was glass, and so on. Jordan used to feel bad about it and wanted to quit, but I explained to him that if we hadn't sold those losers the drugs, they would've bought them elsewhere. After all, nobody forced them to use that garbage, so what the hell did he have to feel guilty about?

Anyway, that's not why I brought this up. It's about Bobby fucking Nickelsen. I knew that guy was trouble the moment I saw him. His hair was always twisted in long greasy strands, his bangs glued to his forehead, his clothes dangling on his frame like rags from a hanger. He reminded me of those spiteful mutts who wanted nothing more than to bite, but tolerated your presence because you occasionally threw them scraps. Still, he had two things going for him. The first was a taste for *cappriciosa*, the second a seemingly endless supply of hard cash.

Bobby had been our customer for about six months when, one day, instead of paying as usual, he and his skank girlfriend pulled a gun on us and made us hand over the pizza. We did, and they let us walk. It was a dumb thing to do, seeing as we knew where he lived. Even if that hadn't been the case, we knew many of his friends and they'd sell him out in a blink if we offered them free samples. I doubt he knew what he was doing. I think his mind was too fried.

The next night, we got a gun of our own, plus some baseball bats for good measure, and went to sort it out. Bobby and his girlfriend were so blasted they didn't even notice us until we were in their apartment, their gun safely in my hand. So we took the baseball bats, and the rest, as they say, is a clusterfuck. We wanted to give them some bruises and crack a few teeth, but we got carried away and Bobby ended up on the floor with his forehead literally beaten out of shape. He didn't die, but... let's just say he won't be identifying us to the cops. Or identifying anyone else, ever again.

Jordan thinks Bobby's the reason we ended up here. He believes we're on our way to be judged. He says that's why nobody dies on this bus—we're past that. *They* want to hear us justify our crimes one last time before they drop the hammer. And they know everything.

Or rather, that's what Jordan thought the last time we spoke. I don't know what he thinks now, or if he's even capable of thinking, anymore. I haven't talked to him in about a day. Or to anyone else, for that matter.

Because...

You see, I...

I'm all alone, here.

The nurse was the first to go. I was reading this notebook when I heard a splash. I spun around, but all I saw was the top of her head sinking into the tar. The teenager went next. He approached Jordan and me, and said he was glad we killed Richie and the bouncer. He had this plastic look in his eyes, like a cheap toy. Then he headed for the open doors. I shouted and got up, but he stepped out before I could reach him.

By then, the station had grown from a bright speck to a fist-sized blaze. If you focused on it for a few seconds, you could discern dark shapes soaring within it. They didn't remind me of anything in particular, yet, whenever I glimpsed them, my skin broke out in goosebumps.

Jordan couldn't stand the sight of them. He'd start wailing every time he looked, letting out this loud, undulating sob that gnaws on your nerves and makes you want to rip your own ears off so you wouldn't hear it anymore. God, I tried, I really, *really* tried to calm him down, but he wouldn't listen. He kept telling me to cut the bullshit, to stop lying to myself. The only way out was the tar.

In the end, Jordan stood up despite my protests and started for the doors. I grabbed him and tried to pull him back, but he dragged me along to the doorway like I weighed nothing. I started begging him to stop, and he put a hand on my shoulder and said, "Come with me. We can jump together." I told him he was out of his goddamn mind.

"You really think you're innocent, don't you?" he said, then looked toward the station. "You can bullshit me and you can bullshit yourself, but *they* know who you are. We're all bad people here, Steve. They gave us a chance to choose nothingness over punishment. It's as merciful as they'll get."

I told him to cut the crap, that that makes no sense, that, even if we did bad stuff, we had good reasons for it. Jordan's face only got sadder. I was still talking when he went limp and let himself tumble out, like his bones had turned to jelly. If I hadn't let go, I would've fallen out with him, face-first into the tar.

Kevin held on the longest. He'd been standing at the front of the bus, staring at the oncoming station, ever since it first appeared on the horizon. Eventually, he turned around and made his way toward the middle doors, leaning on the seats to support himself. His eyes had gone a murky white, like there was fog inside them. He stopped in the doorway, looked in my direction, and muttered something. I didn't catch it, and didn't ask him to repeat. I just sat there and waited for him to do it. It wasn't a long wait.

I'm all alone, now. The last passenger on tar-express, nearing the end of his journey. The station is so close it covers the horizon like a vast fiery cloud. Its light paints the tar orange, making it seem like the bus is sailing on a sea of molten gold. Or lava. The air here is full of soot. It dances in the light like dust particles in a sunbeam, sticking to my face and prickling my skin.

Please get me out of this place.

Help me.

Anyone.

~

I CAN'T JUMP. I can't.

There's nothing after the tar. Everything just ends.

I have to keep going. I can see the dark shapes in the station and I know they're waiting for me and that they'll listen. I'll explain myself. They'll understand. They must.

Because I can't jump into the tar.
I can't face the end.

I've entered the station and the bus is slowing down.

There's burning fog everywhere and the air's so hot it's like I'm in a sauna. Jesus Christ, my clothes are starting to smoke and those dark things are all around me.

They all know me, and I know them. I can feel them looking.

They see me.

Into me.

Oh God, they have so many eyes.

CLICK FOR ASCENSION
BY THOMAS KODNAR

When Sheila took her last breath, she was grateful.

Not because she had been in any rush to die, and not because she hadn't enjoyed living. Her gratitude—which, otherwise, was complete, for all she had left in this final nanosecond was an intense base sense of her emotional state of being, of her*self*—was riddled with tiny specks of fear, too, sensed by her as crimson blotches of imperfection in a blessedly dark, equally empty and full moment: she'd been scared for weeks now, so it was no surprise that some of it would swap over into her time of release, of elation, of severely anticipated, unavoidable death. Who in their right mind was not afraid of this? Of *the end*? Even if the end had been so foreseeable, and the only possible solution to the problem that was a life of sickness, of pain, and of the horror of a body turning, ever so destructively, against itself.

So, Sheila met death with mixed feelings. Death did not care either way. It took her completely and, once it had a hold of her, fast.

There was darkness. For a minuscule blink in existence,

Sheila thought she even intuited a *lack* of existence, a nothing unlike anything a living person could imagine.

Then the darkness lifted.

Sheila wasn't religious. She vaguely remembered going to church with her parents as a child, but she'd never paid attention or understood any of the rituals they'd made her perform. She'd thanked God once in her life, when the doctors had told her that her son had not inherited her disease, but that god who'd received her acknowledgements had been as impersonal as whatever or whoever her gratitude in the face of death had been directed at. And everything she'd expected and hoped for from dying was release from her sufferings, not any further life *after* the end of life —an idea which, to her, had always seemed absurdly illogical.

Yet, here she was.

First, Sheila had the imprecise sense of being within a sort of inconceivably fast current. She couldn't name her form of movement, nor could she be sure it *was* movement: was she floating? Was she being pulled on a string? It was reminiscent of sitting in a rollercoaster, only there was no seat beneath her, and though she believed she *did* feel something like a safety belt pushing against her, this feeling wasn't constant, nor was it strong—and, just like this weight cutting into her at one moment and lifting off her the next, *she*, this *her* allegedly constrained by the weight, seemed to be there only at certain points, gone at others; comparably, the entire idea of *moments* and *points* in something like time seemed, all of a sudden, very farfetched to whatever was left of Sheila's mind, to whatever it was that was swimming, or running, or dragging along with this curious river of pure being and entire non-being.

Before she could begin to think about this new mode of

existence—or even accept that it *was* existence, that *she* was existing—Sheila, simultaneously overwhelmed and, lest she go mad, necessarily unperturbed, began to see. It was unclear to her whether she had herself opened a peculiar set of ocular appliances or had been given sight of a different, eyeless manner from an outside source. She was too busy becoming aware of surroundings which, weirdly enough, did not seem to *surround* her so much as they were, for lack of a better term, part of her; as though she had grown extra limbs, and extra-large ones, at that, limbs which far exceeded the reach of the arms and legs she'd left behind. What she saw, if seeing it was, looked like strange, endless tubes, or maybe threads, or, just perhaps, cables, which formed the bed of the unspecifiable river pulling her along, shaped the shapeless flow of being on which she was drifting. They were all around her, they *were* her, and they were, not so much the tunnel which she might have expected had she ever believed in anything like this, but the largest crossroads anyone had ever conceived of, a junction of paths which were very much and not at all like streets, a merging and splitting and interweaving of lines of every color and no color. She had no better words to describe what she saw, for there *were* no better words, and she couldn't even have sworn to it that she *did* see. She still had no idea what was going on, but she was at least beginning to understand that the reality she had found herself in was beyond mere seeing—and, in truth, beyond understanding.

Next, hearing came. And once she heard the low hum, this vibration pervading everything and slicing right through her being, she wondered vaguely whether she hadn't been hearing this all her life, but had been dumbly, naively unaware of it.

In the midst of all this sensing, which was unlike any

sensation she'd known in her lifetime, she swiftly began to redevelop—as a sort of extension and, yet, in what felt like a necessary implication, or even a logical prerequisite added belatedly, a natural sequitur despite the apparent unnatural quiddity of the situation—that sense of *self* she'd had as she'd lain dying. She became aware of her state as an entity in this entirety, of her own narrow, enclosed existence, her limitedness in this un-world of limitlessness and openness. She wasn't a body, not in the way she'd been prior to her death—but she wasn't detached from all time and space, from matter as such, either. She was not a spiritual, immaterial being of pure thought, let alone of pure love or pure bliss; this was not the rapture of a divine paradise. And yet, it *was* a different state of being, one which in its sneaky, opaque, downright arcane way impressed upon her, confused and dazed and uncomprehending as she was, that it was a *higher* state. What she was was not a bunch of cells arranged into human form, but it was human, alright, and it was constrained to a certain area, if there were areas in this place which was a non-place. She assumed that there weren't, not really; just like she was and wasn't human, did and didn't see and hear and feel, this space she was in was no space, the area of her individual structure neither structure nor locus. It was expanse and it wasn't. It was her consciousness, no longer bound by nerves and muscle, but bound, nonetheless.

Suddenly, forcefully, the auditive took over as the number one impression when the humming first increased in volume, seeming to fill her up like air would a balloon—then stopped abruptly.

What followed was a sound she'd heard hundreds of times before—but one she couldn't place for the life of her. All she knew was that its usual volume was amplified to a maximum on a wavelength beyond the range audible to human ears.

It was a shriek of such proportions that her nails would have crawled into her skin, had she possessed either of the two.

It was a screech like none a living thing can utter.

It was the brief, pointed wailing of a battalion of banshees, in one instance there to shred her—she was all hearing now, and the sound raped her essence—and gone the next, but echoing through eternity as she plummeted, propelled by the strangely familiar yet unknown noise, into another part of this post-reality.

She was now, as though cast down into another realm by that noise, within a whirlwind of fleeting images, strange flickering symbols, and flashes of light that looked like surges of electricity. Sheila was turning with everything around her—horizons of unfathomable information flickered everywhere, and she was in them and with them. It lasted forever and for the blink of an eye.

When it stopped, it felt to her almost as though she'd landed on a floor, falling onto it with a soft thud and, luckily, no pain. The tubes and threads and cables had returned into focus, but, even though they were still all around her and everywhere within her, they were no longer the only thing she saw. Beyond such worldly reactions as astonishment, surprise, or effort now, she didn't try to understand how she came to be outside the church where she'd married her husband. Except that she wasn't really outside it, she knew. Not because it was impossible—though it very much was so, for she was dead—but because it didn't *look* like she was, not precisely. Yes, she saw the beautiful gothic front, the high cast-iron door with the magnificent imprint of a saint slaying a dragon, and the gorgeously colored stained glass of the windows, the high tower housing the bell and the cherry tree which grew to the left side of the ancient building. She saw all of these things clearly and at the same time—and from multiple angles. She was in front of the church and she also stood to its left, seeing the high wall which ran past its main body and protected its yard and garden, where she and her husband had held their agape. Then again, and just as much, she stood on the opposite side of the street from its main entrance, and saw the Italian restaurant next to it, in all its unfashionable inexpensiveness, so stark a contrast to the lovely house of religion, where she'd married not because she'd shared in its faith, but because her husband's family and her own had insisted on a traditional wedding. And beyond it all, behind these impressions as much as overlapping them, were those curious lines running in so many directions but, for the nonce, running without her. She was given a moment of rest at a place where, years ago, she'd made an important choice and said an important word, setting her off on the path which was to be the predictably short remainder of her life.

The last time she'd seen these images, she'd Googled the church as part of the preparations for her funeral ceremony. Were these her memories? She'd heard of people having their life run by them as they expire, but nowhere did she see herself in her wedding dress, beaming exuberantly, joyous beyond words from the fact that the man she loved had decided to marry her despite her sickness. The church doors didn't fly open to spill the happy couple onto the renovated gray steps outside, the lights in the windows didn't flicker, the clouds beyond the church tower were unmoving: these were not scenes from her life, they were *photographs*. They were *literally* the images she'd seen when she'd been searching for the church's telephone number online. If she had embarked on a deathly re-watch of her life, would she really begin by re-checking her latest Google results?

Her ponderings were interrupted when another—a *new* —sound filled this strange world. It, too, was familiar but alien, heard-before but never like this, never this loud or this all-encompassing or this... close.

It was, in fact, two short-lived sounds, a pair of signals, robotic and musical at the same time, a little like notes on a xylophone. *Di-din*! Fleeting and loud and inviting. Then silence.

And, barely daring to believe—and hoping that she was wrong—Sheila *did* believe that she knew what this silence meant. That she knew the preceding signal. Impossible as it seemed to be.

If she had the right of it, she might be able to speak. She wondered if she should try. And she wondered what would frighten her more: if her suspicion were to be proven correct, or if it turned out that she still lacked any semblance of understanding of her new environment...

"Do you have a question?"

The sentence came from the confusion of tubes and lights, and it came from right beside her. It came from every image of the church and from every corner of this unwalled room.

And Sheila knew that voice. Knew it well. It had directed her to many a destination when she would have been lost without it. It had kept her informed on the weather when she hadn't depended on the trustworthiness of her own glance outside her window. It had provided her with recipes and song lyrics and the names of pop idols' spouses when she couldn't come up with them herself. It was the voice of a woman, echoing in the eternal vastness. It was also the voice of a lifeless being, hollowed out, purposeless, and meaning nothing by its words.

And it was the voice of knowledge. Turned up to the maximum and pervading all that was.

Sheila turned slowly to locate the source of the voice, not expecting to find anything. She was right in this expectation. And *now*, she was scared. Now, even though this new scenario was in no way more unnerving, less probable, or more insurmountable than any other since her death (which had been—seconds ago? minutes? days?), she was beginning to feel a disembodied sense of dread. Maybe her disembodiment was why she hadn't been frightened up until now: how does one experience fear if one has no heartbeat to accelerate, no skin to break out in sweat, draws no breath which can come short and clipped?

Now she knew: all that was left was that terrible, almighty chill, which, finding no bones in which to burrow for marrow, dug over her mind instead, leaving her one shivering, speechless, dumbfounded, massless heap of discombobulated ghostly thoughts...

But there was nothing to it. She would have to try and speak. If she wanted clarity, if she wanted to be rid of this soul-gripping fear, she would have to try to find her way through this mess.

Aware that she had no mouth, she tentatively attempted to open one anyway. She fought to concentrate on a thought, struggled to wrestle it from within her, to give birth to its expression. She failed on all accounts. Focusing on one thought was difficult enough—and, really, what thought was there to focus on? What could have done the trick of making sense of all of this?—but getting this bodiless creature she'd become to *say* the words "Where am I?", that was beyond—

Di-din!

"Please specify your question."

The womanly robotic voice again from all around her, tearing at her in its loudness and invasiveness, its unavoidability, its reasonable, inhuman sobriety and, yet, mockingly human intonation.

Sheila realized with a jolt that she must have spoken aloud after all, albeit accidentally. By *not* trying too hard.

The images of the church were losing substance now; they were morphing and warping, swimming away. She let it happen. They had given her no comfort. Their presence had been as insane and absurd as any other detail of this drama playing out before her, with her as the lead actress who had not learned her lines. She ignored the images' disappearance and focused again...

"What is this place?" she said—or thought—to the voice.

Di-din! "Please specify your question."

Her fear abating as her frustration grew, Sheila did something which felt like getting to her feet, though there were no feet to get onto and there was no definite floor to lift off from. Gathering her mental strength—which was the only thing she had never lacked in life—she specified her question: "Am I on planet earth?"

Silence. Then: *di-din!* "Yes and no. This address—" (the voice listed a sequence of numbers which brought Sheila's chill back for a moment because she felt like she knew the sequence, though its familiarity was as wispy and faint as a breath of wind from an unidentified nook in a stranger's house) "—is associated with a specific locality on Earth. But you are not bound to this address, nor are you currently there in any relevant sense, Sheila."

More than anything, it was her name coming out of that invisible, mouthless intelligence which reinforced Sheila's unease. She tried to hold onto the thought that now she at least had the chance to receive an explanation, some sort of justification for her being here, but it proved nigh on impossible: the overwhelming impression was that nothing that voice could tell her would make any more sense than what it had already spoken. The images of the church were fading into darkness around her, rather abruptly at first, as though a computer screen had been inactive for a while and dimmed its internal light in response, then gradually, as though they were dancing on the verge of being forgotten...

In an unconscious act of desperation, as she fought to hold back tears which couldn't fall because there were no eyes to cry them, as her helpless mind flopped about for a way out of here, searching for escape she deemed impossible from a place she could not name, she uttered another question: "What is happening to me?"

The answer came almost immediately.

Di-din. "The connection was successful."

Sheila thought that she must be losing her mind, if she had not already lost it—and she intuited that, here, losing her mind would be losing herself, losing all that she was.

"I don't understand," Sheila lamented at the voice.

Di-din. But no reply beyond that. Merely the receptive, appreciative signal, informing Sheila that she'd been heard.

Not knowing what else to do, Sheila moaned: "I want out of here."

Di-din.

"You can only go deeper," the voice informed her; it seemed cooler now, less female, less casually, laxly well-intending. "Is that what you want?"

It was not. She wanted away. She wanted blissful darkness or, better yet, attribute-less nothingness, as she would've expected to find, as would have made sense. She didn't believe that "deeper" implied either of the two.

But if it was her *only* way...

"I want out..." she repeated weakly.

Di-din. "You can only go deeper. Is that what you want?"

It wasn't. Oh no, it most certainly wasn't.

But what was there to do?

"Yes," Sheila surrendered.

It felt as though a hook caught her somewhere behind her non-existent navel and pulled so mightily that any corporeal thing would have been torn apart in earnest, ripped in half, right down the centre. And, even without a body to tear, she *did* feel something let go, something which had held her together, something which had kept her in one piece. Helpless, she watched as the cables and tubes surrounding her increased in size until they were no longer visible as individual things—if that is what they ever were— and enwrapped her, pulled her through to another world beyond this first peculiar, outlandish beyond which had already been too much for her.

The realization that she had made a mistake, that she should have declined the offer of going deeper—though it did hit her irrevocably—was unremarkable compared to everything else which swept through her, dragging her down, drawing her—deeper. Feeling as though she were soaring again, then as though she were being thrown, then pulled, then as though she were not moving at all, she could do nothing but stare—for whatever species of eyes she was equipped with now, she did not know how to close them— as impressions like none she'd ever hoped to see, none she could understand, washed over her, gripped her—entered her.

All these images.

Not of churches, but of bodies. And of acts. Of crimes so hideous they boggled her as much as they frightened her—mangled limbs, excavated intestines, women and children gagged and tethered to radiators, starved men hanging from ceiling beams—and of scenes so absurd they appalled her even more, so unimaginable that she had no names for what she saw: a fat person crawling naked over a floor infested with scuttling cockroaches, a wall draped with animal skulls and giant male sexual organs, a field of decapitated flowers in which hooded beings poured unidentifiable liquids from head-shaped containers onto a heap of pig feet.

Sounds accompanied the unfathomable pictures: gunshots and screaming and exhalations of agony which could only be the last breaths of the painfully, irretrievably sick; mad laughter and wickedly vulgar exclamations and radioed reports describing crime scenes even more horrendous than any of the visible affronts to life, to hope, to goodness. The visions were cruel, but these noises—they were hell.

True, seemingly everlasting hell.

What was left of her was splintering. She could feel it. It was a condition so horrid that even the images and sounds faded before it. Not that the afterlife was real, not that *hell* was real, not that *she* had been cast into hell was what was worst and hardest to stand, but that she should be torn apart like this, this feeling of being pulled in every possible and impossible direction at once. She tried to force herself to stop, to put an end to the misery of being stripped, not limb from limb, not even cell from cell, but thought from thought, piece of soul by piece of soul, if soul was what she was...

She gathered all her strength, all her energy, and willed

it into this command both to herself and to this un-world, the command to *STOP*—

And it was then that she finally realized: she *had* an ounce of control. A semblance of mobility in this strange place. For it *had* stopped. Instead of switching to another monstrosity, the last image she had tried and failed to close her sight against, a picture of a man cutting out his own appendix, hovered before her, still and silent. No sound issued from it, or from anywhere. It was then that she knew: the reason the world around her had been altering at such breakneck speed, that every horror was replaced by a new one before she could even begin to try and cope with the first—was *her*. She wished to flee, she begged, albeit silently, in perceived defencelessness, to escape the terror—and, obeying her, this non-world tossed her right into the next terror. For down here, at this level—*deeper*—there was nothing but terror.

Staring at the man and the blood gushing forth from the wound he'd opened in his own stomach, Sheila gave herself a moment to cry. But still no tears would come, of course, for there were still no lachrymal glands, no eyes. And what use was crying anyway?

Defying the desire to wish the picture away, ignoring the will to go on even if it meant another horror, more from the soundtrack of Hades, she used the little strength she found within herself to think or speak or hope one word into existence: "... Siri."

Di-din.

Sheila might have laughed, had she had the body to do so, and had she not been the most exhausted and most scared she'd ever been.

"Please," Sheila repeated, her gaze never wavering,

bravely facing the madman operating on himself. "Take me out of here."

Di-din. "Certainly. Where do you wish to go?"

Relief surged through her, eradicating the fear. Sheila finally managed to close whatever she had that went for eyes down here, blocking out the revolting sight after all. She knew that she could do that now without fear of the next abomination.

She whispered her final word: "Nowhere…"

Du-dun.

ABOUT THE AUTHORS

C.W. Blackwell was born and raised in Northern California, where he still lives with his wife and two sons. He has been a gas station attendant, a stock broker, and a crime analyst. His passion is to blend poetic narratives and pulp dialogue to create evocative genre fiction. He writes mostly crime fiction and horror. His recent work has appeared in *Pulp Modern*, *Shotgun Honey*, *Switchblade Magazine*, and *Rock and a Hard Place Magazine*.

Harvey Click, author of *Realms of Night, Night Conjurings, A Traveler from an Antique Land, Demon Frenzy, Demon Mania, Magic Times, The Bad Box* and *The House of Worms*, earned an M.A. in English from Ohio State University, writing a novel for his master's thesis. He has written six other novels, four of them in the horror genre, and two collections of horror stories. He has taught English and creative writing for Ohio University, Ohio State University, the James Thurber House, and OSU's Creative Arts Program.

Tom Garback (he/him) is currently pursuing an M.A. in Writing and Publishing at Emerson College, where he is President of Wilde Press, a non-profit that publishes four titles a year. His fiction, poems, and essays have been featured in *Cabinet of Heed, Blind Corner, Oddball, Polaris, Sonder*, and a dozen other publications.

Find out more at tcgarback.wixsite.com/website/writing

Julie Hiner spent endless hours during her childhood lost in books. The only thing that took precedence was her Walkman. Julie is still a hardcore 80s rocker at heart.

Julie secured a solid education and career in computer science. She switched paths to finish her non-fictional book, an inspirational story of facing fears, cycling, and massive mountains.

Fueled by a long-time fascination with the dark mind of the serial killer and inspiration from a talk by a local homicide detective, she flung herself into writing her first novel. She now runs KillersAndDemons.com – Tales of Dark Crime and Horror.

Thomas Kodnar, born in 1992, prefers horror in both his reading and his writing. Studied philosophy at the university of Vienna. Has published short stories in a variety of anthologies and magazines, e.g. in *&Radieschen*, *Zwielicht*, *HORLA – The Home of Intelligent Horror*, *phantastisch!*, and *ParABnormal Magazine*. Writes stage plays in cooperation with the glashaus collective. Likes coffee, Stephen King, vegan cake, Donna Haraway, Digimon (the TV-series) and Pokémon (the video games). More on his German website and his Instagram

Find out more at thomaskodnar.at or @thomaskodnar on Instagram.

Daniel R. Robichaud lives and writes in Houston, Texas. His work has appeared in numerous markets, including *parABnormal* magazine, *Eldritch Dream Realms* anthology, *Hookman and Friends* anthology, and more. A portion of his short fiction has been collected in three volumes: *Hauntings & Happenstances*, *They Shot Zombies, Didn't They?* and *Gathered Flowers, Stones and Bones: Fabulist Fictions*. He writes weekly reviews of fiction and film for the Considering Stories website.

Find out more at consideringstories.wordpress.com, or find Daniel on Facebook @daniel.r.robichaud, or on Twitter @darktowhead

New Jersey born and raised, **Paul Stansfield** spent decades as a field archaeologist for his day job. Surprisingly, even though he professionally disturbed hundreds of graves, he has yet to suffer a haunting or zombie attack.

By night he likes to write horror stories. He's had over 20 stories published by magazines, including such publications as *Bibliophilos*, *Morbid Curiosity*, *Cthulhu Sex Magazine*, *The Literary Hatchet*, and *Horror Bites*. Currently he has stories available in 11 anthologies, including "The Prison Compendium" (EMP Publishing), "Cranial Leakage Vol. 2" (Grinning Skull Press), "Hidden Menagerie Vol. 1" (Dragon's Roost Press) "Welcome to the Splatter Club" (Blood Bound Books), and "Shadowy Natures" (Dark Ink). He's an Affiliate Member of the Horror Writers Association.

His hobbies include watching professional football and baseball, drinking craft beer, tandem unicycle-spotting, and translating ancient Esperanto books into Silbo Gomero (sometimes all at the same time).

Find out more at paulstansfield.blogspot.com

J. Thorn has published two million words and has sold more than 185,000 books worldwide. He is an official member of the Science Fiction and Fantasy Writers of America, the Horror Writers Association, and the Great Lakes Association of Horror Writers.

J. co-hosts the Writers, Ink podcast with J.D. Barker and has interviewed some of today's most successful authors including Hugh Howey, Josh Malerman, Joanna Penn, Chuck Palahniuk, Blake Crouch, James Rollins, Steven Pressfield, David Baldacci, and James Patterson.

Thorn earned a B.A. in American History from the University of Pittsburgh and a M.A. from Duquesne University. He is a full-time writer, part-time professor at John Carroll University, co-owner of Molten Universe Media, podcaster, FM radio DJ, musician, and a certified Story Grid nerd.

Find out more at jthorn.net

Mijat Budimir Vujačić is an economist by trade, storyteller at heart. He is a published author of three horror novels written in Serbian: *Krvavi Akvarel*, *NekRomansa*, and *Vampir*. His stories appeared in *SQ*, *Serial*, *Devolution Z*, *All Worlds Wayfarer*, *DBND*, *Turn to Ash*, *Crimson Streets*, *Encounters*, *Acidic Fiction*, *Double Barrel Horror*, *Creepy Campfire Quarterly*, *Under the Bed*, *9 Tales*, and *Infernal Ink* magazines, as well as in professional anthologies *Infinite Darkness*, *Toxic Tales*, *Silent Scream*, *The Nightmare Collective*, *Down With The Fallen*, and *The Worlds of Science Fiction, Fantasy and Horror Vol1*. He believes a strong work ethic is the root of all success, and that it is best to err on the side of action. A fan of all things horror, he is also an avid gamer, occasional blogger, hookah enthusiast, and a staunch dog person. He lives in Belgrade, Serbia.

Find out more at mbvujacic.blogspot.com, or get in contact at mbvujacic@gmail.com

Daniel Willcocks is an international bestselling author and podcaster of dark fiction. He is the CEO of Devil's Rock Publishing, one fifth of digital story studio, Hawk & Cleaver, co-producer of iTunes-busting fiction podcast, 'The Other

Stories,' as well as the host of the 'Great Writers Share' podcast, and the 'Next Level Authors' podcast.

Residing in the UK, Dan's work explores the catastrophic and the strange. His stories span the genres of horror, post-apocalyptic, and sci-fi, and his work has seen him collaborating with some of the biggest names in the independent publishing community.

Find out more at danielwillcocks.com

Heinrich von Wolfcastle writes by candlelight from the seclusion of his castle in the foothills of the Carpathian Mountains. His debut anthology of short stories titled Screams Before Dawn was called "an engaging page turner" by *Scream Magazine*. He is an affiliate member of the Horror Writers Association and a member of the Great Lakes Association of Horror Writers. Though he lives the life of a recluse, some say he emerges from the shadows for Trick-or-Treaters on Halloween night.

Find out more at heinrichvonwolfcastle.com, or find him on Facebook @HeinrichvonWolfcastle and Instagram @Heinrich_von_Wolfcastle.

DEVIL'S ROCK PUBLISHING
A NEW HOME FOR HORROR

If you enjoyed this title, find more A-grade horror and dark
fiction at
www.devilsrockpublishing.com

OTHER TITLES BY DEVIL'S ROCK PUBLISHING

Serial Fiction, "When Winter Comes"

The First Fall (Episode 1)

Buried (Episode 2)

Black Ice Kills (Episode 3)

Masks of Bone (Episode 4)

Into the White (Episode 5)

Winter Comes (Episode 6)

Anthologies

The Other Side: A Horror Anthology

Keep up-to-date at

www.devilsrockpublishing.com